Here's what critics are saying about
Leslie Langtry's books:

"Brilliant! Leslie Langtry has once again penned a 'gotta read every page' drama. I loved it, and the end as brilliant…Agatha Christie would be proud!"
—*Kings River Life Magazine*

"Darkly funny and wildly over the top, this mystery answers the burning question, 'Do assassin skills and Girl Scout merit badges mix…' one truly original and wacky novel!"
—*RT BOOK REVIEWS*

"Those who like dark humor will enjoy a look into the deadliest female assassin and PTA mom's life."
—*Parkersburg News*

"Mixing a deadly sense of humor and plenty of sexy sizzle, Leslie Langtry creates a brilliantly original, laughter-rich mix of contemporary romance and suspense in *'Scuse Me While I Kill This Guy*."
—*Chicago Tribune*

"The beleaguered soccer mom assassin concept is a winner, and Langtry gets the fun started from page one with a myriad of clever details."
—*Publisher's Weekly*

BOOKS BY LESLIE LANGTRY

Merry Wrath Mysteries:
Merit Badge Murder
Mint Cookie Murder
Scout Camp Murder
(short story)
Marshmallow S'More
Murder
Movie Night Murder
Mud Run Murder
Fishing Badge Murder
(short story)
Motto for Murder
Map Skills Murder
Mean Girl Murder
Marriage Vow Murder
Mystery Night Murder
Meerkats and Murder
Make Believe Murder
Maltese Vulture Murder
Musket Ball Murder
Macho Man Murder
Mad Money Murder
Mind-Bending Murder
Mascots Are Murder
Mosquito Bite Murder
Manga and Murder
Mayor for Murder
Mardi Gras Murder
Munchies and Murder
Memories Are Murder

Greatest Hits Mysteries:
'Scuse Me While I Kill This
Guy
Guns Will Keep Us
Together
Stand By Your Hitman
I Shot You Babe
Paradise By The Rifle
Sights
Snuff the Magic Dragon
My Heroes Have Always
Been Hitmen
Greatest Hits mysteries
Holiday Bundle

Aloha Lagoon Mysteries:
Ukulele Murder
Ukulele Deadly

Other Works:
Sex, Lies, & Family
Vacations

MEMORIES ARE MURDER

A Merry Wrath Mystery

USA TODAY BESTSELLING AUTHOR

Leslie Langtry

MEMORIES ARE MURDER

CHAPTER ONE

———

My poor, unsuspecting target had no idea what I was about to unleash on him. I carefully eased up on the toggle. There was no point in giving away our position or letting him know we were watching. Hopefully the drone would maintain silence as it carried out my sinister work.

"Gotcha," I whispered as I looked at the screen. *Now you can't hide.* I reached for the switch that would deliver the payload. "Almost there…" I said softly.

Someone tapped me on the shoulder. I ignored it. Damn! My target must've heard the drone, because he looked up.

"Now!" I shouted as I hit the switch and dropped the payload. I studied the screen and shouted, "Direct hit!"

I did a little endzone dance to celebrate.

"Mrs. Albers!" a voice called out. "Mrs. Wrath isn't sharing the drone!"

I re-checked the screen. Olaf the goat was gleefully eating the dog kibble that mysteriously dropped from the sky. My Scout troop was at a farm the girls had bought with their proceeds from the *WHO'S THERE? BIGFOOT!* merchandise. I thought it was a great time to teach them the proper way to use drones.

Why? Because Betty's parents complained. Well, Betty's neighbors did anyway. Apparently the girl was doing some massive surveillance on every house within a one-block radius. Rex informed me two days ago that not only did she not have a license, but her neighbors might sue her parents for invasion of privacy.

"She doesn't need a license to use it recreationally," I insisted.

Rex's eyebrows went up. "Betty was monetizing this, which was not the worst part of it, by the way."

I guess blackmailing your neighbors for money probably crosses a line. Especially if word got out that Clovis Jenkins, the hard-line evangelical minister, enjoyed wearing hard-core S & M leathers as he lounged in his backyard, or that Dorinda Higgenbottom operated an illegal duck breeding operation out of her garage.

"Why did you say that wasn't the worst part?" I asked my husband.

Rex ran his fingers through his hair. "Because rumor has it she's looking into ways to *weaponize* it."

"Okay," I decided. "I'll talk to her."

Which had resulted in us spending the day at Sunshine Rainbow Glitter Princess Pony Farm, learning about drones and their *legal* use, which didn't include extorting money from religious hypocrites and duck brothels.

"Merry…" Kelly gently took the controls from my hand and passed them off to one of the Kaitlyns. "You have to let the girls try it."

"Okay," I grumbled. "It's just so fun! I mean, the technology has advanced so much! If I'd had something like this when I was in the CIA, I could've avoided some in-person undercover and done this from a safe distance.

Spies today were so lucky. They could sit off-site and take pictures of a black bag drop miles away. That would've come in so useful when I was undercover with Carlos the Armadillo in Colombia. Instead of following Henrietta the Hernia all the way into Medellin to see if she was reporting to the rival gang about Carlos's drug mules and getting caught along the way, I could've followed her with a drone. Even though I escaped, it would've saved me a black eye, a bruised ulna, two broken fingers, and half a tank of gasoline.

As more dog food rained down on a deliriously happy goat, I thought about the next step in this process. We were planning to talk to the girls about when they could use drones and when they couldn't. Unfortunately, other than spying on people and feeding goats, I wasn't exactly enthusiastic about the other options.

Kelly had made a list that included delivering gifts to shut-ins and taking pictures of a sunrise, but I wasn't buying it. And if I wasn't, then my troop wasn't either. They were too savvy for their own good. Betty had already found ways to blackmail her neighbors, and rumor had it she was thinking of adding weapons. Would she be satisfied with just doing *nice* things? Unlikely.

My name is Merry Wrath Ferguson, and I used to be a spy for the CIA. I say *used to be* because after seven years of service, I was "accidentally" outed by the vice president as a way to get back at my senator dad. My real name is Fionnaghuala Merrygold Czrygy, but as soon as my name and face were splashed all over the media, I changed it to a combination of my middle name and my mother's maiden name and moved back to Who's There, Iowa to help my best friend Kelly start a Girl Scout troop.

Oh, and I also got married to the town's detective. It seems important to mention that.

"Don't touch that button!" Betty shouted at the Kaitlyn, who looked at her curiously.

"Why not?" all four Kaitlyns asked in unison.

I had four Kaitlyn M.s in my troop, and they all looked exactly alike. After seven years, I still couldn't tell them apart.

Betty had the girl guide the drone back to us—but stopped it about fifty feet away. Then she hit the button.

"You modified that with a flamethrower?" I asked as I gaped at the now burning pile of hay. "How did you get it so small?"

Kelly ran into the barn and returned with a fire extinguisher and put the flames out. She shot me a look.

"That is *so* bad!" I said while secretly giving Betty a thumbs-up that Kelly couldn't see. "You'll have to tell me what you did so I can make sure no one ever replicates it," I insisted. *Except me.*

Perhaps reading my mind, Kelly ordered everyone into the barn for a brownie break. This was our go-to distraction tool. Everyone liked snacks. Even the Huns and Visigoths loved snack breaks. As we filed into the barn, Kelly discreetly took the drone and handed it to me. The look on her face told me to deactivate it and that I wasn't getting any snack until I did.

Grumbling as I stomped outside, I sat down at a picnic table to examine the mechanism. They'd better save me a brownie. I was starving. I very gingerly poked around the small device, trying not to trigger it by accident. These things could be touchy. I'd seen flamethrowers embedded in toy cars, Swiss army knives, and once in a Yakuza member's pet hermit crab shell (which came as a brief and fiery surprise to Pete, the hermit crab).

The little nozzle must've receded back inside the drone. I could hit the button on the controls, but then it would burst forth, literally guns blazing. However, if I just found the right spot to pop it open without it shooting fire, I could disable it. It couldn't be that hard, right? I mean, a *child* installed it.

My cell buzzed. Riley's picture appeared on screen, his good looks marred by the addition of horns and a beard, drawn in sharpie. I took the call and hit the speaker.

"Hey Riley, you're on speaker and there are little girls around. FYI."

I continued to prod the underside of the drone. Maybe I should take the batteries out? No, then the mechanism wouldn't work.

"Merry." Riley's voice had an edge to it. "You're with the girls?"

"Yup." My fingers slid over something, and I examined it closer. "We're teaching them the rules of the road, drone-style."

"Oh yeah? I just ordered a huge commercial drone for my private eye business."

I looked at the phone. "I should probably vet it for you, just to make sure it's safe."

He sighed. "It'll have to wait because we have a problem."

"We?" I asked as I turned my attention back to the drone. "How does this involve me?"

Riley had been my handler during my years with the CIA. He retired some years ago and followed me here, where he set up a private investigation firm. Since I tended to solve a number of his cases before he did, I was surprised that he'd actually want to include me in his *problem.*

"Did you hit on one of your married clients?" I continued. The charming, drop-dead gorgeous man was his own worst enemy sometimes.

"No," he said slowly. "We have a visitor. From the past."

"Well…" I found a hinge and began working it back and forth. "If it's one of the many bimbos you seduced over the course of your career, you can handle it on your own."

The mechanism was about to give! I almost had it!

"I wish it was that simple," Riley said. "Unfortunately, it's an old contact of yours."

My eyebrows went up at this news, but I kept working the mechanism. "I've been visited by Russian spies, Chechen strongmen, and the Yakuza. Most died, some were arrested, and two of them married my twin sisters-in-law. Who's left to find me?"

"Merry," Riley snapped. "Will you take this seriously? This isn't a joke!"

Oh, this baby was about to pop. I pulled out my camping knife and slid it into the crevice to give it a little help. "Okay, fine, who is it?"

There was a pause that made me a tiny smidge nervous. "It's Teo. From your days with Carlos."

The hinge sprung and the flamethrower activated, setting the picnic table on fire. I stepped away, snatching my phone before it could burn.

"Teo? Teo the Tapir? Is here?" I squeaked.

Carlos the Armadillo gave everyone a nickname because he didn't like his. It was given to him because when afraid, he could jump three feet in the air, straight up. Like an armadillo. It didn't stop him from getting hit by my car. Or maybe that's why I hit him with my car years back.

You can kind of guess the meaning of most nicknames. Henrietta the Hernia had two bulging hernias that made it impossible for her to wear a bikini. Paco the Packrat hoarded twist ties and wine corks. Most of the nicknames were harmless. And you might think Teo the Tapir would be too.

It wasn't.

"He is. And Merry," Riley added, "he's looking for you."

CHAPTER TWO

"Who's Teo?" Betty asked.

"What's a tapir?" Inez added.

Lauren, junior zookeeper, replied, "A tapir is a pig elephant."

"Okay." Inez seemed satisfied with that explanation. "Pig elephant. Makes sense."

I was busy beating out the blazing picnic table with an old rug I'd found in the barn, because Kelly had used up the fire extinguisher on the haystack. "How did you hear that?" I asked over my shoulder.

"Betty's listening," Ava said. "She's *always* listening."

The fire was out, and I dropped the singed rug. "On my phone? Betty tapped my phone?"

Ava shrugged. "Of course. It's part of the city's new security measures."

Eleven-year-old Ava was our mayor, the youngest in Who's There, Iowa's history. And Betty was her much more competent G. Gordon Liddy.

"You can't tap my phone," I insisted. "It's illegal."

Ava looked away thoughtfully. "Then I'll just make it legal."

The four Kaitlyns nodded.

"You can't," I said. Could she? I had to admit that I wasn't familiar with town ordinances. I decided to stick to my guns and handed my phone to Betty. "Remove the tap."

"Okay," Betty said. "But that will cost you. My hourly rate is $60."

I threw my hands in the air. "Why should I pay for you to remove something I didn't want on there in the beginning?"

"Of course you didn't *want* it." Betty rolled her eyes. "It was a clandestine tap. It would take all the fun out of it if you'd *wanted* it."

I shook my head. "Take it off the phone. For free. Now."

The girl blinked at me. "There's no such thing as a free lunch. That's what my dad always says."

Huh. Betty listened to one of her parents. That was new.

"But your dad gets a free lunch every day," Ava countered, reminding us of Betty's dad's new very lucrative city job. "It's in his secret shadow contract."

Betty nodded. "That's different." She looked at me. "Do you want to Bettymo it, or should I just charge your credit card?"

"Neither." I paused. "Wait, Bettymo?"

"It's like Venmo, but way Betty-er," Inez explained. "She gets 45%, and you have to sign an NDA, whatever that is."

I put on my best intimidating leader expression and hoped it would work. "Nope, not paying. You are going to take it off now."

Kelly appeared. She looked at the burnt remains of the picnic table and sighed.

Betty gave in. "Fine. But just this once. I'm giving you a freebie cuz you're like, an okay leader and all." She pulled up an app I'd never seen before, tapped it twice, and handed it back. "Here."

"Mrs. Wrath," one of the Kaitlyns said. "You never told us who Teo the Tapir is."

The other seven little girls and my co-leader looked at me expectantly.

Should I tell them that Teo was a stone-cold killer who had survived so many stabbings they called him the Tapir because of the animal's unusually thick skin? Or that like a tapir, he seemed to have a prehensile nose that could snort an impossible amount of cocaine? Or that Teo had allegedly killed more than two hundred people? Okay, that wasn't related to the tapir thing, but it seemed like something I shouldn't leave out.

"He's a pig elephant," I said finally.

"Don't worry," Betty stage-whispered to the others. "I'll find out and report back."

Teo was here and looking for me. That was a problem. The two of us had never gotten along—not since he accused me of cheating at the Tenth Annual Llama Calling Competition and Fun Fair. I beat him handily in that (the trick is in the way you stress the letter *G*, as few people know that's a llama's favorite letter), the sack race, and the guinea pig costume competition (hint—you'll never lose if you go with Elvis). The only thing I didn't beat him at was body count.

During the four months I'd spent with Carlos's cartel, Teo never took a shine to me. In fact, I'd say he went out of his way to be hostile, like setting fire to my shoes…while I was wearing them, eating all of my Easter candy before I could even eat the ears off the chocolate bunny, and blowing up my bed with C-4. Okay, some of those are worse than the others, but I really like Easter candy.

After dropping off the girls, I carefully drove home, making sure I wasn't tailed. I was just pulling into my driveway when a white SUV raced up behind and blocked me in.

Crap! I didn't have my gun! I'd promised Kelly I wouldn't have one in the van anymore because of a few incidents with my troop. The first time Betty found my .45, she took out all the bullets and replaced them with pebbles that she somehow managed to squeeze into the magazine. That gun didn't work right after that. And then there was the time she professionally field-stripped it, hiding all the tiny components around camp for a scavenger hunt (I never did find that firing pin). And then there was the time Betty and Inez managed to shoot the air out of two tires in my minivan with one shot— which was, I must say, pretty impressive.

Personally I thought Kelly had overreacted the last time. The kid was *joking* about holding up a bank. She never would've seen it through. She was the mayor's right hand. Even Betty would know that robbing a bank in a town where you work for the mayor is probably a bad idea. Of course, she might have been thinking of robbing a bank in another town, but I couldn't prove that.

I stayed in my van, trying to come up with a way to protect myself. Philby, my cat who looked like Hitler, was sitting in the window, staring back at me as if to say *you've brought this on yourself.* She was probably right.

The doors to the SUV opened, and my Chechen brothers-in-law, Ron and Ivan, got out. I relaxed and joined them.

"Merry!" Ivan picked me up and crushed me in a bear hug before handing me over to Ron, who did the same. "Is good to see you!"

"You guys literally see me several times a week," I croaked as I strained for air.

Ron set me down. "Yes. We are always happy to see you!"

"Except for when we are not," Ivan corrected.

I straightened my clothes. "When are you not happy to see me?"

Ron and Ivan had worked for Wally, the Chechen strongman who's gang I'd infiltrated. They came to the US a few years ago and ended up marrying Rex's twin sisters, Randi and Ronni.

Randi and Ronni were professional taxidermists who owned Ferguson Taxidermy—Where Your Pet Lives On Forever! The diminutive, raven-haired women were a bit older than their husbands. Randi, Ivan's wife, loved and adored me. Ronni, Ron's wife, hated me with the hot radiation of a thousand nuclear power plants. No matter what I'd tried, the woman despised me.

And now they were pregnant. A secret they'd recently shared with only me, asking me to keep it from my husband until the time was right. I hoped that time was coming soon because keeping the secret was killing me.

"Wives are crazy," Ivan continued. "They want to eat strange things at all hours of night."

Ron nodded. "Last night they ask for squeezy cheese on pineapple. Is too weird."

"And unhealthy." Ivan flexed his muscles to demonstrate how in shape he was.

Both men had huge muscles to make up for their tiny brains.

"We need to get out of house," Ron said. "Can we hang you?"

"Hang out with me?" I wondered.

"Yes!" Ron clapped his hands. "That is the one. We would not want to hang you."

Hmmm…maybe these clowns could be useful.

"Have you guys ever heard of Carlos the Armadillo?" I asked.

"Yes! I have heard of. You killed him." Ivan puffed out his chest as if he'd just won a prize.

Ron gave me a wink and thumbs-up as he seemed to believe my killing Carlos was a good thing.

"Well, one of his henchmen, Teo the Tapir, is in town looking for me," I began. "Teo is a very dangerous man. I don't know why he's here or what he wants."

The men's demeanor changed, and they scowled.

"If this Tapir kills you," Ron said, "we will kill it."

Ivan nodded solemnly before asking "What is a tapir?"

Ron held his hand about three feet off the ground. "Is pig elephant."

"I'd prefer it if it didn't get that far," I said, addressing the idea of killing the man. "I don't know what he wants, but we weren't as close as I was to you two."

"But if pig elephant does kill you," Ron said again, "we will avenge."

"No"—I shook my head—"it's a man. Tapir is his nickname."

Ron considered this. "Good. I do not like to kill animals. But a man I will kill in your memory because you are dead."

"Um, thanks?" I replied.

Ivan looked at me curiously. "Does that not make you feel better?"

"Oh yeah," I assured them. "Much better."

The two men stepped close together for a moment and began whispering. I used the opportunity to clear the troop stuff out of my van and put it away in the garage.

"We will do it!" Ron shouted from the doorway.

"Do what, exactly?" In cases like this, it was good to know precisely what was being agreed to.

"Guard your body!" Ivan said.

"Before it was dead…hopefully," Ron added.

"Oh, good," I said as I moved a stack of empty boxes. "I…" I froze.

A relaxed hand lay palm up, fingers curled slightly as if it was beckoning me forward. I shoved more boxes aside and sighed heavily. A corpse lay on her back, eyes closed, not breathing—like corpses do. I checked for a pulse anyway. Nope.

Ivan and Ron, sensing something was up, came up behind me.

"We will not guard *that* body," Ivan said.

"No"—Ron nodded—"we only guard family. That body will need someone else."

"No, she won't," I said. "It's too late for her." I reached into my pocket, pulled out my phone, and called Rex. After telling him I'd found a dead woman in our garage, I hung up and did a little examination and took some photos. There wasn't much time before the police arrived.

The victim was in her thirties, with a short, brunette bob. She was wearing camouflage fatigues and desert combat boots. She kind of looked like that Russian villain played by Cate Blanchet in the last Indiana Jones movie.

"Do you want us to dispose?" Ron ventured.

I shook my head. The woman looked familiar, but after racking my brain, I came up empty. Who was this woman, and why was she dead in my garage?

"Ivan," I said, picking the smarter of the two, "go to the end of the driveway and warn me when Rex gets here."

Ron looked over my shoulder. "She was murdered."

I glanced at him curiously. "How do you know?"

"Because she is in garage owned by you. If dead body appears near Merry, it is murdered."

I quickly pulled on a pair of latex gloves from a box on the shelf above. A brisk search turned up no wallet, no dog tags, no ID of any kind. I pulled her collar away from her neck but found no ligature marks. There was no blood on the floor, which meant she hadn't been stabbed or shot. I carefully felt the back of her head but didn't find any lumps. I wiggled her head, but her neck wasn't broken.

"I can't figure out how she was killed," I muttered.

"That isn't your job, is it?" Rex's voice said behind me.

I stood up, holding my hands behind me so he wouldn't see the rubber gloves.

"Hey Merry," Ron said from behind my husband. "Rex is here with officer who eats a lot but never gains the weight."

Rex walked over and looked down at the body, while Officer Kevin Dooley found the brownies from the troop meeting and began to eat. For once, I didn't stop him. Kevin and I had gone to school together. This mouth breather had a knack for finding food and was only recently learning not to contaminate the crime scene with crumbs and Cheeto dust.

I said nothing as Rex inspected the scene. The weird sense of déjà vu grew stronger—as if this dead woman was someone I'd just been thinking of.

It hit me like a ton of bricks. *Of course!* I knelt down and started opening her jacket.

"Merry," Rex warned, "you aren't supposed to touch the body."

"It's okay," I said as I undid the last button and ripped open the jacket. "I'm wearing gloves."

"See if she has any snacks," Kevin requested. "I just ate your last brownie."

My husband continued to protest as I ran my hands over the body's abdomen. When I found what I wanted to know, I stood up.

"Why did you do that? And why right in front of me?" Rex asked.

"Because I thought I knew her and wanted to make sure."

"Make sure of what?" Rex wondered.

"The bulges in her abdomen." I pulled the gloves off with a snap. "That's Henrietta the Hernia, from my days with Carlos the Armadillo."

CHAPTER THREE

———

Riley pulled in just as Dr. Soo Jin Body, the super smart and unfairly beautiful medical examiner, arrived.

"Hi Merry!" Soo Jin sang out as she and Riley joined us.

"Huh." Riley whistled as he leaned over the body. "That looks a lot like Henrietta the Hernia."

Riley had been my handler in Colombia, but while I was in the field, he held court in the office in nearby Medellin. He'd never really met Henrietta or Teo but knew who they were from my photos and reports.

"I don't know why I didn't recognize her right away," I mumbled. "I think it's the short dark hair. Henrietta was an ash blonde."

"The fatigues might have tripped you up too," Riley added. "Wasn't she a bit of a girly girl?"

Soo Jin and Rex listened. They knew of my CIA past. Kevin was rooting through a chest freezer where Rex and I kept overflow food. He pulled out a frozen ham and began sucking on it.

"Do I need to call the CIA?" Rex asked.

Riley shook his head. "I'll do it. Soo Jin can go ahead and examine the body. I don't think the agency will care though. That mission was declassified years ago." He took out his phone and walked away.

I hoped Betty hadn't tapped his cell too, or soon every girl in my troop would know about this. It would probably be better if I didn't mention that.

The medical examiner got down on the floor and crawled around while I filled Rex in on Henrietta. He knew about Carlos, as it was one of his first cases in Who's There. In fact, it was how we met. This was the second time the two of us were standing over a Colombian cartel member. The first time we'd met was over Carlos's body, and I felt a little twist of romantic nostalgia.

"Hmmm…" Soo Jin sat back on her heels. "This is a tricky one. I can't find any sign of physical trauma or poisoning. I'll take her back to the morgue and see what I can find out."

Riley came back. "The Agency isn't interested. They said something about this happening all the time to Merry and *a dead terrorist is the only good terrorist* or something to that effect. They were, however, concerned about Teo."

Rex's eyebrows went up. "Teo? Should I be expecting more dead cartel members?"

"I wish," I muttered under my breath.

"Teo is no joke, Merry," Riley reminded me. "He didn't like you when he thought you were a cartel member. If he knows you were actually CIA and that you killed Carlos, he could be pursuing a vendetta."

"Will someone please explain what is going on?" Rex asked.

"We are to guard Merry's body," Ivan spoke up. "If Tapir kills her, we will avenge her possibly untimely death."

"Yes," Ron added. "And we will be sad while beat him to the death."

"See?" I pasted on a fake smile. "Nothing to worry about."

Riley wasn't convinced. "Teo is bad news! He really hated Merry."

"Hate is a strong word," I said as I tried to downplay this in front of Rex.

"He blew up your bed with C-4!" Riley argued. "And he was mad you weren't in it at the time!"

"Merry…" Rex sounded grave. "It sounds serious. And this guy is here?"

Riley spoke before I could. "He's been seen around town, asking blatantly about Merry but using her old name. No one has said where she lives yet, but it's only a matter of time before he finds the right person."

"How do you know he's been asking about me?" I pressed.

"I have informants," Riley said.

"You"—I pointed at him—"have informants? This is Who's There, not Gotham!"

This town of around five thousand didn't have the kind of crime you needed for informants.

My former handler adopted a mildly defensive tone. "Yes, I have informants. And they give me excellent intel."

Rex, the peacemaker, held up his hands. "Fine. Merry's in danger. Riley, you know this guy. What do we do?"

"*I* know this guy," I snapped. "And if he murdered Henrietta here, Teo knows where I live."

"This could be a coincidence," Soo Jin suggested. "Maybe this Teo doesn't know where Merry lives and Henrietta came to warn her? We don't know for sure she was murdered. She could've died from natural causes."

Ron's eyes went wide. "No one dies in such way around Merry. It is *always* murder."

Ivan agreed. "Always!"

"Guys." I held my hand up. "Not helping."

"And"—Ron held up one finger—"what if *Merry* murdered dead woman on floor? Then this Tapir would not know where she lives."

"I didn't do it," I growled.

Ivan shook his head. "You are only one who knows her in whole country, maybe. Must be you."

These two numbskulls were starting to get on my nerves. "I was with my troop all day. You guys arrived at the same time I did. I'm alibied."

Kevin looked up from his snack. "Watch out. Did you know someone tried to frame me for murder? Can you believe that?"

We all turned to look at him. "Yes, Kevin," I said evenly. "I'm the one who solved the case and saved your neck."

"Oh. Thanks." The paste-eater went back to his frozen ham. Or rather, *my* frozen ham.

I turned back to Riley. "Can you find out if Teo is staying at any of the hotels in town? Actually, that rundown dive motel outside of town is the most probable place."

"I have informants," Riley started.

I cut him off. "Good. Then get on it. And let's relax a little. It is possible that Teo doesn't know where I live yet. So I'm probably safe…"

Boom!

Across the street, the garage of my old house exploded. Well damn. Either the girls had learned how to blow things up or I guessed Teo knew where I was after all.

"I just had that garage redone!" I said later as I watched the fire department hose down my old garage. It looked pretty bad, but fortunately, the house wasn't damaged.

"Twice," Rex added, reminding me that recently, the girls had damaged the garage during an unauthorized sleepover when I was at a bachelorette party in Niagara Falls. "I'm going to go talk to Ray."

Ray Goldensoph was the fire marshal and chief of the department. A tall, thoughtful, quiet man, I respected him enough to know he'd discover the truth. Hopefully he'd find out that it was something else, like if I'd left some of my old CIA-grade plastique on top of a Bunsen burner for no apparent reason.

What was I thinking? Of course this was Teo's work. Who else could it be? He had to be responsible for Henrietta and must've found out I had two houses. He planted the corpse in one garage and blew up the other.

Something seemed off though. Why just blow up the garage? Either he thought he was taking out the house, or he didn't want to kill me…yet. It would be just like that psychopath to toy with me. He'd probably want to torture me to death. Well, I wasn't going to fall for that!

Rex walked back across the street. "Ray says it could be faulty wiring. From the recent contractor's work. He doesn't know why that would make the structure explode, however." My husband lowered his voice. "You didn't keep any of your old CIA stuff in there, did you? Anything explosive?"

"It was an accident?" I stared at him. "That's kind of better. It doesn't explain Henrietta, but maybe it's just a coincidence."

"He said it might be an accident. His statement wasn't conclusive." Rex gave me a look. "You didn't answer my question."

"Well…I might have…kept something…" I struggled to answer. "I mean, I moved some stuff out there to make room for the troop's T-shirt inventory…but I don't remember leaving anything *too* dangerous in there."

He folded his arms over his chest. "Define 'too dangerous.'"

I couldn't help but shrug. "More dangerous than usual, I guess. It's not like I left plutonium in the garage."

"You have plutonium?" Rex sighed. "That might be grounds for divorce, actually."

I rolled my eyes. "Why would I keep plutonium in the house? It's such a pain in the butt to store, and in some places you have to have a license for that kind of thing…and then you really need to know what you're doing because one wrong move, and *blammo*! And then there's the girls. How irresponsible is it to keep plutonium around *my* troop?"

Was he really asking me this? Just because I may have the stuff to make a bomb didn't mean I'd actually do it. Well, at least not until the troop was older. It was important to me that they had a healthy respect for explosives, but at the moment, they barely had a healthy respect for matches, so I was waiting.

Rex turned his attention back across the street. "Well, Ray will find it, whatever it is. And then I'll have to explain why you have some probably illegal equipment. At least the ladies weren't here."

My husband was referring to a group of elderly Girl Scouts who we'd found hiding out in an old Scout camp since it closed in the 60s. I was letting them live in my old house, but they were such a curiosity and the Girl Scout Council felt so bad that they'd lived in the woods for several decades that they were treating the women to stays at Disney World and the like. Currently they were at a donor's mansion in Branson.

"And the house is unscathed," Rex was saying. He paused. "You don't think your troop had something to do with that, do you?"

I shrugged. "It's always possible, but they usually own up to things like this for extortion purposes. I like Ray's idea that it's an accident."

Two orderlies were wheeling Henrietta away on a cart. Half the neighborhood was on the sidewalks. When they saw the body being wheeled from my garage on this side of the street and the remains of an explosion at my house on the other side of the street, they shook their heads.

We probably weren't going to be invited to any neighborhood potlucks anytime soon.

Riley appeared at my side. "You really know how to alienate a neighborhood, Wrath."

Rex smiled and walked back across the street to shoo Ivan and Ron away from gawking at the wreckage.

"The fire marshal thinks it might be a wiring problem," I said way too loudly in hopes the neighbors might hear. I lowered my voice and turned to Riley. "Do you think Teo killed Henrietta?"

"It's probable," Riley mused. "How did they get along back in the day?"

My mind reeled back in time. "Carlos had a lot of people working for him. I'm sure they crossed paths, but I never heard that they hung out or even knew each other."

Riley nodded. "Carlos's cartel was immediately absorbed by a rival cartel once he died. His men and women split up and went to work for different drug lords. I can see if there's anything on Teo since you've left."

"Thanks," I said and meant it. "Meanwhile, Ron and Ivan are going to be my security."

We turned our eyes across the street, where Ron and Ivan were in some sort of muscle-flexing competition that ended with fisticuffs and them rolling around in the grass, punching each other.

Riley ran across the street and helped Rex pull the men apart. I went back into my *unexploded* garage, where Soo Jin was climbing out of her jumpsuit.

"You really found nothing?" I asked quietly.

"Nothing except for what appear to be a couple of hernias on her abdomen." Soo Jin ran her hands through her hair, and it fell perfectly into place. "It's so strange." She bit her lip. "It has to be a heart attack or something similar. I wonder. What were her eating habits like?"

That wouldn't help. "As much as I'd like it to be natural causes, I think she was a bit of a health nut. Ever since she got those hernias in her twenties, she became super healthy. She worked out, drank lots of water, and became a vegetarian."

"Well…" Soo Jin folded up the jumpsuit. "Healthy and young vegetarians have heart attacks too. It's rare. Maybe this is one of those cases." She placed her hand on my arm. "At any rate, she's someone you knew once, and I am sorry for your loss."

"Thanks." I wondered if I showed up in her office in a few hours and turned on the waterworks, would she tell me what she discovered?

Soo Jin left with Kevin loping after her. He'd left the ham on top of the freezer with a little note on hamster-shaped stationary that said *Get better snacks.*

Across the street, Rex and Riley were standing close to each other, talking solemnly. Every now and then, one of them looked at me. If there was anything I hated, it was overprotective men who didn't think a woman could take care of herself.

"Merry." Ron and Ivan appeared at my side. "We will need big guns."

Ivan tapped his chin. "Really big guns."

"No way," I reasoned.

"But we have to protect you!" Ron protested.

That was it.

"Go home to your wives. I'll call when I need you."

The two men hesitated before getting into the white SUV and driving away.

Rex walked over to me while Riley made a call. "Do you think those two are acting stranger than normal?"

"Than normal?" I grimaced. "No. Why?"

"Because they asked me where they could buy squeezy cheese in bulk for the twins," my husband said. "My sisters hate that stuff. Do you think they're having marital troubles?"

Dammit. Randi and Ronni still hadn't told Rex. Well, *I* wasn't going to do it.

"Ron and Ivan are addicted to the stuff," I lied. "They're dumb enough to think if they overwhelm your sisters with it, they'll give it another try."

I hated lying to my husband. Not about things like plutonium, but about almost everything else.

CHAPTER FOUR

Rex and I spent the rest of the evening sorting through the rubble across the street. There was very little left to salvage…a set of aluminum sushi camping dishes and tongs from Okinawa, an asbestos trophy from the 2nd annual Let's Pretend Pickles Are Knives And Fight competition in Grozny (where I came in third) and, rather ironically, a working mini flamethrower made out of North Korean Letgo that I'd bought at a garage sale in Uzbekistan.

Rex turned it over in his hands. "It's made out of Legos? They misspelled it."

I took the blackened block from him. "No, it's a North Korean knock-off brand of waffles called Letgo. Most food in North Korea is inedible, especially the waffles. Which is really the only reason it works." I looked around. "The fuel tank should be around here somewhere."

"Merry…" Rex started to speak. "Was this some sort of accelerant?"

I waved him off. "Don't worry. It was empty. I haven't been able to get *Dear Leader Maple Syrup* here for it. Which is probably a good thing since it's so dangerous. They do have a low-fat version. Then again, all food is low-fat there."

My husband stretched his arms. "Maybe we should call it a night. And I'm thinking that in the next week, you and I should inventory your knickknacks before someone gets hurt."

"You may be right," I agreed. "I haven't seen a couple of things in a while, and I'm worried the girls found them."

If Betty found the high intensity electrical disrupter and used it, I'd never hear the end of it. Maybe Rex was right. We should go through my stuff. I just had to go through it first to hide the things I didn't want him to know about.

Rex appeared to read my mind. "You're going to have to tell me everything you have."

"Of course, babe!" I said a little too brightly.

He held out his hand. "Pinky swear."

Uh-oh. He wasn't going to leave me any wiggle room on this, by going straight to the dreaded pinky swear—an absolutely unbreakable promise that kept my girls in check.

I walked toward him and feigned running into a dangling plank. His concern (and the fact that I might have overdone it and was now bleeding) put the oath aside, and I was in the clear for now.

The next morning, the whole mess had me completely distracted, as I gave Leonard cat food, Philby and Martini frog food, and Rufus blinked disappointedly at his dried dog kibble. I even poured orange juice on my Lucky Charms. Then I dumped it out and did it again before deciding on toast.

Teo showing up out of the blue didn't make sense to me. Oh sure, I'd had visits from his type before, and almost all of them were unfriendly. Why did he wait until now to come looking for me? I was done with him seven years ago. I'd heard the old saying that revenge is a dish best served cold, but this seemed ridiculous.

The one thing I was sure about was that this wasn't going to be a pleasant visit between old colleagues. If he did murder Henrietta and blow up my garage, it would be worse when we met in person. Maybe having Ron and Ivan around wasn't such a bad idea.

Rex had gone to work after I'd insisted I was going to be fine. I wasn't sure he believed me after I poured orange juice on my cereal twice in a row, but he went anyway. Once he was gone, I wandered through both garages again.

Unfortunately, it didn't take long before I determined that there wasn't anything in our garage to tell me why Henrietta was there or how she died. So I started kicking through the debris across the street. Rex had called one of those companies that clean up after a fire to come over first thing. I wanted to check it out first.

The fire marshal believed that it was faulty wiring that somehow exploded, but I wasn't sure. On the one hand, if it was that, then there was the chance that Teo hadn't found me yet. On the other, how could Henrietta be dead in my garage without Teo's involvement?

It wasn't long before I finally gave up. The stuff in my garage, mostly Scout camping gear, was easily replaced, and I was certain the cleaning company wouldn't find any classified spy documents or weaponry.

I sat down on my stoop to think. It had been a long time since I'd seen the Tapir. Maybe he wasn't here to destroy me. Maybe he was just on a nostalgia kick, in town, and decided to look me up for old times' sake. It didn't seem like something a killer cartel member would do, but I hung on to the idea of maybe.

"I heard what happened." Betty's voice made me jump.

"Yeesh! What are you doing here?" I put my hand over my heart, as if that could slow the pounding.

Inez joined us. "I heard it on the scanner. You were all over that thing last night with bodies, explosions, and stuff! It was awesome!"

I held up my index finger. "One body. Not bod*ies*. One. And the fire marshal thinks this was an accident." I waved my arm in the direction of my former garage.

"It's Teo the Tapir," Betty said. "Isn't it?"

I looked her in the eye. "You didn't answer me. Why are you here?"

"We thought we could help." Inez pulled a set of brass knuckles out of the pocket of her pink sundress and clapped them onto her fist.

Betty nodded. "You're kind of a menace to the community and all that. The mayor got a bunch of calls from your neighbors last night complaining. She called me to come over and straighten you out."

"So that's how you found out," I sighed. "I think I'd rather you'd both heard it on the scanner with Inez."

"That's Inez's job." Betty shook her head. "I'm the fixer. People want you to move away."

"Great," I moaned.

"Okay," Betty said after a moment. "We'll help you."

"How are you going to help me?" I asked warily.

"We could plant more bodies and explosions in other parts of town," Inez said. "That'll take the heat off of you."

Betty appeared to agree. "The explosions will be easy, but I'm not sure where we'll get the bodies."

"Nope" was all I said.

"I didn't say I *couldn't* get them. I just said I wasn't sure where to get them," Betty explained. "I could call Hilly…"

I cut her off. "Don't even think about it. Look, while it's really nice that you want to help me by blowing things up and dropping bodies everywhere, it's not a great plan and it might land you in juvie, and I don't think they have Girl Scouts in juvie."

"Ava will pardon us." Betty pulled a piece of official-looking parchment out of her pocket that read *Whoever reads this, Betty is immune from prexecution. The Mayor.*

"It's persecution," I corrected. "Or rather, prosecution."

The little girl squinted at the document. "I like this better. The misspelling could be interpreted for that or for execution." Betty stuffed the note back into her shorts.

Inez nodded. "Betty's very smart."

"Okay, smart kid, tell me what I should do next?"

Betty considered this for only a minute. "You should take the fight to him. Don't wait for him to blow up your other garage or kill anyone else. Go find this tapir pig guy."

I jumped to my feet. "You're absolutely right!"

Inez seemed surprised. "She is? Her parents and none of our teachers ever say that."

"Well, you are this time." I gave both girls a hug and asked if they needed a lift.

"Nah." Betty waved me off. "We thought we'd visit your neighbors for a little talking to."

The two girls walked away, with Inez smacking her brass-knuckled fist into her other hand. I probably should've stopped them, but I kind of wanted to see if they got results.

They were right. I should find Teo before he found me. What if he attacked my house and one of my poorly fed animals got hurt? No, I was taking this fight to the streets! I grabbed my bag, got in my van, and drove away.

"Riley," I said on speakerphone as I started up Main Street. "Any word about where Teo is staying in town?"

He sighed. "You're taking the fight to him, aren't you?"

"Of course." I decided not to say the girls suggested this. "It's a solid plan. It worked for us in Fiji."

He stifled a laugh. "That was just a couple of sailors who were drunk when we found them. It was easy dealing with them. This will be different. Teo is actively looking for you. Not like a few guys you'd insulted at a bar."

The sailors in question were Russian and were taking leave in Fiji, when Riley and I were on a brief break between gigs in Colombia and Okinawa. The sailors had been very rude to a couple of tourists at a bar. They thought they were hilarious since they believed no one spoke Russian. I insulted them in Russian, and they lost it. Maybe it was because I called them Putin's prison purses. The sailors threatened to beat me up, and I said something like "bring it on" before the bartender threw the sailors out and banned them from coming back.

The tourists had caught up with us later and said the sailors were out looking for us. Riley and I took the fight to them. It wasn't much of a fight. They'd had enough vodka to drown a small village. At any rate, they came to two days later in the streets of Bangkok, dressed like circus clowns with *kick me* on placards around their necks. Riley picked Thailand, but the rest was my idea. I wonder what ever happened to them.

"Pick me up. I'm going with you." Riley hung up before I could protest.

I really didn't want to do that because I didn't want anyone else getting hurt from being in my proximity. Then again, Riley was in the CIA with me. He might be able to help. At best, I could use him as a human shield.

Crap. I forgot my gun. I pulled into the parking lot and texted Riley to bring a couple.

Kelly followed him out and walked up to my window. The former ER nurse was now getting her PI license and working as a researcher.

"This is a terrible idea, you know," she told me.

"Blame Betty," I replied. "It was her idea."

Kelly looked away for a moment then back at me. "I will. Where is she?"

"Last I saw her, she was heading towards my neighbors' houses with Inez and a pair of brass knuckles." I hit the gas, and we flew backwards. As I stopped to shift into drive, I called out, "Good luck!"

"I had no luck with the hotels," Riley admitted once we were on the move. "I figure we should go there in person and show the management a photo of Teo."

"We might not have to do that," I said, my eyes locked on the windows of Feeling Lucky's House of Delights—an ice cream parlor in town.

"Why is that?" Riley tried to follow what I was looking at.

"Because he's right there." I pointed. "Having the French Tickler Naughty Éclair. The bastard."

CHAPTER FIVE

"Hi Teo," I said as I pulled out a seat and sat down.

Riley pulled up a chair on my right, between us. The Tapir looked different. Gone was the angry scowl I'd thought permanently etched into his face. He'd lost weight and was framed with lean muscle. Instead of fatigues, he was wearing a black polo shirt with cargo shorts and sport sandals. The long, wild black hair I remembered was now short and neatly trimmed. He had a mustache and a goatee that made him look more like a South American hipster than a gangster.

Teo brightened into a huge, sincere-looking smile as we joined him. "Finn! I've been looking for you, and here you are!"

"Here we are," I said casually as if I didn't have a care in the world. "This is Riley. We worked together back in the day."

The men exchanged greetings as Kayla, one of the teenage druids from the ineptly named Cult of NicoDerm, slouched over to take our orders.

"Bird Goddess," she said using my nickname. "The usual?"

"You have a usual?" Riley asked me.

I ignored him because that was a silly question. "Yes, thank you, Kayla. And bring me an Is That A Banana In Your Pants Banana Split for Riley here."

In case you're wondering, yes, this is an unusual ice cream parlor. Feeling Lucky's was opened by a retired copywriter for both the Victoria's Secret and Frederick's of Hollywood catalogs, who brought her old jobs with her. There were a few protests when she opened about immoral desserts with decadent names, but the ice cream was superb, so eventually the Lutheran Ladies for the Wholesome shut up about it.

"Bird Goddess?" Teo seemed intrigued.

"The kids in the Cult of NicoDerm think I can talk to birds," I said dismissively. "It's nothing."

"You live an interesting life here." Teo sat back in his seat, appearing to appraise me.

"Even more so with this unexpected visit from you," I replied. "To what do I owe the pleasure?"

Teo smiled warmly. He seemed different. Friendly. It was kind of terrifying. Years ago, I knew what to expect when we crossed paths. But this…was something different, and I wasn't sure if it was real.

He shrugged. "I wanted to see you after all these years. It's been too long, my old friend!"

Riley made eye contact with me and scratched his left ear. He was telling me to watch out. It was a nonverbal body language we'd developed back in the day. Or maybe he was telling me that the aardvark was ice skating at the nuclear plant again. It had been a long time. I might have been a tad rusty. Still, it was good advice, as you should never allow an aardvark to do *anything* at a nuclear plant.

"This is a friendly visit?" My eyebrows went up.

"Relax," Teo said softly. "I'm not in the business anymore. I started a rival cartel when you killed Carlos and made millions. Now I'm looking for a place in the States to retire to. And I thought if Finn can do it, and Riley also picked this place, so can I!"

So he knew who Riley was. He'd done some research.

"You don't think the CIA would react badly to a known drug lord settling down in small-town America?" Riley asked amiably.

"No," Teo laughed. "I sold out ten other cartels and made a deal. I'm good." He cocked his head to one side. "Isn't that what Americans say? I'm good?"

He *was* good. This sincere bestie stuff was a good act.

"So, how have you been?" Teo patted my hand.

It took all of my concentration not to rip it away. "Not bad."

"I hear you got married and your name is Merry now!" Teo nodded as Kayla deposited our desserts. "And you have a cult and talk to birds! How interesting! Perhaps I should look into membership!"

Kayla froze, eyes wide as she studied the man. No one ever wanted to join the Cult of NicoDerm. The kids had tried for years. She was just about to open her mouth when I cut her off and asked for more napkins. I'd have to explain later that she did not want this guy.

I dug into my Hot Fudge Hottie Sundae. Riley didn't touch his. He insisted on always eating healthy—which was boring. I only ordered it because I knew I'd get it after he rejected it.

"And you want to retire to Who's There, Iowa," I said.

"Why?" Riley asked what I was thinking. Not that we expected a truthful answer.

"Because it's good to know people in the place you plan to settle down in," Teo said.

"Teo." I set down my spoon. "We were never friends. You tried to blow me up. So forgive me if I'm not buying it."

"I know." Teo nodded. "But time and circumstances have changed. I don't hold it against you that you were a spy in our midst. You shouldn't hold my past against me. What's done is done. In fact, it was your connection that made it possible for me to make such a sweet deal. I should probably thank you."

"While that's a great philosophy and all," I said, "I'm still not buying it. Surely you know other people in other towns. What about Mateo the Matador? You guys were close."

"Dead," Teo said. "Gored by a bull."

Okay, that was fair. People in cartels didn't have the same lifespan as most folks, especially if they engaged in deadly hobbies like Mateo. "How about One-Handed Tim? Or Pedro the Pimple?"

"Accidentally shot himself trying to clean his gun left-handed," Teo answered. "Pedro died from one of those flesh-eating viruses."

"Chloe the Clownfish? Sharkface Shawn?" I continued.

"Poisoned by a sea anemone while spear fishing, and eaten by a shark…on the same trip. All dead. There's no one left. You are all I have now."

I saved the best for last. "How about Henrietta the Hernia?"

Teo's face turned red. "I couldn't stand that woman! She was a huge gossip, always twisting what anyone said and turning people against each other. I hope to never see her again."

Huh. I didn't know that about her. I wondered what she'd said about me.

"Well, she's here," Riley said smoothy. "In town. Just like you are."

We watched him carefully as I added, "Isn't that a not terribly believable coincidence?"

A look of horror crossed Teo's face. "Oh no! She's found me!"

"Found *you*?" I gasped.

Teo looked around nervously. "Well…I…that is…I owe her child support that I may accidentally have not paid for a few years."

"You had a kid with her?" I shook my head in disbelief. "Someone you hated?"

"Well…" He picked an invisible thread from his khaki shorts. "She was attractive. And you know how drunk everyone gets at the bi-monthly Capybara Roundup."

I did know that. The Capybara Roundup isn't so much about rounding up the world's largest rodent as it is a social weekend of drinking, debauchery, and shuffleboard. It was mandatory family fun for anyone in Carlos's crew. I avoided drinking to stay sharp, but I did play a lot of shuffleboard.

What was happening here? This wasn't what I'd expected. I thought the man was here to kill me, but he was acting like he was my best friend and confidant.

"We only knew each other for four months, Teo," I said evenly. "And we didn't get along during that time. Why would I believe you're here to develop a friendship?"

Teo thought, his face struggling for an answer, before he let out a breath. "Look, I know it doesn't make sense. I get that you're concerned. But the fact is, it gets lonely killing the people you know all the time. And while I didn't kill the friends you've mentioned, I'm serious about this. I don't know anyone else, and a lifetime of meaningless violence gives you a certain perspective."

I started scarfing down my sundae to stall, and to finish it so I could get started on Riley's. Teo must be pulling a fast one. He seemed sincere, but I didn't trust him.

"I know you don't trust me," Teo said as if reading my mind. "And you're right not to. I know I'll have to earn that trust to build a friendship. And I'd love it if you gave me the chance to try."

I didn't know what to say. This was too bizarre. Maybe I could try to give him a chance, at least long enough to find out what's going on. He was being polite. And I liked to reward politeness…

"Are you going to eat that?" Teo pointed to Riley's sundae.

Riley slid it to him. "Have at it, pal. Merry knows I don't eat like this. She does it to mess with me."

Hey! I wanted that sundae.

Teo laughed heartily. "I'm so looking forward to experience such things in a way where one prankster does not end up dead!"

The bell above the door tinkled, causing Kayla to sigh heavily at the thought of doing work.

Two large shadows loomed over us. Ron and Ivan stood behind me, arms folded, giving Teo the death stare.

"Merry, Mr. Riley," Ron said without taking his eyes off Teo. "Do you need your bodies to be guarded?"

"Is this bad guy?" Ivan asked.

Completely oblivious to the threatening cloud of toxic masculinity, Kayla sauntered over. "What'll ya have?"

Ron and Ivan smiled at her. "We will both have the Twin Pasty Hot Cream Pastries," Ron ordered. "Thank you, nice cult girl!"

They turned back to Teo, again looking menacing.

Teo smiled and offered his hand. "Teo ManTeo, a friend of Merry's. Any friend of Merry's is a friend of mine."

The two men broke into smiles and pulled up chairs. "Oh good!" Ivan said. "You are friend. Not dangerous pig elephant."

Teo looked at me curiously. "Pig elephant?"

"Otherwise known as a tapir," I said.

"Oh"—he waved us off—"that life is behind me now. I'm moving here to be near my friend Merry." He looked at the two men. "And you are?"

"I am Ron!" Ron shook Teo's hand. "And this is Ivan. We are from Chechnya. Also worked with Merry and came here when boss wanted to kill her. But he died, and we married sisters-in-law. Now all close family."

Teo slapped his hand on the table. "Yes! That's exactly what I'm doing too! It's so nice to see that it worked out for you, which means it will work out for me!"

Crap. The guys were right. I'd been spying on them, embedded with their gang, and they came here, presumably to help Wally get even, and ended up family. I hope Rex doesn't have another sister he hasn't told me about. We really shouldn't pair up our family with all the terrorists I used to know.

The pastries arrived, and while Teo ate Riley's sundae and the guys ate their desserts, they slapped each other on the backs as if they were old friends. It seemed so very wrong.

Riley scratched his right cheek. Either he was saying we were screwed or that someone had not cleaned their AR-14 in a while and as a result it might rust soon. At this point it didn't matter. Because now we had to figure out if Teo was telling the truth.

And I was going to need new bodyguards.

CHAPTER SIX

We left Ron, Ivan, and Teo behind to get acquainted. Back in the van, neither Riley nor I said anything for a few minutes. We just stared at the three former bad guys laughing it up inside.

"What the hell just happened?" I blurted out.

Riley shook his head. "I have no idea."

"We had him on the ropes," I continued. "Do you believe his ridiculous story?"

Riley took out his cell phone. "No messages from Ahmed at the CIA. Until we know the whole story, we need to be vigilant."

I agreed. "I just can't believe he's serious. The guy only knew me for four months and *hated* me."

"We have to consider all the possibilities." Riley massaged his temples. "There's the tiniest fraction of a percent that he might really be doing what he says. I need to find out if he's telling the truth about the deal."

I shook my head. "It's too far-fetched."

"Would you have ever guessed Ron and Ivan would come here and live?" Riley asked.

"No, but that's different. The three of us really were friendly in Chechnya. They thought of me as a little sister. It's a different story with Teo." I stared off into the distance. "I can't believe Chloe the Clownfish is dead. I mean, I get Sharkface Shawn. He was an idiot. But Chloe was kind of cool. She was impervious to poison ivy. Did you know that? That's how she got the nickname. I guess she wasn't impervious to sea anemones though…"

"Merry," Riley interrupted. "We can't rule out that Teo might have killed them all. When I hear from Ahmed, I'll run all those other names too. If they died the way he said they did, then we might consider he's telling the truth."

"What about Henrietta? Now we know he actually had a motive for killing her. And he was in town. I should've asked where he's staying."

The passenger doors opened, and Ron and Ivan hopped in. "That is easy. He said he is staying at boardinghouse."

I stared at them. "There aren't any boarding houses in Who's There! What is this, 1945?"

Riley spoke up. "Maybe they mean that he's staying at an Airbnb." He pulled up the app on his cell. "Look, there are ten houses for rent this month, with four that say they are booked. He might be in one of those."

"Send me the list," I said. "And guys, way to cave to the criminal in there."

Ron seemed surprised. "But he is nice."

"And like us," Ivan said. "He says he does not want to hurt you."

"Go home," I demanded.

The guys left the car dejectedly.

I told Riley, "I'll drop you back at the office. I want to look over my garage again. It's possible we all missed something."

I dropped Riley off and drove home. But when I pulled into my driveway, I noticed something else happening.

"Guys!" I shouted at the three druids dressed in robes. "What are you doing here?"

"We are going to do a cleansing spell," Heather explained.

Stewie and Mike were standing off to the side, pouting.

"We didn't want to do a stupid cleansing spell," Stewie, the short, rotund redhead squeaked. "That's ridiculous! I am the Dred Demon Odious!" He threw his hands in the air and wiggled his fingers in what most people would call jazz fingers. "I am the night!"

"Yeah." Mike slouched sullenly.

Heather's hands clenched into fists at her side. "Look! You morons said Kayla and I could do white witch stuff now and then, and you're gonna help!"

"The other Dred Demons will laugh at me!" Stewie despaired.

"Yeah," Mike said a little louder.

"Everyone laughs at us anyway!" Heather shrieked. "I'm tired of scrubbing graffiti off the Doom Chariot!" She motioned at an old hearse covered in chalkboard paint that was meant for hopeful suggestions but usually just had the word *Stewbutt* written all over it.

"I told you before," Heather insisted, "that we need to build our brand, and we can't do it if the same old crap isn't working."

"Hey." I stepped into the fray. They might be awkward adolescents, but they were *my* awkward adolescents, and I didn't like to see them fighting. "Let the ladies have their white…um, magic. Heather's probably right, and something new could help get recruits."

"No!" Stewie shouted, sounding like a tiny pug puppy. "We aren't going to change anything!"

"Well, I'm one of you," I reminded them. "And Heather, Kayla, and I can outvote you."

"You can't vote!" Stewie cried with more fear than confidence. "You're the Bird Goddess! You can't vote!"

"What? I didn't know that!" I was getting riled up.

Stewie gulped. "It's in the by-laws. You aren't a druid. You're just a goddess. Goddesses can't vote." He took a step back from me in fear.

"How does a demon overrule a goddess?" I asked.

"Yeah!" This time it came from Heather.

"You can't go!" Stewie sputtered at the girl. "We need you!"

"What about what I want to do?" Heather shrieked.

Stewie and Mike had been developing some rather misogynistic tendencies lately, and frankly, I was sick of it.

I folded my arms over my chest. "You let the girls come up with rituals, or I'm leaving."

Stewie stuck out his chin petulantly. "No!"

I did not like being told no by a teenager. "Then I quit!"

"Me too!" Heather stripped off her druid robe and dumped it on top of my garbage can. "And furthermore, Kayla quits too!" She did a pantomime of Kayla dropping her robe…if she weren't here and serving a known killer at Feeling Lucky's.

"No! You can't!" Stewie's voice rose to a pitch only dogs could hear. "You signed the blood oath!"

Heather walked over and towered over him. "That was ketchup! So it doesn't count!"

Mike's Adam's apple trembled. "You know Stewie faints at the sight of blood!"

The girl took the keys from her purse, got in the Doom Chariot, and drove away.

"How are we gonna get home?" Mike asked.

"Walk," I said as I turned and crossed the street, going into my house and slamming the door.

"Bird Goddess!" Stewie's face was plastered to my front window. "Don't forsake us in our hour of need!"

"Yeah!" Mike's nose was smashed against the glass.

Philby raced out of the room and returned moments later wearing the werewolf mask. She'd been waiting for this moment all of her life. She jumped into the window, hissing violently.

The two teenage boys screamed and ran away.

I high-fived her. The fat feline führer had my back.

Our garage was tidy, and it was not because of me. I took more of a *disaster in a third world country* approach to garage organization, which probably resulted in the fire across the street. I wasn't a slob or anything. It was just easier to dump stuff in the garage with the vague promise of organizing it later. I was always going to get around to it. Now, considering the burned-out shell across the street, it seemed like I'd have that opportunity. Hey! This now seemed like a glass half full type of situation. It's always easier to organize a garage when you've lost everything in it to a fire.

Rex was a bit of a neat, orderly guy. I tried not to hold that against him, and deep down inside I kind of liked it. As I stood there, measuring things up, I had to wonder why there wasn't more of a mess. If Teo tracked Henrietta here and they fought, which Henrietta would do to avoid being killed, why wasn't everything in a shambles?

At least there wasn't any blood. That stuff was impossible to clean up. I moved a few boxes around, peeking inside in case I should find the weapon neatly stored away. Then again, I had no idea how she died, so how could I know what the weapon was?

It could be a hypodermic needle. Perhaps an air bubble was injected into her veins. If I'd wanted to kill someone without a mess, that's what I'd do. I became more careful in my search, slipping on a pair of thick rubber gloves used for cleaning gutters.

I was just moving the last box when I heard a ping, like something metal hitting the ground. In a garage, that could mean anything from a nail to a wing nut. But what if it was a clue?

Nothing was on the floor that I could see. Maybe it rolled under the workbench. Getting down on my hands and knees, I lowered my head and looked under. There was something there. Maintaining eye contact with the item, I reached underneath, and my fingers closed on something round.

I withdrew my hand and looked. It was a ring. A heavy, silver ring, with a long arrow carved around the outside. There was some sort of inscription on it, but the engraving was faded from years of wear. Rex kept an old magnifying glass out here. Where was it?

A few minutes later, I found it and held it up to the inside of the ring. There was script inside, but it was still too worn down to read. It wasn't mine. And the size made me think it belonged to a man.

I opened up a folding camp chair and sat down to think. The ring wasn't Rex's. I was sure that I'd never seen it before. It could have been the killer's or Henrietta's. Sliding my finger through it, I realized it could fit a man or a woman. This seemed to be a clue of some sorts. But whose finger did it belong to?

Grabbing my bag, I jumped in the van and headed to the hospital for answers.

"Hi Merry!" Soo Jin greeted me the minute I walked into the morgue. "I'll bet you're here about Henrietta, right?"

I handed her the ring. "I found this and wondered if it was hers. It could've fallen to the floor in a struggle."

Soo Jin put on latex gloves and then held the ring up to the light. "The arrow is interesting. The script is very worn down. I doubt if we can figure it out, but I'll send it to the lab anyway."

I made an appeal. "I want to know if it fits her hand. It could belong to the killer."

Soo Jin left the office for the lab, and I followed. She walked over to a cooler and opened the door, sliding out Henrietta's body.

"As you know," Soo Jin said, "when it's colder, rings can be loose and slip off. So bear that in mind."

I watched as Soo Jin lifted the dead woman's hand and placed it on her ring finger. It slid on easily and was loose. Next, the medical examiner put the ring on the middle and index fingers. The ring went on, but in each of these cases, it wasn't a perfect fit. Finally, she tried the thumb, which appeared to be an exact fit. Then she tried the other hand with the same results.

"I guess you have your answer." Soo Jin frowned.

I took several photos of the ring, feeling a little guilty that I hadn't told Rex first. I'd have to let him know that I'd found it and it was already headed to forensics. At least I saved him a step. That seemed like a small win.

That was only part of my reason for coming here. But I think she knew that.

"It's enough. People wear rings that are too big for their ring finger. And this seems like a man's ring."

My friend nodded. "I'm glad you brought it in. It could belong to the killer—whose DNA I haven't found yet."

My eyebrows went up. "You're ruling out natural causes, then?"

"It was murder all right," Soo Jin slid the body back inside and closed the door. "I found a needle mark on her right arm. "Venous air embolism. She was injected with an air bubble. It found its way to the brain, and she stroked out."

I was right! I wanted to high five Soo Jin but thought that might look bad.

"Was there anything in her clothing? A wallet or ID of some sort?"

Soo Jin shook her head. "Nothing. Are you sure you know the deceased? If it's been a long time since you've seen her, we might need a second identification."

"Riley and I both thought so, and he'd only seen pictures of her. The hernias are a tell. I think I know someone else who can help," I said slowly. "But he might be the killer, so that might not be the best idea?"

I filled her in on Teo, from our contentious relationship to his wanting to be my friend.

"I don't know if he'd be considered reliable, but we should give it a try." She held up one finger. "But you have to tell Rex. Merry, is this the guy who Riley thinks wants to kill you?"

"Yes," I said quickly. "But I'm not convinced that's what he's here for. Can I bring him in to ID Henrietta?"

Soo Jin gave a rare warning. "You have to tell Rex. And don't come back without him. I know I let you do a lot of things that would get someone like me fired. But this could mean your life is in danger, and I won't put up with that."

"Thanks!" I threw my arms around her and then left before she could change her mind.

She wasn't wrong. For years, Soo Jin has given me all kinds of intel, and I'm guessing Rex told her he was mostly okay with it. If she had an ultimatum this time, I was going to follow it.

I called Ivan when I got in the car. Sure enough, he had Teo's phone number, and he invited Rex and me to a cookout. I crossed my fingers, hoping this would be the moment that the twins would tell Rex they were pregnant. I wasn't sure I could keep this secret much longer, and I didn't think it was fair of Randi to insist that I do so. I was already lying to my husband about a bunch of stuff. I didn't want to lie to him about this.

Using the number Ivan gave me, I called Teo. He didn't answer. I left a message asking him to call me as soon as he could.

By the time I got to the police station, I'd decided to come clean about everything, in hopes that Rex would allow me to be there when Teo ID'd Henrietta. I waved hello to Troy Wallace, Rex's competent officer, and passed by Kevin, who was eating a whole box of Hostess cupcakes while filling out some form that was now covered in chocolate.

"How's Hamlet?" I asked.

Kevin looked at me with hooded eyes and cream filling on his nose. "Okay."

"Who's Hamlet?" Troy asked, probably hoping to finally get some personal insight into the enigma that was Kevin Dooley.

"About one hundred hamsters," I said as I breezed past.

Recently, I'd learned that Kevin had a lot of pet hamsters, all named Hamlet, living in tanks in his apartment.

"Hamlet's good," Kevin said slowly. "So's Hamlet, Hamlet, Hamlet, Hamlet…"

I went into Rex's office before he could finish. My husband greeted me with a smile, and I plunked down in the chair opposite him. Kevin's voice carried as he was still saying the name Hamlet over and over. Glancing through the doorway, I spotted a confused Troy, who was most likely now very sorry he'd asked.

"Did you get hold of Troy's friend?" I turned to Rex.

Officer Wallace had been trying to find a job for a friend of his, and Rex was hopeful he could make it happen. Troy was a competent cop, which was the exact opposite of what my husband experienced with Kevin. The idea of having two good officers working with him had been irresistible.

"I talked to her this morning to set up an interview. But this is all contingent on waiting for the mayor to give budget approval. Can you put in a good word?" he wondered.

This was something I could do for him. "We have a Scout meeting tomorrow, so I'll make sure of it. Although, greasing Betty's palm might make it go faster."

"Bribes of elected officials are illegal," Rex reminded me.

"Yeah, well, if there's a way around it, Betty's found it by now." I got up and closed the door. "I have news. Riley and I found Teo."

Rex didn't look happy. The man knew I could take care of myself, but I could tell he wasn't thrilled that some guy who'd once tried to kill me had tracked me down. I continued, telling him about the ring in the garage. When I finished, he steepled his fingers.

"You found a piece of evidence and took it straight to Soo Jin?"

"Of course I did." I tried to look insulted.

"Wow," my husband said. "While I should give you a hard time for not bringing it straight to me, I'm impressed that you didn't just keep it for yourself."

"Why would I do something like that?" Besides the fact that I'm always doing something like that?

Rex just gave me a look that indicated that he wasn't buying it. I apologized and promised to do better—hoping I would actually follow through next time.

"Do you think," Rex mused, "that Ron and Ivan befriended Teo to keep an eye on him or because they actually think he's their friend?"

"Sadly"—I shook my head—"I'm pretty sure it's the last one. Ivan and Ron are too friendly for their own good. They once made friends with a Russian who was just cozying up to them so he could kill their boss. Fortunately, Wally had me and I figured it out before Vlad had a chance to kill him."

Rex appeared to be confused. "Weren't they Wally's muscle? Wasn't that their job?"

I laughed. "No. I mean, yes, they were his muscle and very good at beating people up for him, but they were terrible at security. Anyone who smiled at them could get past them."

Rex looked out the window. "Well, that's good and bad, I guess."

I changed the subject. "I called Teo and left a message. You'll want to meet him, so I'll arrange it."

"No need." He waved me off.

"Really?" I leaned forward eagerly. Was he going to let me take Teo to identify Henrietta's body?

My husband looked wary. "Yeah. He's going to be at the cookout at my sister's place tonight."

CHAPTER SEVEN

"You look worried." Rex reached over and held my hand as I sat in the car in front of Randi and Ronni's place, holding a bowl of potato salad. "I don't think he'll try anything here."

"I'm not." I was. "If Teo so much as moves funny with you, Ron, and Ivan there, I don't think he'll survive to try dessert. Well, unless Ronni tries to help him. But I think I can take her. Especially since…" I froze.

I was going to say since she's pregnant. We were going to an event where everyone but Teo and my husband knew his sisters were both knocked up.

For some reason, Rex acted as though he hadn't heard the last part. He got out of the car and came around to help me out. Steeling myself with the potato salad as my armor, I headed up the steps to Ferguson's Taxidermy.

I'd knowingly walked into potentially dangerous situations before. I once accompanied Wally, Ron, and Ivan to a warlord retreat on the Black Sea, knowing that some of the members of the Yakuza I'd just been undercover with would be there. Fortunately, the vodka at the event was so strong I was able to convince Botan and Dai that I was merely a hallucination. They played tetherball with me for two hours one day and still believed I wasn't real. I won all four matches too.

This, however, was different. This was even scarier. Because this was *family*.

Teo was already in the backyard in a Hawaiian shirt, khaki shorts, and flip flops. He looked relaxed. Too relaxed. He was drinking a beer and joking with Ron while Ivan flipped burgers on the grill.

"Merry! Rexley!" Randi ran over and hugged us both. "So glad you could make it on short notice!"

I hugged her back and asked her what to do with the potato salad, while Rex went over to introduce himself to Teo. He'd told me on the way here he wanted to meet him without me so he could get a sense of whether or not I was exaggerating. Whatever that means.

"Let's get it inside." Randi pulled me into the back of the house to the kitchen.

The tall, Victorian house was the first home built in Who's There, by the Peterson family who'd founded the town with a bar and a lumber business, in that order. The twins didn't change it much, except to turn the entryway and living room into a display area for their anthropomorphized taxidermy.

It took a special person to appreciate the work Randi and Ronni did. The twins specialized in taking animals and creating scenarios where they behaved as humans. At the moment, there was a wildebeest in a black suit, stovepipe hat, and bifocals, teaching five sheep, sitting at desks, about the Louisiana Purchase. Next to that was a group of moray eels dressed as retirees playing pickleball while an angry llama refereed.

They weren't all large dioramas. On a table just before the kitchen was a small building that appeared to be on fire, with dozens of mice in lab coats running out, arms up, screaming.

"What's that one for?" I asked my sister-in-law as we passed into the kitchen.

"That's for a business. They wanted scenes depicting their safety policies. This one is called *No Matches on the Floor of the Ether Factory, Please*. It turned out really good, didn't it?" She frowned. "Oh wait, something's missing. Hold on."

Randi reached around behind the building and brought out a lop-eared rabbit dressed as Godzilla who was aiming his laser eyes at the building.

"Client in Japan?" I asked. In spite of having an actual store, most of their clients ordered online and were from, you guessed it, Japan.

"That's right." Randi pushed a strand of hair out of her face. "They didn't ask for this, but we thought it would be a fun touch. Nine times out of ten, they request a Godzilla."

I followed her to the fridge, where I shelved the potato salad. Glancing out the window to make sure Rex was still with the boys, I lowered my voice.

"When are you two going to tell Rex?" I asked. "This is a really hard secret to keep."

"Soon." Randi smiled and patted my arm. "We just want to wait for the right time."

I stared at her. "And when would that be?"

"When our parents are home, of course. They're in Greece right now."

Oh. I didn't know that. Rex's parents owned a Greek restaurant in Des Moines. They were the nicest people you'd ever want to meet, which explained why Rex and Randi were so good-natured. I always wondered if Ronni had been a changeling sired by the devil.

Speaking of the devil, guess who chose this time to walk into the kitchen? Ronni spotted me, and her glare turned icy.

"I guess we had to invite you if we wanted Rex to come," she grumbled. "I don't know what my sister, Ron, and Ivan see in you, or that Teo for that matter. I think you're the absolute worst!"

"Yes, I know. It's nice to see you too," I said.

"Ronni," Randi chastised. "You leave Merry alone. She's never been anything but nice to you!"

Randi always stood up for me. It never helped. Ronni just hated me. I never really knew why, although my friend Hilly told me it had something to do with the fact that these older women somehow found themselves pregnant at a late age.

"What do you think of Teo?" I ventured.

Randi turned to me as she chopped up some watermelon. "Oh, he's lovely. It's nice for the boys to meet someone like themselves."

Out the window, I noticed that Ron and Rex were now sitting, chatting with Teo. Rex was smart. He'd have this guy's number and tell me if he thought I had something to worry about. He was very good at reading people.

I was too, but in cases like this, where I had a past with the person, things got fuzzy. When espionage turned into friendship, things got a little squiffy.

"I don't know why he didn't kill you in Colombia!" Ronni snapped.

"Then we never would've met our husbands," Randi reminded her sister. "If it wasn't for Merry, we'd be single still."

That stopped her in her tracks as she struggled to find a way for that to be bad. "It's her fault we're knocked up!"

I looked at Ronni with surprise. "You're not happy about the pregnancy?"

"Of course we are," Randi said. "It's a miracle! We never thought it would ever happen."

"*I* never thought it would happen," I said without meaning anything by it. "Pregnant. Wow."

Rex walked into the kitchen at that moment, and I thought that now the jig was up and the girls would have to tell their brother. He had to have heard them. But his face was a mask of casual indifference—a look he saved for interrogations when he wanted the perp to confess.

"Rexley!" Randi fanned herself. "You startled us! How long have you been there?"

He shrugged. "I literally just walked in. Ivan says he needs his special spices?"

Rex gave me a very brief glance that convinced me he'd heard us and would be asking questions later. I gave him a tiny nod.

Ronni hugged her brother, and over his shoulder, she narrowed her eyes at me, kind of resembling the rabbity Godzilla in the other room.

I grabbed a jar on the counter that had a label with Ivan's Special Spices handwritten on it. Then I dragged my husband into the other room.

"What do you think about Teo?" I whispered.

"Teo?" Rex asked for just a moment before he recovered, no doubt his mind was on hearing the news that his sisters were pregnant. "Oh. He's being very charming, but I can't quite get a read on what his intentions are."

I nodded. "It's hard, isn't it? I mean, part of me really wants to think he's come in peace and means what he says, but my spydy senses are a bit off."

"Not tingling?" Rex pulled me into his arms and gave me a very long, passionate kiss.

I pulled away, gasping. "Well, they are now! How long do we have to stay here?"

My husband grinned. "At least until after we eat. Besides, it's very important to me that I know you are completely safe. I'll need more time with Teo to do that." He held me at arm's length. "No matter what happens, we'll get through this together." Then he pulled me into a hug.

That was nice! I mean, I didn't need a man to protect me from Teo, but it still gave me a warm feeling to know Rex had my back. We pulled apart when Ronni barked from the kitchen that she needed help carrying things outside.

Dinner was served at two picnic tables pushed together.

"Teo." Rex passed him the salt. "Are you serious about living here?"

Teo smiled warmly. "Of course! It seems that I have already made lots of friends! It's like I have a family. Just like the old days, right Finn...I mean Merry?"

Yeah. Just like the old days where you tried to kill me, I thought to myself.

"Have you thought what you'd like to do as a job?" I asked.

Ron shook his head. "You cannot work as guy who hurts people. They do not like that here."

Ivan agreed. "You have to find wife with great business so you can help! It is interesting. I lifted whole wildebeest yesterday." He frowned. "Sadly, it was dead. But my wife will make into something nice!" He put an arm around Randi and kissed the top of her head.

Randi responded by giggling.

"I suppose"—Teo poured ketchup on his burger—"I will get bored not doing anything. I really don't need the money. After I've been here a while, perhaps I'll find some sort of job."

"You don't need the money?" Rex asked.

Teo laughed. "No. I'm set for life, really. Kind of like Merry when she retired."

He obviously didn't want to tell Rex his money came from drug distribution, and I wasn't about to correct him.

We chatted about nothing through dinner, with Ron and Ivan telling Teo about all the things they thought were weird when they got here.

"Nice bathrooms," Ivan said. "They have very few goats though."

Ron agreed. "Is not a bonus. But there are hundreds of TV channels!"

Ivan brightened. "Yes! That is good!"

"And when they say 'I am going to kill you,'" Ron added, "they do not mean it."

"That is odd," Ivan agreed. "But there are many houses, and if you do have goats, you do not take them inside with you."

"I thought I'd get a little cottage of sorts," Teo said. "Nothing fancy. Nothing too big. Just a little house with a yard like this. We didn't really have nice yards. Too many chickens and not enough lawn care, I'm afraid."

"Did you know that they do not use chickens to wake you in morning?" Ron asked. "Is a thing I miss."

"I'd like to have a garden," Teo continued. "And a couple of chairs and a table. That would be nice. Especially not hearing gunfire every day."

"You won't hear much of that around here," Randi soothed. "It's a very quiet little town."

"It would be," Ronni sneered, "if Merry would quit killing people!"

Teo looked at me with interest.

"Don't mind Ronni," I sighed. "There are *some* murders now and then, but I've never killed anyone here." *Well, no good guys.*

Ron put his arm around his wife to calm her down. I had no idea what the man saw in her. Then again, I wasn't sure what the twins saw in the Chechens.

"We have had comic book cons," Ivan said. "Merry was Beetle Dork." He held out his phone, showing a picture of me as a giant beetle. "And we had conspiracy people."

"And Big Foot!" Ron added. "And there was a war in the country."

"A Civil War re-enactment," I corrected. "The Battle of Idiot Creek."

"And Merry runs a troop of little girl militia fighters," Ron said. "One of them is mayor!"

Teo looked at me with interest.

"Girl Scouts," I corrected a bit more strenuously this time. "They have Girl Guides in Colombia. Not militia. But yes, one of them is the mayor."

"Is not true," Ivan challenged. "Betty is in troop, and she is scary!"

"Training to be assassin," Ivan said.

"I guess it's hard to stop doing what you love." Teo grinned at me. "A militia! Made up of little girls! And one of them is a strongman!"

"No," I started. "That isn't true…"

Ivan clapped. "Yes! Betty is like Wally except for he was bald and old and sold weapons to terrorists. Betty is just as scary but very small and a girl."

I was starting to take exception to the idea that girls couldn't be despotic leaders. Wait…what was I thinking?

Randi, Ronni, and their husbands got up to clear the table while Rex got the firepit ready for s'mores. I pulled Teo aside to where Rex was. Anticipating what I was going to say, Rex stood and studied the man's face.

"I have to tell you something," I said quietly. "I wasn't lying about Henrietta being here."

Teo flinched too quickly for it to be faked. "I would like to avoid her. Do you think she would get Riley to serve me with papers?"

I shook my head. "I doubt it. She's dead."

Teo fainted clean away.

"That didn't go how I expected," I mumbled to my husband as he bent down to rouse the man.

"What do you think?" I asked Rex back at home.

My husband scratched Leonard, our Scottish deerhound between the ears absently. "It's complicated. If he's lying, then he's very convincing. On the other hand, he seemed sincere. He answered my questions immediately, taking no time to pause and think of what to say. His reaction to hearing about Henrietta was convincing, and frankly, his body language was spot on."

I slumped next to him on the couch. "Yeah. It's really hard to tell, isn't it? I hate that. It's so much easier when they act more true to their original nature." I sat up straight. "We can give him a polygraph! I think I've got one in the basement across the street." I frowned. "Of course, I haven't kept up with the latest advances in the technology, but I think I could pull it off."

"You should add that to the list of things you're hiding from me." He waited a moment. "Maybe he's really changed?" Rex suggested.

"Lana hadn't changed," I said, mentioning an old adversary. "She'd fooled me."

"Yes," Rex said, "but Ron and Ivan worked out." He thought about this for a moment. "Mostly, anyway."

"I guess it's possible that Teo could be like them." I tapped my chin absently. "But if I'm wrong and let my guard down…" I made explosion sounds, throwing my hands in the air for emphasis.

Rex frowned. I didn't like it when he did that. He was still as handsome as ever, but it meant he was seriously worried. My husband was a calm, relaxed person who made people feel at ease. The frown did not put me at ease.

"I'll take him to identify the body. Then I'm going to bring him in for questioning," Rex decided.

"Okay. I'll watch from the observation room!" This was going to be like working a case together!

My husband held up his hands. "No."

My mouth dropped open. "No?"

Rex seemed a little surprised that I needed to ask. "This guy may have tried to murder you and frame you for the murder of Henrietta. Technically speaking, I should remove myself from the investigation due to my involvement with you."

"Who'd investigate?" I wondered. "Surely not Kevin. And you wouldn't want the Feds brought in."

"Troy might be able to handle it…" He seemed unsure.

"You've never recused yourself from a case because of me before," I pointed out. "Why now?"

"Because I'm the only detective this town has. And Sheriff Carnack is busy dealing with another issue."

I held up my hands. "Don't recuse yourself. I won't watch the interrogation. But if you want, I have some things we used in the CIA that might make Teo talk. I'm sure my rubber hose, electrodes, and lucky waterboarding gear weren't in the garage."

He shook his head. "No thanks. I'm not going to waterboard him. He's just a person of interest. And if you are serious about staying out of this one, I'll keep working on it."

"Fine." I grabbed my cell, feigning getting a message. "Uh-oh! Kelly has a Scouting emergency. Don't wait up!" After a quick kiss, I ran out the door.

Once I got in my van, I drove away without any real destination. Kelly hadn't texted. I just didn't want Rex to make me pinky swear to keep out of the investigation.

I drove to a random neighborhood, parked on the street, and turned off the engine because I just needed time to think. Rex was absolutely right. Pressuring him to involve me in the investigation was a bad idea.

Teo's behavior and decision to retire here was messing with my mind. There was no comparison with Ron and Ivan moving here because they liked me in Chechnya, and they weren't as smart as Teo. I didn't like how easily he'd cozied up to my family. They'd accepted him far too easily, which was another problem.

Maybe I was being too harsh. It could be possible that Teo was telling the truth. The problem with that theory were the coincidences of his arrival and Henrietta's murder. It just didn't make sense unless he was the one who killed her.

Would it really be that awful if he was legit? If he wanted to live here like he'd said? Was Who's There big enough to become a terrorist expat community? I'd better keep that to myself. It would be bad if the CIA caught wind of it. They'd want to move everyone here.

"What's up?" Hilly Vinton opened the passenger door and slid in.

I looked around. "Where did you come from?"

Hilly cocked her head to one side. "The other side of this door, obviously."

"Don't you ever work anymore?" I asked. It seemed like a fair question.

Hilly was always popping into the middle of Iowa for no reason, and she still worked for the CIA. Hilly was an assassin who wasn't an assassin because that is illegal and the CIA doesn't do that, except for the fact that they totally did. It's a disclaimer I had to make even in retirement.

"Of course I do," she laughed. "I just had a job in Honduras. This was on the way to my next gig in Iceland, so I thought I'd drop by for a visit."

"Who's There is hardly on the way between Honduras and Iceland," I deadpanned.

Hilly looked at me as if I was crazy. "It is if you go the most obvious route."

It just wasn't worth arguing about. She'd used this argument with me before. Who's There, many geographers would be startled to realize, was in the middle of a direct route between Alaska and Russia, Disney World Florida and Disney Land Paris, and in one I still disagreed with—Kansas City, Kansas and Kansas City, Missouri.

"Betty called. Said you needed some straightening out," Hilly said, interrupting my thoughts.

Betty was going to get some straightening out. "Did you ever do any work in Colombia?" I asked.

Hilly rolled her eyes. "Of course! And I heard Teo the Tapir is in town."

"You know him?"

She lifted her hand, palm facing down, and wiggled it. "Sort of. He was one of my assignments back in the day. CIA called it off though."

That got my attention. "Why did they call it off?"

"Because you were there." Hilly shrugged. "They thought it might make you look bad."

That seemed uncharacteristically nice of the CIA. "They didn't reinstate the assignment after I left?"

Hilly appeared surprised by this as well. "If they did, they didn't give it to me."

"Do you recall why you were supposed to take him out?" I couldn't believe I didn't know this.

The assassin thought about this for a moment. "It had something to do with Carlos the Armadillo. I can't remember what it was."

That was strange. The CIA wanted to kill Teo because of Carlos but rescinded the assignment because of me. That almost never happened as far as I was aware.

"So?" Hilly studied my expression.

"So what?"

She rolled her eyes. "Do you want me to finish the job?"

It was tempting. But if Teo really was trying to turn over a new leaf and was of no threat to me… "No. At least, not yet."

"Well…" Hilly stretched her arms. "I'll stick around in case you change your mind."

"You really don't have to. I'm fine."

She opened the door and got out. "See you tomorrow!"

"What's tomorrow?"

"Your troop meeting?" Hilly rolled her eyes again. "Man! You really are losing it!"

And with that she left.

CHAPTER EIGHT

———

The troop met at my old house in the summers and sometimes during the school year. Fortunately, only the garage was in tatters, and technically the fire marshal hadn't condemned us, so we could still meet in the house. The next morning, I went over early to get set up. And since I wanted to make sure no one blew up any other part of the house with us in it, I decided to set up two card tables in the backyard. Kelly was bringing the all-important snack, and I was responsible for any materials we needed.

We'd discussed social media usage with the girls before, but now they were older and going into sixth grade, so we thought we'd revisit the topic. Saying that the Boy Scouts had monkey butts was one thing when they were eight. Now, on the verge of being teenagers, we'd decided to touch on some subjects a little more seriously. By the way, Boy Scouts do have monkey butts. It just isn't a good idea to say that on TikTok.

The girls arrived almost all at once. Kelly didn't even raise her eyebrows when she spotted Hilly. She'd given up on keeping the quirky assassin out long ago, mainly because Hilly completely ignored the request. Besides, Hilly could use the socialization. She was like a puppy who didn't have a filter, if that puppy was a stone-cold killer.

Kelly had the girls sit in a circle. "We are going to talk about using social media, and later we are going to set up a troop page."

"We are?" I inadvertently said out loud.

"You knew about this," Kelly muttered under her breath.

"Oh right. Of course."

"See?" Betty said to Hilly. "She's losing it."

Hilly nodded.

One of the Kaitlyns raised her hand. "Mom says we're too young to have Facebook accounts."

Kelly nodded. "It's best to wait until you're older, but most kids don't, which is why we are talking about this now."

"As mayor," Ava announced. She announced everything these days, as if she was making a public statement to *60 Minutes*. "I have a social media platform. I'm on Facebook, Twitter, Instagram, and Betty Vision. And we are looking into TikTok."

"Betty Vision?" Did Betty have a social media platform of her own?

"It's new," Inez said. "It'll be a hit."

"It's not ready," Betty said. "And we can't tell you anything more about it because you are old."

"We're not too old," I protested. "We are just the right age for…Betty whatever."

"This is exactly why we need to talk about this," Kelly insisted. "The question is, are you old enough to handle social media? You not only think the answer is *yes*, but that you can invent a social media platform."

"Yeah," I said. "I'm not too old. You're too young."

Hilly raised her hand, and Kelly nodded at her. "Why can't they start their own social media platform?"

"Excellent question," Kelly said. "We've talked about social media before, but I want to think about what the platforms have to offer girls your age. Let's get into four groups of two."

The four Kaitlyns divided themselves into twos. Ava and Inez partnered up, leaving Lauren and Betty together. Kelly told them they each had a platform to look at and analyze, and we'd discuss it in ten minutes.

"I don't have a partner," Hilly complained.

"You're not in the troop," Kelly said.

"Can you believe they think we're too old for Betty's thing?" I grumbled.

"Merry, focus," Kelly said calmly. "We need to get the girls thinking critically about this. It's important."

"Sorry," I apologized. "I'm just a bit distracted. Remind me why we are doing this again."

"Because of what happened a couple of weeks ago…" Kelly wiggled her eyebrows as if that would jog my memory.

"Oh. That."

"What happened?" Hilly asked.

"Betty created a Facebook page for the Cult of NicoDerm," I said quietly. "And ended up summoning a demon."

Hilly whistled. "That's impressive!"

"Fortunately, it wasn't a real demon," I explained further. "Just a really creepy guy named Willard."

"He *thought* he was a demon and got a bit too interested in the two teenage girls," Kelly reminded me.

"He's gone, so it doesn't matter," I insisted.

Betty had set up the Facebook page and, as a recruitment technique, invited people to join the cult. Only one person accepted—Demon Willard, a very strange thirtysomething guy with tattoos everywhere. He really did look like an actual demon. Stewie and Mike were thrilled, but Heather and Kayla found Willard too weird for words and threatened to quit.

To make a long story short, after a lot of complaints by people in town, Rex had a little chat with Willard. Then I had a "little chat" with him in my basement, which may or may not have included promises of things that have electrodes and attach to sensitive places. He ended up leaving town—and the state, according to the tracker I put on his car, if it's still working. Apparently, he's in Florida now.

"A demon, huh?" Hilly mused. "Might come in handy in my line of work."

Before I could ask her how, Kelly spoke up. "What's going on with the Teo situation?"

I filled her in on how Teo went from being confronted at Feeling Lucky's to becoming one of the family at the cookout.

"You invited someone who tried to kill you to a cookout?" Hilly's eyebrows went up.

"No." I lowered my voice. "Ron and Ivan did. And Ronni was a little too happy to comply. Pregnancy hasn't softened her up any."

"The twins are pregnant?" Kelly's jaw dropped open.

"I didn't tell you?" Now I felt bad. Kelly was my bestie. "Well, I was told to keep it under wraps from Rex, so I just kept my mouth shut with everyone, I guess."

"You should've told your best friend," Hilly glowered.

I held my hands up defensively. "You're right. I should have."

"I mean," Hilly continued, "I get why you didn't tell Kelly, but me?"

"What are you talking about?" I asked the assassin. "You already knew about this because they told you!"

"Huh," the assassin said. "I forgot about that."

"At their age," my co-leader mused, "it's kind of a miracle."

I fidgeted uncomfortably. "I'm feeling pretty guilty about not telling Rex. He's going to be disappointed that I knew before he did. For a moment at the cookout, I thought he'd overheard me talking to the twins about it, but I guess he didn't."

Kelly stifled a smile. "So that's why he asked me if I knew any reason why you might be acting strangely."

I looked at her curiously. "What do you mean?"

"Hey!" Hilly spoke up. "Merry's not acting any weirder than she normally does."

Kelly began to laugh. "He must've overheard something, because I'm guessing he thinks you're the one who's pregnant!"

Hilly took a step back and looked me up and down. "You can't be!"

Rex thought I was pregnant? Oh no. He must really feel betrayed if he thinks I'd talk to his sisters before telling him!

"Merry's not pregnant," Kelly hissed. She grabbed me by both arms. "You have to tell him."

"It's not my news to tell!" I protested.

"You owe your husband more loyalty than your in-laws." Kelly shook her head. "I told you before I told my family, but Robert knew right after you. Trust me on this."

"Ronni will hate me even more than she does now…" Something I didn't think was even possible.

"You have to tell him," Kelly said. "Or I will."

I perked up. "Hey! That could work for me! I told the twins I wouldn't tell Rex, but they didn't ask me not to tell *you*."

Kelly looked me in the eye.

"Okay," I said, backing down. "I'll tell him."

"What are you going to tell who?" Betty asked. "And why are your fingers crossed behind your back?"

The girls had come into the room quietly and were standing around us in a circle.

"Nothing," I said. "Let's get back to the meeting. Time for your presentations! Who's first?"

Two Kaitlyns got up.

"Facebook," one of them said, "is where old people can see pictures of their grandkids and talk to other old people. It's useful so that we don't have to constantly send pictures to our grandparents and they aren't lonely anymore."

The other Kaitlyn held up a picture of two old women hunched over and knitting while they talked to each other about their grandkids.

"Those women are really old," one of the Kaitlyns felt the need to explain. "They're like, forty."

"But it isn't just for old people," Kelly protested. "I'm on it. So are my friends."

The two Kaitlyns looked at each other but wisely said nothing.

I clapped my hands. "Who's next?"

The other two Kaitlyns got up, and one of them said, "Twitter is where politicians get into arguments with regular people. It isn't useful because who cares what politicians have to say? And you can only use one hundred and forty characters, which is way lame."

"Hey!" Ava complained. "I'm a politician!"

The other Kaitlyn spoke up. "All politicians are lame except for Ava, who is awesome."

This seemed to appease the mayor, because she gave a short nod and sat down.

These two Kaitlyns showed a picture of a tall, bald, angry man in a top hat and a button that said *Politician*, yelling at a bunch of people who were on their computers.

"We did this before we thought about the Ava thing," the first one acknowledged.

"Interesting interpretation," Kelly said. "Very clever of you to see that politicians use Twitter a lot."

Inez and Ava were next. Inez stood up.

"We had Instagram, which is supposed to be about pretty pictures but is kind of like the new Facebook. Lots of celebrities use Instagram. We consider it useful because we like movie stars."

Ava held up a picture of herself wearing a sash that said *Mayor*, being admired by a roomful of people.

"How does that portray Instagram?" I asked.

The mayor looked at me as if I was an idiot. "Because Instagram likes pictures, and this is a good one."

The other girls nodded, so I went along with it, just to show them I wasn't old.

Kelly said, "You are right…Instagram started out being about photos and is used by a lot of celebrities. But the picture isn't really germane to the assignment."

"Ava insisted," Inez said. "I wanted to draw a picture of a girl with a selfie stick falling off a cliff as she tried to take a stupid picture. I was going to have another picture of her bloody body with the words *Instagram Kills*!"

"People die for Instagram," one of the Kaitlyns said.

"So it's not useful," the other Kaitlyn finished. "Unless the dead selfie girl was a bad guy. Then it might be useful."

"Betty and Lauren," Kelly said. "You're up."

Both girls got to their feet.

"TikTok is fun, with lots of cool animal videos," Lauren said. "And that's useful because people learn about animals they didn't know about before, like cats and wombunnies."

"Wombunnies?" Kelly asked.

"Cats?" Hilly asked.

Betty stood there, arms folded across her chest, but contributed nothing.

"TikTok also teaches you things," Lauren went on. "Like how to dance, what's a good book to read, or how to defuse a bomb."

"There's a video on defusing a bomb?" I asked. Maybe I should look into that. Even though I was retired, it was always good to keep up with the latest technological advances.

Betty finally spoke. "Betty Vision will do that. It'll show how to do that, stalk people, black hat hacking, and will have groups where they can network."

Hilly nodded. "Sounds like ClinkedIn."

"You mean LinkedIn," Kelly corrected her.

She shook her head, "No, I don't. ClinkedIn is like that one, but for professionals more in my line of work."

"Why haven't you invited me to join?" I asked.

"Because you don't work in the field anymore." Hilly shook her head.

"Why is Betty inventing something if it already exists?" Inez wondered.

"Because BV will be better," Betty promised. "Way better."

Hilly nodded. "I'll join it."

"I don't think it's a good idea for you to start a social network based on black bag drops," Kelly said.

I stared at her. "Look at you, rocking the lingo!"

"You *do* agree with me," Kelly said.

"Of course!" I said quickly. "I don't want to be part of something that considers me too old to join!"

"That's not exactly where I was going with that…" my co-leader started.

Hilly turned to Betty. "I can hook you up. I know a couple of really good hackers in Peru who could get the word out."

"No," Kelly said. "This is getting away from us. We need to focus on the task we started."

Betty nodded. "Sounds good." She produced a business card and handed it to Hilly. "Have them get ahold of me."

"Do something," Kelly hissed to me.

I took the card before Hilly could accept it. "No one is starting any social media platforms without talking, at length, to *me* first. Got it?"

Two of the Kaitlyns raised their hands. I acknowledged them, and in unison they said, "Is it snack time yet?"

"Good idea!" Kelly said. "There are cookies and milk in the kitchen!"

The stampede into the house included Hilly, who immediately got out the cups and began pouring milk while Ava handed out plates and Lauren passed the cookies.

"That didn't go how I expected." Kelly sat down on the couch in the living room, looking defeated.

I joined her. "That went exactly how I expected. Actually, I'm kind of surprised that Betty hadn't started Betty Vision long before this."

"The girls are in sixth grade," Kelly said. "In a year they'll be teenagers."

"*That* is terrifying," I admitted.

"It just seems like they are getting out of control," Kelly said. "They used to be cute and fun. Now they're political leaders, starting social media networks, and running covert ops."

"Yeah." I nodded. "I wish they'd had something like this for us back in the day."

Kelly lightly punched me in the arm. "You're not listening."

"Oh, you're right. Sorry. I'm a bit distracted."

Kelly sighed. "So about Teo the Tapir. Want me to follow him? I just had a class in stalking techniques."

I grinned. "I'll make a spy out of you yet! When do you get licensed?"

This time, she smiled. "Next month if everything lines up right. I can't believe it. From emergency room nurse to private investigator!"

"It's very cool." I patted her on the back. "You'll be able to investigate anything! Rex won't even let me be involved with his interrogation of Teo."

Kelly's eyebrows went up. "Why don't you become a private investigator? I'm sure Riley wouldn't mind. You solve half his cases anyway. I'm sure he'd take you on."

I shook my head. "Riley as my boss? No thanks."

"But he was your handler for years," Kelly said.

"True." My gaze drifted into the distance. "We did work well together. But he'd never cough up the money for my salary. And I don't need the job. Independently well off, remember?"

"Maybe you could work pro bono?" Kelly suggested.

"He'd have to pay me *something*," I reasoned. "He won't respect me if I work for free. And I don't think I'd respect myself."

Kelly stood up, looking a bit happier than she had when she sat down. "Think about it. I'll start talking to Riley about it after the meeting."

"I will," I promised. Maybe she'd fixate on this idea and forget about my earlier promise to tell Rex about the twins.

We wandered into the kitchen to find the girls and Hilly deep in discussion.

"And you should consider a presence on the dark web," Hilly said before she saw us. Out of the corner of her mouth, she said quietly, "We'll talk more later. The *old* people are here."

"Are you gonna kill this tapir guy?" Betty asked. "If not, I could hire someone."

"Nope, uh-uh"—I cut in—"you are not taking out a contract on Teo."

"I'd do it for free," Hilly admitted before taking a stack of five cookies and shoving the whole thing into her mouth.

"He could be innocent," I said halfheartedly. "Maybe someone's framing him. It's kind of turning my life upside down."

Hilly put her hand on my shoulder. "And don't forget that your husband thinks you're pregnant."

"Alright, girls." Kelly clapped her hands for their attention. "Let's get back to the discussion."

It felt like a blanket had dropped over the room as Kelly and the girls got together to work on a page for the troop. I heard the buzzing of conversation, but it was background noise compared to the idea that my husband believed I was pregnant and hadn't told him.

Why would he think that? Was I acting more unusual than normal? Maybe that was a loaded question. At any rate, I needed to clear this up as soon as possible. It broke my heart to have him think I didn't tell him. I loved and adored Rex. He would be the first person I'd tell. Then Kelly. By then, Betty would've found out by bugging my house or something and it would be all over the world.

The fact of the matter was, I had no intention of having kids. These girls were my kids. And believe me, that was enough for five lifetimes of reincarnation. But I couldn't help wondering…did Rex feel the same way? We'd discussed it years ago, and he was fine with not having children. But had his feelings changed?

I shut these thoughts out of my mind as my cell vibrated in my pocket. I pulled it out to find a text message from an unknown caller.

Meet me at noon. Come alone, or else! Corn Hole parking lot.

Now what was that about?

CHAPTER NINE

It wasn't the clandestine nature of the text or the message that got me thinking. Believe me, spies get all kinds of funky messages on their phones.

Keep your mouth shut or you die!
I know who you are!
Putin is super sexy, not old, and can fight a bear with his mad judo skills! This is not from Putin!

The meeting ended with me still deep inside my own mind, trying to get past the Rex revelation and trying to remind myself that Teo the Tapir might be out to kill me. I set my alarm for an hour and a half in time and helped Kelly and Hilly clean up. When we were done, I went back across the street and sat in the minivan, forcing myself to clear my head, but unfortunately, something else took its place.

Kelly's suggestion was interesting. Should I consider becoming a PI? The idea had merit. Rex had used Riley a few times on parallel investigations when his resources were limited. And Rex couldn't really get mad at me for investigating if it was my job.

Or would my husband think of me as competition? Probably not. My husband was very supportive of me. He'd probably love to see me occupied with a job.

On the other hand, I really liked my freedom. The ability to come and go as I pleased. Take the girls to camp for a week…run up to my house in northeast Iowa…visit Belize…that kind of thing. Next year would be their last year in elementary school. One more year, and they'd be middle school teenagers.

Whoa. That was a scary thought. Kelly was right. We could barely handle them now. What kind of horror would happen when they were older?

I put that thought out of my head. That was still a year off. For now, the idea of being a PI was more interesting. That, and I really didn't want to dwell on what might happen in two years when the girls got their driver's permits and became interested in boys.

I shook my head to clear it. Okay. It was decided. I would seriously consider this option. But first, I needed to bounce it off Riley.

Riley shared his thoughts after my explanation. "I couldn't pay you a salary."

"I could do it on an as-needed basis. Like a contract worker," I suggested, sounding more optimistic about the idea than I really felt.

"I'll give it some thought," he said. "But right now, I have some intel. I heard back from Ahmed."

"How is he doing these days?" I asked.

"They've promoted him to a key administrative job."

You could've shocked me with a cattle prod. "You're joking. Ahmed? Cookie Ahmed?"

Don't get me wrong. Ahmed was a great guy, and I used him for information myself. But he was also an idiot and easily blackmailed with peanut butter sandwich cookies. And he was terrified by the dominatrices who ran HR. For good reason. Those women were super smart, powerful, and scary.

Riley nodded. "HR made a very enthusiastic case, and Administration took him up on it."

"Seriously?"

"Apparently HR adores him," Riley explained. "Kind of like a pet."

"So they're promoting him as a puppet," I said.

Riley shrugged. "Anyway, it appears that Teo was right about the deaths of the others."

"Really? That seems like good news." If Teo didn't kill the people we used to work with, maybe he didn't kill Henrietta.

"I wouldn't say he's out of the woods yet," Riley warned. "Sure, Mateo was gored, but Teo was in the stadium."

"Could just be coincidence," I offered. "And how could he control how a bull behaves on the floor of the arena?"

Riley continued, "One-Hand Tim died cleaning a gun."

"Which happens all the time," I added.

"But it was Teo's gun."

My optimism started to dim. "Oh. But it could still happen. Accidents like that happen all the time with those bravado guys."

Riley continued, "Pedro the Pimple caught a flesh-eating virus in the hospital shortly after Teo visited him, according to the visitor's log."

This time I didn't say anything.

"And Chloe the Clownfish and Sharkface Shawn were on vacation together with a couple of other guys, including Teo."

My heart sank. I was really hoping that Teo was innocent. "And he was here when Henrietta was killed…in my garage."

"Teo could be setting you up to take the fall," my former handler reasoned. "Maybe he figures that it's just too much of a coincidence that he was at each murder scene."

"What did Ahmed say about this?" I wondered.

"Oh," Riley said.

"You didn't point it out?" Seemed like shoddy detective work. Maybe I didn't want to work for him.

"No," Riley explained. "I did. He said 'Oh.'"

"I don't get it," I insisted. "Why come to town and make a big fuss about looking for me when he was planning to murder Henrietta? Seems kind of idiotic."

Riley's eyebrows went up. "Like being at the scene of five other people's bizarre deaths?"

Yeah. Like that. "Then Teo isn't playing with a full deck."

"I've thought of something else." Riley held up his index finger. "What if he really is here to kill you?"

I threw my arms up in frustration. "We're back to where we started! We don't know anything more than when we first found Henrietta dead."

"That's not true. We know now that he was present for five deaths of his other colleagues. That's something."

"Fair point," I agreed. "You know, I was really hoping he was legit. Now I have to call Ron and Ivan."

"I'll have Kelly look into those five deaths," Riley suggested. "Maybe she can find something that the CIA missed."

I got to my feet. "And I'll ask Rex how his interrogation went."

"Report back, and I'll think about the idea of bringing you onboard," Riley winked.

"First I have to meet with someone." I held out my phone to show him the text.

Riley frowned when he'd finished reading. "I'll go too."

"No. I need to go alone." I pointed to that part of the text.

"Why? Whoever it is won't even know I'm there."

He had a point, but I wasn't taking him with me. "I don't want to spook whoever it is."

"You don't know who it is!" Riley threw his arms in the air. "That's a huge red flag. It could be an ambush."

"That's right. But it also could just be an information exchange. I did this all the time alone when we worked together."

"You need backup," he insisted.

"I'll be fine. I'll check in with you when I'm done so you'll know I'm safe." Why on Earth did I show him the text?

Riley grinned. "Just like old times, eh? You going out on missions and me worrying about you. This is what it will be like to work with me."

I shook my head. "Maybe it's something unrelated. Like the Scots want me to stop Betty pushing independence, or Randi needs me to help her find dead mice in the dumpster."

He waved me away. "Yeah. Sure. Whatever. Just be sure to text when you're done."

I drove to the nearest fast food place and ordered a double cheeseburger, fries, and a chocolate shake. Fun spy tip—never go anywhere hungry. Fun Girl Scout tip—always be prepared! It's hard to fight or basically do anything on an empty stomach, so it's best to overload.

I knew an agent who refused to eat between meals and ended up nearly starving to death in a Yugo on a stake-out in Moldova. Fortunately, a rural woman spotted him sitting in his car, felt sorry for him because he was in a Yugo, and brought him roasted goat testicles. From then on, Norman Nuts, as we called him after that, always had food on him, just in case.

My thoughts turned to who this might be and what they wanted. It felt like this was about Teo and Henrietta, but it could be something else, like Heather and Kayla wanting me to team up with them to oust Stewie. They would definitely be this mysterious about it.

Or maybe Ronni hired Hilly, and today's *that day* where I end up in the dumpster without ever being able to tell Rex I'm not pregnant and I'm thinking of getting a job.

The trick with showing up to something secretive like this was to get there early and unseen. If it was a trap and you walked right into it, you only had yourself to blame. I drove out of town half an hour before our meeting.

The Corn Hole was a dive bar and an Iowa Hawkeyes–only place, and you were dead meat if you showed up in anything other than black and gold. The barfights kept the hospital emergency room busy several times a week. Rex was relieved it was on Sheriff Carnack's turf, even though most of the perpetrators broke into fights at the hospital later and ended up in his cells.

The exterior was plain with a simple gravel lot. Inside was depressing, with rough tables, patched-up chairs, and a cement floor that I was once told was there because it was easier to get blood out. That, by the way, wasn't true unless you have a significantly powerful power washer. But that was a story for another time.

Beer was the only thing on tap, although there were stronger spirits that usually came in unlabeled bottles. They did have wine once. The menu said they had "red" and "yellow." But they got rid of that because the wine drunks caused more fights than the beer drinkers. Fortunately, the bar was closed during the day, so no one would see my clandestine meetup.

I pulled into the driveway of an abandoned farmhouse not far from the place and parked. From there, I'd head through the cornfields until I got close to the Corn Hole, which was naturally surrounded by, you guessed it, cornfields.

As I got out of the car, I noticed a white, rusted out conversion van on the other side. Had someone bought this place and tried to fix it up? Just in case, I decided to see if anyone was around. The last thing I needed was for a handyman to call the sheriff on my minivan. That would be awkward.

Sneaking over there would be silly. This was broad daylight, and any slinking around would be viewed suspiciously. So I just walked over to the van and checked it out. The vehicle was locked, and I didn't see anyone through the windows.

The house was next. It was a rundown, abandoned, one-story ranch house, which was good because I'd been in Victorian two-story versions of this before, with mixed results due to huge holes in the floor and unstable staircases.

The door creaked as I opened it and shouted hello. Then I froze and listened. Nothing. I waited longer. Five minutes later, still nothing. I shouted something about driving by and expressing interest in buying the property, but there was no sound at all.

This was wasting time. I needed to sneak over to the Corn Hole and see who was lying in wait for me. Upon deciding that the van had been left behind for whatever purpose, I stepped into the cornfield and began to walk between the rows.

I'd bet you didn't know you could get hopelessly lost in a cornfield, did you? If the corn was high, it was easier than you'd think. When I detasseled corn in high school, every now and then there'd be a team of first timers from Des Moines who'd end up lost for hours.

The trick was to stay in one row, breaking a leaf every fifty feet or so, always on the same side. Never cross over without doing something similar. I was in luck because the way the rows ran, I was basically walking in a corn tunnel straight from the farmhouse to the Corn Hole's lot.

As I got closer, I chose my steps more carefully and tried not to so much as touch the leaves on the tall plants. Corn plant leaves are stiff, and they rustle. Anyone with a higher vantage point (which could only be standing on the bar's dumpster) would see the corn moving as I made my way along the row.

I slowed even more as the row curved a bit and I saw a figure up ahead in the same row. Was this my contact? What was he doing here? Obviously, he stole my idea and was waiting for me! The bastard.

Stopping in my tracks, I tried to figure out how to play this. I was close enough that slipping into another row would be heard. Just walking over to him would alert him to my presence, and I needed the element of surprise. He was only about twenty feet away.

So I charged him. I tore through the black soil. It appeared that he'd heard me coming and turned in slow motion.

"What the…" was all he had time to say as I tackled him to the ground.

The man was wearing a ski mask in the middle of a hot summer day. What an amateur! He was dressed in black tactical gear, and I could tell in a moment's tackle that it was a man. I got to my feet and lifted him to his as I tore off his hood.

"You've got to be kidding me," I scoffed.

Kurt Allen Hobbs Jr. Esquire, cub bounty hunter from Bladdersly, stood meekly before me.

"Hi Merry," he said.

CHAPTER TEN

———

"What are you doing here? Was it you who texted me? Did you change your phone number?" A stream of questions flowed out of me as I tried to gauge the situation.

Kurt Allen Hobbs Jr. Esq. was an overly eager and earnest young man from Bladdersly who, once or twice, had sort of helped me with a case. And he was currently dating one of my druids, Kayla.

"And why are you dressed like a ninja?"

The kid removed his long-sleeved black shirt to reveal a red T-shirt underneath. Emblazoned across the chest was:

Kurt Hobbs, Esquire
Bounty Hunter/Private Investigator
No Case Too Small, No Purp Too Large.

"*Purp* is misspelled," I pointed out.

He nodded excitedly. "It's something new I'm starting, spelling *perp* as *purp*. I think it'll go viral because people will think it's cool!"

"Or people will think you can't spell," I suggested.

He had the good grace to look sheepish. "Apparently T-Shirt Pig doesn't fix it if you turned in the misspelling in the first place."

"Why are you here?" I pressed.

If he wasn't the person who sent me the text, I needed to get rid of him before that guy got here.

"I have some information!" Kurt was so excited he began bouncing on balls of his feet. "I think I can help with the Tapir guy." His face brightened. "Or I can arrest him for you and bring him in! Is he violating some sort of bail?"

Kurt was always on the prowl for his first arrest as a bounty hunter. He was so looking forward to this moment that he'd tried to bring me in on occasion.

"No one is looking for him," I said. "Except maybe the CIA."

"The CIA?" Kurt pumped his fist in the air. "That's the big time! I could even afford to get corrected T-shirts!"

In a way, it was a relief that I wasn't meeting someone more dangerous.

"The CIA doesn't use bounty hunters," I told him. "What's the information, Kurt?"

The young man's face fell. "Really? Maybe I could turn him into the FBI or someone else? What's he wanted for?"

"He hasn't been arrested, for one thing," I sighed. "Otherwise, he could be wanted for being a Colombian drug lord."

It was as if the young man exploded. "A drug cartel guy? Like Pablo Escobar? Awesome! An international capture would be amazing!"

"I doubt it. Word is he cut a deal with the CIA and is here legally."

Kurt considered this. "Why did Kayla tell me you and Mr. Riley were upset to find him at Feeling Lucky's?"

So many people already knew that I'd feel bad if I didn't tell him. So I filled him in on everything.

"Whoa!" he said when I finished. "That's crazy! What's with you and murder?"

Time to bring this conversation back to the beginning. "What information do you have for me?"

For a moment, I thought he'd forgotten. Then recognition played across his features.

"Oh right! Kayla found this. That Teo guy dropped it. She thought it was weird so asked me to bring it to you."

"Why didn't she just bring it to me?" I asked.

Kurt stared at me. "Because I needed the experience. It's important to practice these things so when I have a real situation, I'm ready. There's not a lot of call to wear a ski mask in July."

He handed me a piece of paper with my address written on it. There was a drawing of a house exploding with a stick figure with short curly hair lying on the ground outside of it, with little x's where her eyes should be. There was also some sort of oily residue on it. I held it up to the sun and noticed a watermark image that looked like a coiled snake.

This could be a smoking gun, so to speak. First off, I'm in the clear for accidentally blowing up my garage. This seemed like proof that it was done intentionally. Second, it's pretty hard to say you didn't blow up my garage if you have my address, a picture of my house exploding with me dead, and a residue of some sort of accelerant. I needed to make a copy of this and get it to Rex.

I looked at the junior bounty hunter. "I suppose it's silly to ask if you have a plastic bag?"

Kurt grinned. "Of course! A good bounty hunter is always prepared! I have four sizes. Which do you want?"

I accepted a quart-sized bag and slid the piece of paper inside.

"I also have mace," Kurt continued, "zip ties, a knife that folds up like a credit card, water purification tablets, a space blanket, and gum!"

"Why do you have water purification tablets?" I waved my arms around. "The nearest lake or river is about twenty miles from here."

He rolled his eyes. "You're a Girl Scout! You know the answer to this."

"So Kayla saw Teo drop this?" That made her a witness.

"Yeah, sorta," he said.

That gave me pause. "Sorta?"

"He said he needed to use the bathroom before eating. Kayla kind of forgot he was in there five minutes later and walked in to see him shooting up. He looked embarrassed and went back to his seat. She found this on the floor. You know what? I'll bet he was doing heroin or something like that! Isn't that what Colombian drug lords do?"

"Or he's a diabetic and needs to give himself insulin before eating food made up mostly of sugar," I reasoned.

Kurt scowled. "That's disappointing."

No, it wasn't. Because it proved that Teo had access to hypodermic needles—which could be used to give someone an air embolism. Teo was looking guiltier by the minute!

I started walking back to my car. Kurt followed along, muttering to himself about being so close to getting real, acrylic business cards so he didn't have only one. I ignored him because my mind was reviewing the possibilities.

Too bad Kurt and Kayla handled the piece of paper. I suppose Rex would want to fingerprint them to rule them out. But this was good news. Teo screwed up. But then, he must have at the other five killings, or why had he been there?

"Kurt…" I paused. "Why didn't you just drop this off at my house? Why all the cloak and dagger stuff?"

Again, he looked at me like I was an infant. "I'm working on my pre-surveillance techniques."

"There's no such thing as pre-surveillance." Was there? Maybe this was new spycraft? I had been out of the biz for a while.

"I invented it! The idea is to get your purp"—he leaned in—"with a *u*, to go where you want him to go instead of following him to who knows where." He puffed out his chest. "Brilliant, right?"

"That's not a thing," I pointed out "Setting up a meeting is what you did."

"It is too something!" Kurt stuck his chin out defiantly. "And you proved it by coming here!" His smile faded a bit. "Of course, you came in a completely different way and snuck up on me, so I'll have to adjust for that. But they'll be teaching this at Quantico soon!"

We came out into the clearing near the abandoned house. I spun on my heel.

"The van is yours!" I pointed at the creepy white custom van.

He nodded. "And you parked here too! Man! I'm in the big leagues now! Come check out my new ride!"

For some reason, I followed him. He slid open the side door.

"It looks like a serial killer's van," I mumbled as I eyed rolls of duct tape, a baseball bat, a couple of stun guns, and what appeared to be a jail cell in the back.

Kurt nodded absently. "Sweet, right?"

"Uh, okay." I started toward my car. "Thanks for the evidence!"

I heard Kurt climb into the van and shut the door. He must've tried to start because the engine stalled and wouldn't turn over. I listened to him try it twice more before I got into my minivan.

"Hey!" He opened my passenger door and climbed in. I really needed to start locking that door regularly. "I need a ride into town."

I said nothing as I started up the van and put it into drive. We pulled onto the gravel road before he started talking again.

"It's really cool that I could help you out like this. Kayla thought it looked important."

"It is" was all I said.

"Do you think your husband will let me make the arrest? Maybe I could arrange for Kayla to walk by. Should I throw the purp against a wall and cuff him?"

I decided it was better not to encourage him.

"Oooh! I should have a catch phrase!" Kurt bubbled. "Something like, 'You've just been Hobbsed! Or 'Welcome to justice, Hobbs style!"

"Or…" I tapped my fingers on the steering wheel. "Don't say anything." I was trying to think, and Kurt was distracting me.

Back in town, I dropped him off at Feeling Lucky's, where he could bother Kayla until she got off her shift. Then I headed to Riley's office and made a copy of the piece of paper before heading to Rex's office to hand it over.

"Hey babe!" I walked around his desk and, after making sure no one was around, gave him a quick kiss. Rex and I weren't fans of public displays of affection and even more so with me often horning in on his investigations.

Reaching into my pocket, I pulled out the piece of paper in a baggie and set it in front of him, telling him how it came into my possession and about the needle. Then I triumphantly plopped into a chair and waited for him to heap praise upon me.

"I'll get this analyzed immediately." Rex called Troy in.

"Hi Merry!" Troy said happily. "How's it going?"

I liked Officer Wallace a little more every time I met him. For a while, Rex had been worried that he was thinking of transferring. I could understand that, because of Kevin. But it turned out that he wanted to stay and was, in fact, trying to bring in a new recruit that Rex was now preparing to interview.

The Who's There police station was a small one, with one detective, a receptionist who changed so often I stopped trying to remember their names, and one officer. It helped that the sheriff's department was also in town, and Sheriff Carnack had two deputies. But Rex had hoped to expand. While he wasn't exactly a police chief—that job phased out years ago, he did want more staff.

Oh crap. I was supposed to talk to Ava this morning. I made a mental note to do it later.

Troy was in his early thirties, tall with a slim build and a handsome face. He was easygoing and good-natured and had finally realized that Kevin was just an anomaly he had to deal with. I'd been thinking lately of fixing him up with Soo Jin.

Rex gave Troy instructions and handed him the evidence.

"See you around, Merry!" Troy winked and was off.

"So, what do you think about that? Seems like Teo's our guy!" I smiled to show him how brilliant his wife was.

Rex didn't say anything. He just ran his hands through his hair and sighed.

Uh-oh.

"How did the interrogation with Teo go?" I asked after a moment.

Rex gave me a look. "It went quite well actually. He seemed genuinely shocked by Henrietta's death and immediately said he needs to look into custody of his child."

My eyebrows went up. "You believed him?"

"He seemed convincing," Rex said with a nod. "And he has an alibi."

I sat forward. "For Henrietta?"

Rex nodded. "Troy checked it out too. Teo was eating lunch in a restaurant in Des Moines for a couple of hours. Then he went to see a real estate agent regarding homes for sale in Who's There. After that, he drove around Des Moines to see the sights, arriving back in town around eight o'clock at night. We have cameras that show all of his movements."

"He could've slipped away," I argued. "It's only a thirty-minute drive to Des Moines…"

Rex raised his hands. "Actually, we thought of that. It's strange how every minute of his time is accounted for. It's as if he made sure he was always in sight of a public camera."

"Like a coincidence," I mumbled.

"Well," Rex replied. "Like a finely orchestrated and staged alibi."

That sounded familiar. "There's something else you should know." I told him what Riley found out.

Rex shook his head. "I'm not a big believer in coincidence either. You say Riley's looking into those deaths? I don't have the budget or manpower to look into five overseas deaths that may or may not be relevant to the case."

It seemed like an opening I should take. "A private eye comes in handy at a time like this, huh?"

"Normally, I wouldn't say so," Rex admitted. "I've seen private investigators screw up a police investigation. But there are many times when it's very useful. And Riley has helped me a couple of times."

I decided to go for it. "What would you think of me being a private eye?"

My husband's eyebrows went up. "I guess I shouldn't be surprised. You're always snooping in my cases."

"I could help you," I offered. I told him my idea of doing it part time and Riley's response.

My husband sat in silence, considering it. Finally, he said, "Do you want to become a PI?"

"I don't know," I admitted. "I haven't really had time to process it. But with the girls getting older and eventually leaving, I should start something now to keep me occupied. And I'd be working with you…"

Rex held his hand up. "You wouldn't be working with me. There might be one or two cases where I might work with a private eye, but it wouldn't be often."

"I could become a police officer…" I suggested.

Did I imagine it, or did Rex flinch slightly?

"I would have to think about that," he said slowly. "Look, Merry, I appreciate what you're saying. It would be nice to work together. You are an excellent sleuth. But you're used to having free time and doing whatever you want when you want to. If you worked for Riley or for me, you'd be on a nine-to-five schedule most likely. I'm not sure you'd like that."

I probably wouldn't like that. And then there was the idea that I'd have to go through all the training, classes, and licensing that Kelly was dealing with. Huh. I really, really, really didn't want to do any of that. I'd done enough with the CIA. Could I be grandfathered in for that?

Rex interrupted my thoughts. "It appears you haven't had much time to think this through. There's no rush. Why don't you take some time?"

I got up. "That's a good idea. What would I do without you?"

"You'd be that crazy lady across the street with Dora the Explorer sheets as curtains." He gave me a wink.

I was back outside, just sitting in my van, when I got a call.

"Hi Merry!" Teo's voice said. "I wanted to make sure you had my number since we're going to be friends and all that."

I looked at my watch. "I'm glad you called. I have a couple of questions. Have you eaten at Oleo's yet?"

"No," Teo replied. "But it's only four o'clock."

"What's your point?" I asked. This could work. I could interrogate him on what I'd just learned and eat the best burger in the state at the same time. It was a no-brainer.

"Americans eat early!" Teo answered. "Okay! I'll meet you there in five minutes!"

I hung up and smiled to myself. It was time to get some real answers from this guy. Maybe tonight I'd have this thing solved. If Teo was the killer, problem solved! If he wasn't…well, I guess I was going to be stuck with him.

As I started my minivan, I wondered which outcome I would prefer.

CHAPTER ELEVEN

"Merry!" Teo waved me over to a table in the back.

I know I'd just eaten a few hours ago, but the aroma of grilled meat was making me drool. I sat down, and we ordered drinks from the waitress, a glass of wine for me and a beer for Teo.

Teo grinned. "It's so good to see you! I love Who's There. And how is it you don't have chickens everywhere? I thought in Iowa there'd be chickens, like in Colombia."

"There are chickens," I explained. "But they are kept on farms. Some towns have ordinances where you can raise chickens, but not here."

He watched as the waitress delivered our drinks. "I don't really miss them. Chickens are a pain in the ass. But they are delicious."

He wasn't wrong. Carlos had had a thing about chickens, and they had run all over his compound pecking at people, crowing at all hours of the night. I loved animals as much as the next guy, but there had been too many, and I had looked forward to our twice a month chicken barbecue.

"How are you settling in?" Always lead with pleasant small talk so you can catch them off guard later. It worked on everyone. Well, nearly everyone. For some reason, Uzbeks were immune.

Teo visibly let down his guard. "I have looked at three houses and like two of them. And I am thinking of trying to find my child, now that Henrietta is gone." He gave me a sad face, but his eyes were on mine to make sure I bought it.

The waitress asked for our orders, and I ordered burgers and fries for both of us.

"Sounds like you are thinking of doing the single dad thing and settling down." I tried not to shudder, picturing Teo with a little kid. It didn't seem possible.

"I am ready!" He clinked my wineglass with his bottle.

"Have you had lots of experience with kids?"

Teo's face fell. "Not really. I was an only child and had no cousins. But I have watched American TV and have learned a lot from your sitcoms."

"That might not be the best way to learn about kids," I muttered.

"Hey!" Teo pointed at me. "You can give me advice! You have been with little girls for how long?"

I set my glass down on the table. "Since they were five. Now they're twelve years old. So I guess I have a little more experience than you."

The man slapped the table. "What can you tell me about little girls? What is your best advice?"

"Don't give them matches. If you see a spider, tell them it's a baby spider and they won't be afraid of it. Always have access to snacks, and stand back after you've put them on the table or you may lose an arm." Was that it? Was that the culmination of years of working with little girls? "Oh!" I remembered. "Lock up your credit cards, and no matter what, never let them know it's possible to kill a man with one finger."

"Why would anyone kill a man who has only one finger?" Teo cried out. "That's barbaric, even by American standards!"

I held up my index finger. "No, that's not what I meant. I meant kill a man using one finger."

Teo frowned. "Little girls sound dangerous."

I took a drink of wine. "You have no idea."

The waitress brought our food. One thing about Oleo's, they always have burgers on the grill, so you get your food fairly quickly.

Teo poured half a bottle of ketchup onto his burger. "I find ketchup fascinating. We have it in Colombia, but you have sugar in yours. I really like it." He took a bite, and his eyes rolled back in his head. "This is *good*!"

"Best burgers in the state," I agreed.

He set down his burger and sat back in his chair. "I don't think I will have any problems settling in here. Granted, I do not know much about raising a kid. But how hard can it be?"

"Do you know if it's a boy or girl? Your kid?"

"A daughter. But I don't know her name. I think that this will be good for me."

We ate in silence for a few minutes, and I tried not to flinch as he drowned his fries in ketchup. It seemed criminal, but he appeared to love it that way. For a moment, I hoped that he wasn't the killer or the bomber of my garage. Sure, we didn't like each other back in the day, but I liked the idea that this former drug lord wanted to change his ways and spend time with his daughter.

And there was a small amount of pride in thinking I'd brought another person to the place where I grew up and they wanted to make a home here. Ron and Ivan enjoyed it here, married, and were starting families. Sure, it took them a while to figure out that there was no abject poverty, peasants, land mines, or goats, but once they got past that, they really took to Who's There quite naturally.

Could the same be said for Teo? If he was going to get custody of his daughter, I owed it to her and Henrietta to make sure he hadn't killed her mother. Seemed important.

"My *husband*," I said, stressing the word, "said he talked to you about Henrietta."

Teo's serene look became troubled. "It's so sad. He took me to identify the body. I wish I knew what happened."

"You didn't even like her," I pointed out.

Teo nodded. "That's true. But I did not want her dead. I just never wanted to see her again. She is the mother of my child."

"You have to admit," I said, stretching my legs, "it really is an unbelievable coincidence that you were both here. In this small town. In the middle of nowhere."

Teo nodded animatedly. "I know! I can't imagine why Henrietta would be here."

"There are a lot of coincidences," I continued, "regarding the others' deaths. Chloe the Clownfish, One-Handed Tim—all of them died with you in the proximity."

Teo had an unreadable look on his face. "That is a coincidence."

"Coincidenc*es*," I said. "That's six people we used to work with who've died with you right there. I don't believe in that many coincidences."

"What about Carlos?" Teo asked. "You were in the proximity when he died."

I rolled my eyes. "That's because I ran him over with my car. And that was an accident because he was pushed. In fact, he was in my territory, and he was brought here by someone who was trying to frame me."

Teo snapped his fingers "That's it! The same thing must be happening to me too!"

Yeah. Right. "Except for the fact that I lived here. Carlos came onto my home turf. You are a long way from yours. I'm wondering if you brought Henrietta here with you with the intention of killing her in my garage."

The former drug lord seemed to be offended. "Why would I do that when I want to live here too? It doesn't make any sense."

"It makes total sense," I reasoned. "It's not very smart, but it does make sense. More sense than it being another wild coincidence."

"I know what you think," Teo sighed. "And I'll admit that it does seem strange, but I really am innocent of any murders since I was active in the business."

Was that all he'd given up? "Did you know that there's a huge influx of marijuana into this county since you've arrived?"

Teo frowned. "I never messed with that crap. I only peddled cocaine." He sniffed. "I have *standards*, you know."

This was getting me nowhere.

I tried a different approach. "Have you talked to Henrietta's mother?"

It occurred to me that I didn't know much about Henrietta the Hernia. I assumed she was Colombian. Maybe I could call her if he knew where she was and in what time zone.

"She lives in Iowa. Some town called Bladdersly," Teo said.

"Bladdersly? Are you sure?" I was so shocked I set down my burger.

Teo scoffed. "How could I forget a name like *that*? Henrietta was always bragging that she was something called a Raging Bladder! Isn't that horrid?"

"You have no idea…" My voice faltered. "So Henrietta grew up in Bladdersly? Did you know that's only ten minutes from here?"

Teo seemed to be surprised. "My daughter is only ten minutes away? Can we go? Right now?" He got to his feet. "I have the address." He tugged on my arm. "Let's go!"

"Why not?" I agreed. This was an opportunity to find out more regarding Henrietta. "You text and see if she's home, and we'll go right after we finish eating."

He pushed his chair away from the table. "This can't wait!"

"Sit down," I ordered. "There are some things in life you can't rush. And one of those is Oleo's."

"Do you know anything else about your daughter?" I asked as we settled into the minivan ten minutes later.

Teo seemed nervous. "Like I said, all I know is that it's a girl and she's about four or five years old."

"I'm guessing that won't go well for you should you try to get custody," I mumbled.

"I've been a bachelor for so long…" Teo looked out the window. "But with your sage advice, I could be a good dad. Wow! Just think! I retire here, have all these friends already, and can raise my little girl! I can pass down my wisdom to another generation."

Only if that wisdom involved dealing drugs and killing people.

"How do you get along with Henrietta's mom?" I ventured.

"I've never actually met her either." Teo looked at his screen. "But she said she is happy to meet me! This is so exciting!"

"It may not be," I realized. "If Rex knew who Henrietta's next of kin was, he would've delivered the bad news of her murder. I'm guessing she doesn't know."

Teo thought about this in silence. "Do we have to tell her?"

I should call Rex. On the other hand, he might tell me to turn around and come back and to stop meddling in his case.

Then again, I was taking a man to see his daughter and I'd get some unique perspective on Henrietta. I made a decision.

"No. It's likely the police don't know about her mother either. In fact, since we don't know what Henrietta has told her about you, let's keep it simple. I'll let Rex know when we get back, and he can give her the news."

Teo smiled. "Good idea." His smile faded. "But you're right, Henrietta probably didn't tell her anything good about me."

Bladdersly was the other large town in the county. Whovians were not fans. In fact, the two towns were bitter rivals. We considered Bladdersly a seething cesspool of despair with citizens who were voted most likely to eat roadkill. Every year, the Whorish (the high school mascot with an unfortunate amalgamation of the town's name and its earliest settlers) fought the Raging Bladders in a tepid game where the winner was usually decided by the team that made the least mistakes.

Growing up, I never visited. As an adult I have had the misfortune of going there quite a bit in the last few years. And now I was heading there to see if the grandmother of Teo's daughter would welcome him or kill him.

The address was on a nice, quiet, and surprisingly picturesque street full of bungalows. I wasn't familiar with this neighborhood and was, in fact, shocked that there was an area this nice. We pulled up to a light-gray craftsman festooned with flower boxes and a huge, colorful garden.

"Here we go!" Teo shivered a little. "I'm really nervous!"

"Well, she welcomed you, so I doubt she'll meet us at the door with a shotgun. Then again"—I patted him on the arm—"maybe we should be prepared, just in case."

I got out, and we walked up a walkway that belonged in a fairy painting. I pressed the doorbell, wondering how I was going to get intel from this woman.

The door swung open, and an elderly woman who looked like she walked out of a Norman Rockwell painting opened the door. If you asked me to draw the stereotypical granny, I would've drawn Henrietta's mom. She was petite, with short, curly, snow-white hair and little spectacles balanced on the end of her nose. She was slightly stooped and wearing a sweater in the heat of July.

"Oh my goodness!" She clapped her hands as her eyes landed on Teo. "You're very handsome! Come in!"

We walked into the house. It was neat as a pin and very cozy with overstuffed chintz furniture covered with crocheted doilies. On the walls were paintings of coastal scenes mostly, which was weird to find in a landlocked state.

"Please sit down!" the lady said. "I'm Doreen, Henrietta's mother. You must be Teo!" She looked at me in askance.

"I'm Merry. I worked with your daughter for a few months in Colombia."

"How nice!" Her wizened face split with a warm smile. "I haven't seen Henrietta in years. She just showed up with a baby one day and handed her over!" Doreen cackled loudly at that.

Henrietta just dumped the baby here and was demanding child support from Teo? I gave him a quick look, and he gave me an almost imperceptible shrug.

"You're very attractive." Doreen smiled at him. "I swear, Elena looks just like you!"

Teo positively beamed at the news. Maybe he really was trying to go legit. I didn't like the idea of him raising the little girl, but no doubt Doreen wouldn't let her go.

"So," the old lady asked. "You'll be taking her today, then?"

It was like getting socked in the stomach by Ron or Ivan, and we both reeled from this bombshell.

Doreen looked at us expectantly. "Oh, I know, it's a bit of a shock. And I love Elena dearly, but I'm getting old, and she should be with young people. The youngest kid on this block is Norm and Margie's son, Joey, and he's thirty-five."

"Oh!" Teo said. "I don't have a place to live yet. I'm staying at an Airbnb and looking at places, but..." His voice trailed off.

"She'd love to go with you!" Doreen stood. "I'll go get her."

And with that, she disappeared down a hallway.

"What do I do?" Teo's voice was tinged with desperation. "I didn't want things to happen this quickly!"

Personally, I felt for him while I also felt this was some kind of poetic justice. I mean, I had some concerns for the poor girl, but Teo had to face up to his responsibilities, and I was more interested in getting some dirt on Henrietta. Then again, Doreen said she hadn't seen her daughter in maybe four or five years, so she might not have much.

Doreen returned. "She's packing now. It'll be about fifteen minutes. Oh my goodness! I should get you some cookies and lemonade!" she squealed and then fled in another direction, presumably toward the kitchen.

"She's packing?" Teo's face was a shocking shade of red. "You have to help me! I don't know what to do!"

I shrugged. "Why are you asking me? I don't know what to tell you."

"You have little girls! Your troop! You know what to do with them. Can't you take her home until I get to know her better?"

"Absolutely not!" I hissed. "This is your daughter, and you have to step up. Perhaps you can buy some time by asking her if you can start with visits."

Doreen appeared again with a tray of cookies and lemonade. She set it down, and I took a glass and a cookie. Teo watched and followed my lead, although why you needed to follow someone's lead to accept cookies was anyone's guess. Cultural difference between Iowa and Colombia weren't that dramatic.

"Doreen," Teo began. "I would love to take care of Elena. I just thought this would go slower. You know, we'd get to know each other first."

Doreen appeared to be disappointed. "You don't want her?"

"Of course I want her." Teo began to panic. "I just…it's that…" His voice trailed off because he couldn't think of anything else to say.

"It seems sort of sudden," I offered.

Doreen waved us off. "Don't be shy. I love having her here! But she should be with her parents. Or one of them at least."

"You said you haven't heard from Henrietta in years?" I interjected.

The old woman nodded. "That's right. My daughter and I aren't very close, I'm afraid. She didn't like growing up here and wanted to see the world. She used to send postcards from all over the world, but I don't count that as hearing from her because she just signed them with 'Wish I'd been born here!'." Doreen laughed. "She was such a kidder."

"She travels a lot, then?" I asked. "What kind of work is she in these days? I haven't seen her in a while."

Teo shot me a warning look. I'm guessing he didn't want this sweet little old lady to know what Henrietta did for Carlos.

"Oh, she's a drug runner," Doreen said casually. "She's worked all over the world for all kinds of characters. Very successful. I'm so proud!"

To say I was surprised by this would be an enormous understatement. Doreen knew what Henrietta did? And she was proud of it? I looked for cameras. Were we being pranked right now?

"Which is how she met you!" Doreen clapped happily. "My daughter told me you were successful and smart. She neglected to say how good-looking you are."

Was she flirting with Teo?

I tried to steer the conversation back to Henrietta. "Work like that must've made her some enemies."

"Oh yes! She had lots of people who wanted to kill her! That just goes to show how successful she was!" The lady beamed as if this was great news. "Warren Buffet says something like that—you know when you've hit the big time if people want to kill you!"

"Yeah," I said slowly. "I think I heard that…somewhere…"

She clasped her hands in her lap. "Well, like I said, we weren't close. I have no idea where she is or what she's doing right now. For all I know, she's dead in someone's cellar or in a cat-strewn Bogota slum. But the life of a drug runner, eh?" She smiled her bubbly smile.

It was probably a good idea we were taking this little girl off her hands. She seemed to have a rather mixed-up idea of right and wrong.

"What do I feed her?" Teo started a barrage of questions. "Does she need baths? What time does she go to sleep at night, and what time does she wake up? Does she need shots?"

Doreen laughed. "She's just like any other kid. Eats just about anything, goes to bed at night and gets up in the morning. She's had all of her shots and should start kindergarten in the fall."

Something occurred to the woman, and she leaned in. "Oh, and whatever you do, don't let her around sharp objects or turn your back on her for one second." She winked.

I was about to ask why when a beautiful little girl appeared with a Disney princess suitcase in tow. She had Teo's dark hair and eyes, and her features were so perfect she looked like a little doll.

The girl smiled and held out her hand. "Daddy?"

Teo fainted dead away.

"Hi." I shook the girl's hand. "I'm Merry. I'm a…friend…of your parents."

"Very nice to meet you," the girl said. "Thank you so much for coming. It was most thoughtful of you."

Her smile was sincere and her manners impeccable. And yet, her sweet grandmother couldn't wait to get rid of her and even warned us about her. My spydy senses weren't tingling and warning bells weren't going off. Perhaps Doreen had a raging case of dementia.

Teo came to momentarily and got to his feet. "I'm so sorry. I was overcome with joy."

Elena nodded. "I know. This isn't easy, is it?" She gave Teo a shy smile.

The little girl fell asleep in my van before we got a few blocks away.

"Be careful what you wish for, huh?" I said quietly.

Teo gulped visibly. "I didn't think that would happen. I was just picturing an idyllic retirement, and the idea of having a little kid to share it with might have made me overly eager."

"How is the place where you're staying?" I asked. "Is it appropriate for a little girl?"

"It's a two-bedroom ranch house," Teo said. "I think it will be okay. Do I have to cook now? I don't know how to cook."

"Eventually, yes. But just take her out for meals for a couple of days until you get the hang of it. Then it's pretty much peanut butter and jelly sandwiches." At least, that's what my troop wanted at that age.

I kind of felt for him. I really did. Sure, he probably killed Henrietta, was responsible for the new drug trade in my community and blew up my garage, but this was quite a bombshell to drop on him if he was legit.

Meanwhile, my head was spinning. I'd have to tell Rex everything when I got home. At least Doreen hadn't talked to her daughter in a while and wouldn't be completely inconsolable at the news of her death.

My mind reeled back to the short four months I'd spent with Henrietta. I really knew nothing about her. The fact that I had no idea she'd grown up one town over from me was the most unbelievable news. You didn't meet a lot of people from Iowa in my past profession. Well, except for that time when I met a guy from Ottumwa at the Uzbeck Clown Conference and Gun Show. Todd was a clown sniper—a rare profession at best, but he found that the Baltic nations were pretty interested in his very specific skill set.

I dropped Teo and Elena at his car at Oleo's. This seemed a bit wrong. But what could I do about it? What *should* I do about it? This was between Teo and Doreen. One thing had changed in my mind—I no longer wanted Teo to be the killer. What would happen to Elena if that was the case?

Maybe I owed it to him to investigate. No. Scratch that. I owed it to that little girl.

CHAPTER TWELVE

Rex wasn't home when I got back. He'd left a note saying another receptionist had quit because Kevin ate her Lean Cuisine and gave her a hamster in payment, so he had to field calls while calling around to find a replacement. I fed the animals and sat in the backyard with a glass of wine, staring into space as I contemplated the events of the past few days.

Leonard lay happily at my feet. He loved being outside because Philby wasn't there. The fat führer often tormented the poor dog. We'd been working on stopping her. I think she just liked the fact that she could terrify such a huge animal.

After a few moments, I remembered I was supposed to nudge Ava on Rex's funding, and this seemed like the right time. I called her and was surprised to get her on the line. After a quick pitch that included the need to pay a lot of money for a new receptionist, Ava agreed but said that someday she might need a *favor*. I told her to stop watching *The Godfather*, and she hung up. It was a fair Marlon Brando impersonation though.

Doreen turned out to be a dead end as far as information about Henrietta was concerned. I tried to recall anything I could about Henrietta but was having a hard time. How do you go four months living near someone and only know that they had multiple hernias? I couldn't think of a single disagreement that might have kept us apart. It didn't seem like she'd knowingly avoided me. So why didn't I know more about her?

Then there's the fact that she grew up ten miles from me. Of course, she wouldn't have known that because I was deep undercover. But still, my job was information gathering. How did I not know she was from Bladdersly?

And then there was the fact that she slept with Teo at least once to produce Elena. And that she avoided her mother until she had a baby to deposit with the poor woman. It was so strange that Doreen knew her daughter was in the drug business and even mused that she could be dead in a Bangkok alley.

Was I missing something? Granted, my time in Colombia was mostly spent with Carlos. How did Henrietta slip through my radar? It didn't make sense. I texted this to Riley, and he texted back that he was currently with a client. That usually meant in the bedroom sense of the word.

Even more perplexing was the possibility that Teo didn't kill Henrietta. If he didn't, who did? Was there someone here from her past who held a dangerous grudge? Why was she wearing fatigues? Why was she killed, or at least dumped, in my garage?

The method of killing was odd. Introducing an air bubble via hypodermic was not going to imply natural causes. Whoever killed her wanted her to die in that place and in a manner that would be discovered. I remembered that Kayla saw Teo with a syringe. Too bad I wasn't at Oleo's first so I could see if he was a diabetic who had to give himself insulin before eating.

That didn't really matter, did it? He had access to syringes, and that's what killed Henrietta.

What if the killer was trying to frame Teo? That was an interesting idea. Teo was here in town. He and Henrietta had a past. Hmmm… Did someone dump her in my garage because they wanted her to be found? Perhaps they figured Teo would just get rid of the body.

That was a likely scenario. The whole thing was a mess, but it had me thinking… I needed to look at Henrietta's life and who might want to kill her if it wasn't Teo. This private eye stuff was starting to look really interesting. Kelly had access to certain channels of research I didn't. I just had Cookie Ahmed at the CIA.

It was time to talk to someone about this PI idea. And I knew the perfect listener…

"So, you see my dilemma." I dumped a pile of crushed shortbread cookies onto the branch next to me. "I don't know what to do. Should I become a private investigator or not?"

The king vulture blinked at me before lowering his head and guzzling down the crushed cookies.

"I know, it's a tough one, right?" I used hand gestures for some reason to emphasize this. "I haven't had a job in, like, seven years. I'm not used to sitting behind a desk or even committing to forty hours a week. Maybe Riley could hire me on an as-needed basis."

"Mom!" Dickie the scarlet macaw shrieked. "Wearing tights isn't weird! It's totally cool!"

Dickie often had a monologue based on the complaints of his teenage boy handler, who, I suspected, was on his phone a *lot*.

"I'm not a LARPer! I'm gonna be a legit superhero someday!" Dickie screamed.

"I mean," I said, ignoring the large red bird, "I need the freedom to do things on a whim, like visit my parents in DC or run away with Rex for a weekend."

Mr. Fancy Pants raised his head and fixed one googly eye on me.

"That's a fair point." I nodded. "I don't do that stuff now. But I could if I wanted to. And that might be more important."

"There's nothing wrong with my superhero persona!" Dickie shouted. "Newt Man is a totally cool idea!"

Hilly Pants, the chick who wasn't so young anymore, hopped into my lap while her mother snoozed in the corner. I stroked her feathers absently. "But it is nice to have a job, to feel like you're contributing to society and not just to Betty's future as a Sith Lord."

Huh. Was I talking myself into doing this?

"Besides, it's not like Riley has round-the-clock cases. I don't think he has more than one or two a month. And I won't work cheating spouse cases. I have standards. I'm not going to do the minutiae either."

I thought about the time I had to babysit a Chechen strongman's pet turtle. Or the time I had to staple reports for Carlos's cartel quarterly meeting. Then there was the time I had to wax the back of a Yakuza sumo wrestler. The life of a spy wasn't all glamorous.

"You're thinking that I'm not making something of my life and using my time wisely. That without a job I'm not part of my community," I guessed. "But I helped save the world a few times as a spy. Which should account for spending the last seven years of my life doing nothing but running a troop."

Besides, I was shaping young minds. Well, eight of them anyway. When I'd started, the troop was a lot bigger. But over the years, girls and their families moved away or had to leave for various other reasons.

"What I'm doing *is* important," I insisted to the raptors.

Hilly Pants barfed on me and then hopped away. I decided not to take that personally.

I sighed. This wasn't going as I'd hoped. Mr. Fancy Pants was a great listener, but tonight I really wasn't getting that vibe. Then again, he had a wife and a kid, which was contributing to his species' existence. Was his life becoming more meaningful than mine?

"If I did become a PI," I said, "Rex might not think of me as interfering with his murder investigations all the time. Oh sure, we've had a lot of murders in this town over the last few years, but there's no way that's sustainable into the future. I can't see it happening much from here on out."

This made me pause. "If there aren't any more murders, what will I do?"

I pictured myself ten years into the future, with the troop graduated and in college…except for Betty, who'd be doing black bag drops and wet work in a Bengali slum or fighting for Scottish independence. The cult kids would be long gone, with jobs and families of their own. My pets would all most likely be gone. And I'd be sitting there, chasing around Randi's and Ronni's kids, bored out of my skull.

Then I pictured myself murdering people just for something to do.

"You're right." I got to my feet. "I need to build something for my future. Some sort of career where I won't be left alone and won't go crazy. Maybe it isn't PI work. Maybe it's something else, but I need to figure it out. Thanks!"

I patted the vulture on the head and left his enclosure.

"*Newt M*!" Dickie sang. "When you need him, he'll be there! Wagging his tail, but he has no hair! *Newt Man*!"

The parrot eyed me suspiciously as I walked past him toward the door.

"It's a work in progress, Mom!" he shrieked as I went out into the night.

CHAPTER THIRTEEN

———

The next day I swung by Riley's office to see if he had any more information.

"Nothing new on Henrietta," Kelly said. "I got your text about Doreen. I'm going to see if she has anything on social media."

Riley shrugged. "It's kind of strange. The CIA has nothing on Henrietta before or after she was with Carlos. I've got a call into a friend at the DEA to see if he's got intel."

I sat down in a chair opposite Riley. "I'm beginning to wonder if it's possible that she was murdered by someone local."

Riley tapped his fingers restlessly on the desk. "Is there anyone here who knew you and Henrietta were with Carlos?"

"I can't think of anyone. I didn't even know she was from here, so why would anyone else?"

"Then why do you think it was someone local?" Kelly asked.

"I know." I held up my hands. "It's far more likely Teo did it. He knew both of us, and he knew Henrietta was from Bladdersly. But we should look at this from different angles, right?"

Riley and Kelly nodded in agreement.

"Found her!" Kelly grinned. "Doreen Herschmann!"

I ran over and looked over her shoulder. "That's her." I pointed at the grandmother. "Herschmann? How did you find her last name?"

Kelly gave me a look. "I just looked up the address you gave me and cross referenced it with an old phone book."

"Phone books?" I forgot those things even existed anymore. "I guess that's something I'd need to know if I do become an investigator. Is there anything about Henrietta?"

Kelly scrolled through the posts. "Looks like just Doreen and the little girl." She leaned closer to the screen. "Very pretty girl. Is it me, or does it look like Doreen is terrified of her?"

Sure enough, in every photo, Elena is smiling serenely while Doreen either has a fake smile or is watching her granddaughter out of the corner of her eye.

"She does seem frightened." I clicked Kelly's mouse on one photo and blew it up. "She told Teo not to let the child around sharp objects and to keep an eye on her every second."

"Maybe," Riley supposed, "Granny Herschmann is afraid of kids?"

"You might be right." I nodded. "Elena had impeccable manners and was good as gold all the way to her new home. Who knows? She might have been messing with Teo."

Kelly was still looking at the screen. "I'll check to see who Doreen's friends are."

"Kids are scary," Riley admitted. "Especially little girls, and especially your troop."

As if they somehow knew Riley was going to say that, Betty, Ava, and Inez trooped in, hauling the drone we'd been practicing with. Betty put the drone on Riley's desk.

"You decorated it?" I asked. "You've basically thrown stealth and blending in out the window."

The drone had been painted bright pink, with sequins glued all over it. It looked like it was going to a drag show.

"Mrs. Wrath." Betty handed me the drone. "Can you make some modifications to the drone?"

I turned it over in my hands. "It looks like you already did."

"We princessed it some. We think it gives it personality. But that's not what we're talking about. We mean *other* modifications." Inez wiggled her eyebrows suggestively.

I eyed the girls warily. "What kind of modifications?"

"Oh, you know, the normal stuff," Ava said.

"It already has a camera," I pointed out. "And a small cargo bay."

"Yes, but it doesn't have a precision weapon." Betty put her hands on her hips. "How can we intimidate or punish people who don't do what we say?"

"That's not a good idea," I looked over to Kelly for help, but she was too deep into research to notice. "Especially with Ava's position."

"We want lasers," Inez piped up.

"Lasers…" I repeated.

"Yes. We want to be able to zap bad guys and get people to do our bidding," Betty said. "Shouldn't be hard. You just have to arm it."

"Guys…" I was at a loss here because I knew it would be irresponsible to agree. On the other hand, it would be totally awesome.

"Like the military does." Ava apparently didn't care if the mayor was considering arming a weapon to bully people. "You know how they use drones to kill terrorists."

"I am not arming this with something to kill terrorists," I insisted. Although, it might have useful applications against Teo should he turn out to be nefarious.

"Okay." Betty nodded. "Since you're obviously squeamish, how about something else? Like a nuclear bomb."

"Nope."

I looked to Riley, but he mouthed, *See? Scary!*

"What about an acid-spitting gun?" Inez's eyes grew wide with anticipation.

"Or something that fires a harpoon?" Betty punctuated this with the pantomime of a harpoon being fired. It was kind of impressive how she got the sound effects right.

"Nerve agent?" Ava suggested. "To convince people to vote for me?"

I did the only thing I could think of—I raised my hand with the Girl Scout quiet sign. The girls stopped talking and waited. The problem was, I didn't quite know what to say.

Finally, I found some words. "You can't use drones to hurt or kill people."

"Why not?" Hilly appeared out of nowhere. "I use them sometimes. Only problem is, a drone can't dump a body in a dumpster. But if it ever gains that capability, I'm a little worried that this type of automation will put me out of a job."

The girls nodded as if they heard this every day.

"Not a relatable argument," I disagreed and lowered my voice. "And you're not supposed to talk about what you do in front of the girls."

Awareness came over the CIA assassin's face. "Oh. Right. I don't kill people," she said woodenly. "But if I did, I'd use drones sometimes, especially if they could dump the bodies into a dumpster."

"Why is it okay for her to have that but not us?" Betty pointed at Hilly.

"Because she's thirty," I insisted, "and you're…"

"I'm not thirty," Hilly said.

That brought me up short. "What? I thought you were thirty!"

The assassin who wasn't an assassin stared at me. "Nope. You got it totally wrong. Waaaaay far off. I can't believe you don't know my real age!"

"That's messed up, Mrs. Wrath." Inez folded her arms over her chest.

"You're not thirty?" I repeated.

Hilly shook her head. "Not even close."

"How old are you?" Could she really be a lot older than me? Or a lot younger?

It didn't seem possible. However, the way she really pushed that she wasn't thirty and that I was way off made me think she was closer to forty.

"I'm thirty-one," Hilly said.

The girls gasped collectively.

"I was only off by one year!" I protested.

"Yeah." Hilly rolled her eyes. "But by a *whole* year!"

"You probably don't know how old we are!" Inez challenged.

"Of course I do." This was almost insulting. I knew how old my girls were! "You're twelve."

Inez shook her head. "Nope. I'm eleven and nine-tenths."

"Nine-tenths? What does that mean?" I quietly did the math in my head, just in case they were right. "There are twelve months in a year!"

"Betty is twelve and four weeks…" Inez went on.

Now that's just splitting hairs. "Why not just say twelve and one month?"

"And Ava is eleven and eleven-tenths," Inez finished with a scowl.

"That's not even a number." These kids were just making stuff up to confuse me. "How do you have eleven-tenths?"

Hilly nodded at the girl. "I get it."

"There are twelve months in a year," I attempted to explain. "Therefore, everything has to be in twelfths. If you are eleven and eleven-twelfths, then you are one month shy of your twelfth birthday."

Betty turned to Ava. "It's sad how some adults forget how to do math."

Ava scrutinized me. "Well, Mrs. Wrath is really old. Not like Hilly."

I threw my hands in the air. "I'm one year older than Hilly!"

The girls studied me curiously. "Really?" Inez asked. "Are you sure?"

"Yes," I said, but at this point, I wasn't anymore. "What were we talking about originally?"

"You were telling us," Betty declared, "that you're going to add acid lasers to our drone."

Hilly brightened. "That's cool! I want you to do that to mine too!"

"I'm not going to do that. I never agreed to that." I decided to leave out the fact that I couldn't do that. Apparently they believed that while incapable of simple math and the ability to count to twelve, I was fully capable of adding acid lasers to a drone.

Ava squinted at me. "Are you sure? I mean, you were wrong about Hilly's age and all of our ages and fractions."

Betty, Inez, and Hilly all nodded in agreement.

I picked up the drone and held it back from them. They took my actions to mean something else.

"She's gonna do it! Yay!" Inez punched the air with her fist.

Ava began jumping up and down, which seemed rather undignified for a mayor.

Betty gave me the stink eye. She knew what I meant.

"All right!" I shouted. "There's important work being done here, and you're disrupting it. Head home, and I'm taking the princess drone."

"She's totally gonna do it," Inez whispered to the others.

"Absolutely," Ava agreed.

"I'll check with her later to see how she's doing," Betty offered.

At times like this, it was best to keep my mouth shut, take my drone, and go home.

Back at home, I tried to find a spot to hide the drone where the girls wouldn't find it. The last thing I needed was a pink, sparkly drone launching a series of attacks on the citizens of Who's There. I ruled out my old house because the girls were always breaking in there. I needed to hide it here, where Rex might notice if the girls broke in to steal it.

I was just contemplating tearing out the bathroom wall to hide it when my doorbell rang. I stuck the drone in the tub and pulled the shower curtain shut for good measure before going downstairs.

My spydy senses went haywire. Not because I was expecting something bad to happen but because Philby and Martini were racing around in circles by the front door. I'd never seen either of them do that before. In fact, Martini was usually asleep twenty-three hours a day. But here they were, mother and daughter, acting like maniacs.

Meooooooooooooooow! Martini yowled.

Philby began spitting and hissing while clawing at the door.

My stomach dropped. Something was wrong. Seriously wrong. And I did not want to open that door. This was scarier than the girls wanting me to rig a drone to kill people. Scarier than the thought that I'd forgotten how to do math.

Whoever was out there banged on it again. They weren't going away anytime soon. I took a deep breath and opened the door.

Kevin stood there holding a large aquarium with maybe fifty hamsters inside. They were all standing, some on top of others, front feet pressed against the glass, staring at me.

"What is happening right now?" I didn't remember asking Kevin to bring an insane number of hamsters over.

Philby and Martini tried to claw past me through doorway. To keep my legs from being shredded, I backed up and allowed Kevin to walk in.

"Can you hamster-sit?" Kevin asked as he walked into the dining room and plunked the aquarium onto the table. "Thanks. I appreciate it."

The cats jumped up and glared through the glass at the little creatures, who suddenly decided they were no longer interested in me or my place. Almost all of them managed to pile into a clear, yellow pineapple hut. Squished together like that, they resembled a furball with dozens of beady eyes. I'd had nightmares that started like this.

One hamster had remained outside of the pineapple. He walked up to the glass and pressed his nose to it. Philby began pawing frantically at the glass in a deluded attempt to break through it somehow.

"That's Hamlet." Kevin pointed at the sole rodent. "He's not afraid of anything."

"They're all named Hamlet," I said drily.

"No." Kevin shook his head. "They're all different. This Hamlet has a silent 'a'."

I motioned to the aquarium. "Why are there fifty hamsters on my dining room table?"

Kevin's normally hooded eyes opened wide, and it was terrifying. "There's one missing!"

"Relax," I said. "I was just guessing at the number."

His face reverted to his usual stoned reptile look. "Oh. That's good. I was worried it might be Hamlet. He's an escape artist."

Martini walked around to the other side of the glass as fifty pairs of tiny black eyes watched and followed her. Then she dropped onto the tabletop and passed out cold.

"Something's wrong with your cat," Kevin pointed out.

"Yeah, she's like that. Why did you bring me fifty-one hamsters?"

"Huh?" He stared at me blankly. "Oh right. Can you hamster-sit these ones?"

I kept my eye on Philby, just in case she tried something I hadn't thought of. "No, and why?"

He looked to my kitchen and licked his lips. This may be the first time in a while I hadn't seen him with food. "My landlord visited me. He kinda freaked out when he saw all of my hamsters. I mean, who knew someone wouldn't like lots of hamsters running around?"

I got between him and the kitchen. "I did. In fact, I recently warned you about this."

"You did?" He looked at me as if seeing me for the first time. "That was nice of you."

Philby gave up on pawing the glass and began licking it as if it was made of bacon. Hamlet the Brave appeared to laugh. Some of the other hamsters piled out on Martini's side and began inspecting her through the glass to see if she was dead.

"I can't take them in." I motioned to Philby. "My cat is trying to lick through the glass to eat them."

"Nah." Kevin shook his head. "She's just trying to be friendly."

He retrieved a backpack I hadn't noticed on his back and pulled out a large, pink plastic ball. With one deft movement, he managed to open the tank, reach inside, and grab Hamlet the Brave. Kevin plopped him into the ball through a small hole. After sealing that up, he set the ball on the floor.

Philby was on the floor in a flash as Hamlet took off running. Leonard came in from the other room and stared at the fat feline führer as she tried to keep up with the hamster-operated ball. Leonard walked over to the table and sniffed the tank before heading into the kitchen for a lie-down.

The orb crashed into various pieces of furniture as the cat tried without success to grab it between her paws. It was like watching someone throw gasoline on a fire as Philby's pupils now took up her entire eyeballs and she began to drool. If there was any chance of the little door coming off or the orb breaking, hamster steak would be on the menu…immediately.

"See?" Kevin said. "No problem."

Upon noticing that Philby was gone and the other cat appeared to be dead, the hamsters came out of the pineapple and formed a sort of impressive hamster pyramid to try to see the action on the ground below.

"Do you have to move out?" I asked with a sigh. Somehow I knew that I was going to be watching fifty-one hamsters tonight.

Kevin watched the action on the floor. "Yeah. I figured I'd move into Mom's house, since she's out of town for a few years."

A few years? His mother was doing time for murder. Her house was now his house.

"Why not take the hamsters *there*?" I pointed out what I believed was the most logical option. "Why do you need me to hamster-sit?"

"They need time to adapt to a new setting." Kevin looked around. "They don't like new places."

I tapped on the tank. "But in light of what you just said, isn't bringing them here and then taking them to the house even more disruptive?"

Kevin looked me in the eye. "You obviously don't know anything about hamsters."

"You're right," I agreed. "I don't. Which would make me a terrible choice to take care of them."

"The most important thing," Kevin continued, ignoring what I'd just said, "is that hamsters are solitary, and you should never put more than one in a tank or they'll kill each other."

I stared at the rodent pyramid. "But *you* have them all together."

He actually rolled his eyes. "That's because I mapped the genome and bred them to be more social. You know, for a smart person, you can be kind of stupid."

Grrrrr! "You just said never put two together, and you have fifty in there!"

His eyes opened wide. "Again? How did he escape again???" Kevin desperately looked around until Hamlet in the ball ran over his foot. He pointed at it. "You should've told me you put one in there."

"I didn't," I said with my fists clenched at my side. "You did."

Kevin's eyebrows went up. "Did what?"

My head was beginning to hurt. "Never mind. I'm not taking the hamsters. You should just take them to your house."

"Uh…" He rolled his eyes again. "You heard me say I can't do that because they don't like change."

"But this is…I would…it doesn't…" Words failed me. Maybe I wasn't too smart. "Fine. But only until tomorrow so you can figure whatever this is out."

He dumped a bag of kibble on the table. "Okay. See you in a week." Kevin walked over to the door and opened it. He turned back to me. "Remember. Solitary animals. Never put two together in one tank." And with that he was gone.

I sat down at the dining room table, trying to figure out what to do with these guys. If I followed Kevin Logic, I'd need fifty-one aquariums. I didn't have more than one—which was currently occupied by a golden poison tree frog, who wisely decided to remain hidden in the foliage.

I did not have time for this. I had a murder to solve. It was time to make an executive decision. I made a call.

"Free hamsters! Yes!" Lauren squealed as the girls crowded around the tank.

"No, you're just hamster-sitting for a little bit." Besides, I thought to myself, Kevin would notice if one Hamlet was missing.

"There are eight of us and fifty-one hamsters." Inez stuck her tongue out as she tried to work out the math.

"Fifty," I said. "I'm going to hold on to Hamlet the Brave." I pointed at the rodent in a ball running around the room.

The rodent had taken to finding Philby and just running toward her until she dove out of the way in a weird game of hamster chicken. He was starting to grow on me.

"Okay," Inez corrected. "Fifty. That's six and a quarter hamsters each."

"How do we divide up a quarter of a hamster?" two of the Kaitlyns asked simultaneously.

"Why don't we liberate them?" Betty asked.

"We can't let the hamsters loose," I insisted. "Two of you will have an extra hamster." I paused. "See? I can do math!"

"I'm going to make little outfits for mine," one of the Kaitlyns said.

This was immediately adopted as a great idea by the other three Kaitlyns.

"I'm going to teach them how to ride around in little cars," Inez decided.

"Mine will help me with my re-election campaign," Ava said. "Animals are people pleasers."

"You don't have to run again for three more years," I reminded her.

The mayor shrugged. "When am I going to get a better opportunity to use campaign hamsters?"

I couldn't find any argument with that.

Betty was quiet. That seemed like a bad omen.

"As long as you keep them safe," I intoned, "whatever you want to do is probably fine." I pointed to Betty. "And you?"

The wheels and gears inside her head were apparently spinning, as she said, "I'm going to train them to do stuff."

I frowned. "What kind of stuff?"

"You shouldn't ask questions you don't want to know the answers to," the girl said.

"What are their names?" Lauren, the junior zookeeper asked. "Hamsters like names."

"They're all named Hamlet." I felt a little idiotic saying that and waited for the questions I was sure would be fired at me.

"That makes sense," Lauren said as the others nodded.

Betty looked around. "I think we should see if they want to fly in the drone."

I thought of the drone in the bathroom. "Not happening."

"Mrs. Wrath," one of the Kaitlyns said, "we don't have stuff to keep our hamsters in!"

I hadn't thought of that.

Lauren spoke up using her vast well of animal knowledge. "They need an aquarium so we can watch and make sure they don't set up an illegal fight club."

"Not a problem." Betty whipped out her cell and began typing. After a minute, she put it back in her pocket. "I just ordered eight aquariums with huts, wheels, and water bottles. We can pick them up in ten minutes from Farm and Fleet."

All eight girls looked at me meaningfully. I was guessing I'd just paid for those aquariums and accessories.

I sighed. "Okay, let's get in the van."

CHAPTER FOURTEEN

———

I should've known that ten minutes was a mere pipe dream. Of course eight little girls wanted to stop for lunch on the way because Lauren said you couldn't take care of hamsters on an empty stomach for some reason. After lunch, picking up the aquariums, and carting them back to my house, we spent one agonizing hour as the girls carefully picked out their six hamsters (with an additional one for two of the Kaitlyns).

Of course, the girls couldn't walk home—laden as they each were with a tank holding six hamsters, so I drove them home. Finally, I returned home to Hamlet the Brave, who I deposited back into his aquarium so he could eat, sleep, plot my murder, or whatever hamsters did. At least with only one, I didn't have to worry about a hamster fight club.

Once I made sure he was secure and Philby couldn't get him out, I took out my phone and called Kurt Hobbs.

"Hey Merry! I'm so glad you called!" the kid said cheerfully.

That sounded like good news! "Why? Do you have something for me?"

"Um, no." There was a slight hesitation. "I'm just glad you called."

"Kurt," I said, diving right in, "you know almost everyone in Bladdersly, right?"

"Well sure. I'm probably related to half of them!"

I don't know why I didn't think of this before. "Do you know Doreen Herschmann?"

There was a strange silence on the phone.

"Hello?"

"Sorry," Kurt said slowly. "Did you say Doreen Herschmann?"

"Yes" was all I replied.

"Meet me at Ella's in fifteen minutes," he breathed. "And come alone!"

"Which one? There are two Ella's across the street from each other."

In another example of idiocy, Ella's and Ela's were two diners of rival relatives who served the same exact food on Main Street in Bladdersly.

"Ella's, with two *l*'s" he said before hanging up.

I walked into Ella's, not particularly hungry just having had lunch with the girls a short time ago. But the aroma of meatloaf made me change my mind, and I sat down in a booth and ordered. The door opened, and a man in a long trench coat, fake red beard, and fedora walked over to me and sat down across the table.

"Kurt," I sighed. "Why are you dressed like that?"

"Shhh!" He looked around wildly, and once he was convinced no one was listening, continued, "It's Irving! One of my aliases! I don't want anyone to know I'm talking to you about Schmoreen Schmerschmann!"

"Um, okay, *Irving*." I was just going to go along with it. "What do you have for me?"

The waitress brought me an iced tea and asked Kurt/Irving what he wanted.

"Oh, the usual," he said in his normal voice.

"Right, Kurt," the teenaged girl, who didn't seem surprised at his appearance, walked away.

"You know," I said as I squeezed my lemon wedge into the tea. "Undercover only works if you go in one hundred percent."

Kurt looked at me and then at the waitress, who was loading napkins into dispensers at the counter. "That's just Bailey. She knows me."

"Everyone here knows you, *Irving*," I said. "Why even try to disguise yourself?"

Kurt motioned to the door. "Because you never know who will walk in next! It could be an al-Qaeda terrorist, a Chinese spy, or Merle Abner!"

I hadn't heard of any terrorist groups with that name. "Who's Merle Abner?"

He slurped his drink before answering. "A guy I owe money to. Now, do you want the lowdown on Schmoreen or not?"

The waitress returned and set a plate of meatloaf with fries in front of me and placed a huge chocolate shake with a piece of cake on top and the biggest silly straw I'd ever seen in front of Kurt.

"Way to maintain a low profile," I said as I started cutting up my meat.

"What?" He slurped noisily. "Everyone gets this here. I'm totally blending in."

A middle-aged woman with ramrod stiff posture and a huge pair of glasses entered the diner. She spotted us and walked over.

"Hey Kurt! How's your new job going?"

Kurt sat up straight. "Great, Mrs. Murphy! Thanks!" As she walked away, he pointed at her. "That's my second-grade teacher, Mrs. Murphy."

"Yeah, I got that. What do you have for me?" I took a bite and closed my eyes. It was so good. This *was* the best meatloaf ever. Of course, I'd never tell anyone in Bladdersly that.

He leaned closer, lowering his voice. "She's lived here all of her life. Housewife and widow. Member of the Methodist Altar Guild for sixty years running. Has one daughter. Can allegedly make a passable tuna noodle casserole…"

I held up my fork to stop him. "So, she's normal. Okay. You could've led with that."

Kurt shook his head. "That's just it. She's not normal. Everything looks that way on the surface, but she's not what you think."

Now I leaned forward because this just got interesting. "What is she?"

Kurt leaned back. "What's in it for me?"

I sighed. "I already introduced you to Kayla, and you're dating now."

That's what he'd wanted last time he helped me.

He shook his head. "I hear you're going to be a PI and work for Riley Andrews."

So, this was about a job. "I haven't decided on that yet. You're misinformed."

Kurt looked around the diner again. He needed to stop doing that if he didn't want people noticing him. "If I help you, you help me. Squid Go Pro." A smile settled on his face, as if he was the cleverest man on Earth.

"It's quid pro quo," I corrected. "And there are limits to what I'll do."

He seemed surprised. "There are limits to what you can do?"

I forgot I was talking to someone who was an idiot. I rephrased it. "No, to what I *will* do. Can you hurry this shakedown up, please? I have a brave hamster to return home to."

"I want you to"—he paused dramatically—"give Riley my resume."

Kurt reached into his coat and pulled out a folded piece of paper.

I took it from him. "That's all? Okay."

"Really?" He got very excited. "You'll do it? Wow!"

An old man in a suit and fedora walked in, looked at us, and said, "Hey Kurt. Hi to your mother."

"Thanks Farley!" Kurt responded cheerfully.

"Your beard is slipping," I pointed out. He adjusted it. "Kurt, you know Riley. You can give it to him yourself."

He frowned. "Should I go dressed like this? It'll be one way to show him my undercover skills."

I was about to tell him no, but this was really getting on my nerves. "Yes. Absolutely. I'll even tell him you're coming so you can see how he won't even recognize you."

"Yay!" Kurt jumped up from the table and started doing a little endzone dance complete with moonwalking.

Bailey looked at him for a moment then turned back to her cell phone.

"Sit your butt down!" I hissed.

Kurt had an *aha* moment and sat. "Please don't tell Riley I did that."

"Believe me, I won't. Now, what is"—I turned to look at Bailey and lowered my voice—"Doreen really?"

Kurt leaned forward again. "There's no record of her anywhere. She's never been written up in the paper for birth, wedding, or her husband's obituary. She belongs to these things but never goes. The Methodist Altar Guild says she never attends meetings. As far as I know, she doesn't have any friends. There are no yearbook photos of her. Nothing. In fact…" he looked around again. I wanted to smack him. "It's possible she can't even *make* tuna noodle casserole."

"Same with her daughter, Henrietta," I mumbled. "We can't find anything on her either, and I don't remember much from my four months with her."

"You know her daughter?" Kurt seemed confused. "Oh right. That Henrietta chick from your garage."

"How do you know all of this about Doreen?" I asked. Kurt didn't know I was going to come by and ask about this one person.

He sniffed. "It's my job to know about everyone. Doreen is maybe the first person I ever knew with a mysterious past. I made a little file that I keep in my bedroom, just in case." Kurt grinned. "You should tell Riley that."

I stared out the window. "Maybe she's not really from here…"

Kurt poked the table with his index finger. "Oh, she's from here alright. My parents and grandparents know her. They just don't *know* her, if you get my meaning." He touched the side of his nose for emphasis.

"Someone like that stands out in a small town," I mused. "Even the most isolated hermit is usually well-known in their community."

"She comes across like a sweet little old lady, and maybe she is," Kurt added. "But she's not really like a hermit. We have one of those, Hermit Kermit. Lives just outside of town in a barn. Nice guy. But even though we see him maybe once a year, we know who he is, what he's like, and that he will not eat brown M&M's. Doreen is sort of like a vague person you think you remember but just can't put your finger on."

I sat back. "That is an excellent assessment. Good job!"

Kurt preened. "You'll tell Riley that too?"

I nodded. "Absolutely. And you're telling me, if I went to the newspaper archives or the school library, I wouldn't find a thing on Doreen?"

He shook his head. "I didn't."

I leaned back, thinking to myself quietly as I finished my meal.

"You know what this means, right?" Kurt asked.

"Yes. But do *you* know what this means?" I fired back.

"Let's say it at the same time, on three," Kurt suggested.

Why not? "Okay, one, two, three…ex-spy!"

Kurt shouted, "Disgraced circus clown!"

We looked at each other until he slumped. "Well, it's probably your idea, but mine is at least fun."

He may have had a point there. With what little we knew about Doreen, it would be better if she was a disgraced circus clown. Way better.

CHAPTER FIFTEEN

———

Rex came home for a quick dinner. He asked why there was a rodent in a ball running around the house and why Philby was on her side, passed out. After filling him in on our new boarder, he headed to the sheriff's office. Carnack needed an assist with the marijuana issue, and I had a feeling that particular problem wasn't going away anytime soon. Unless Teo was behind it. The sooner I solved this thing, the better it would be for our corner of the world.

After meeting with the Bladdersly know-it-all, what did I know about Doreen? Not much. In my experience, someone with no record who flies under the radar is either in witness protection or a spy. I didn't really know much about disgraced circus clowns, but I'd seen enough bizarre things in my short career with the CIA that I wasn't going to rule anything out.

Was Doreen a former witness in hiding? It didn't seem likely since she'd lived in Bladdersly all of her life and Kurt's grandparents knew her. Which left spy. Then again, perhaps she was just one of those people who liked to live off the grid. I knew a guy like that in Chechnya. He didn't like cameras, had no friends and, in fact, refused to give me his name. I later found out it was Khatu.

Khatu delivered goat's milk to the strongman I was undercover with. He never spoke to us or made eye contact, and no one was sure where he lived. It was said he had two dozen female goats and kept their names to himself too. Ron and Ivan tried to be friendly, but Khatu wasn't having it. It became such a mystery that I followed him one day back to his farm.

Turns out he had fifteen goats named after American film stars of the 1940s. There was Bette, Joan, Katherine, Ingrid, Elizabeth, and so on. How did I know this? Each one had a nametag on her collar. Khatu also had four Hungarian wives and fifteen children who served as goat herders. He also had three PhDs in animal husbandry, agriculture, and folk wrestling.

My point was, he was a hermit, and I ended up knowing everything about him.

Even though Kelly was investigating Doreen and Henrietta, I decided to see what I could find out. Turned out, you should never, ever google Henrietta the Hernia. My old colleague wasn't there, but I found a disturbing amount of hernia porn. I should've known better.

I typed in Henrietta Herschmann. You might be surprised to know that *a lot* of CIA work is done researching online. Field work is still important, but at Langley there are rooms full of analysts who do nothing but read papers, watch news reports, read minutes of governmental meetings, scan social media, and listen in on conversations.

Not really my speed but extremely useful information when returning a Chechen strongman's missing cat to ingratiate yourself. It's how I ended up working with Wally, Ron, and Ivan. Of course, Mittens ran away again and, that time, disappeared for good. Maybe we both got what we wanted. Wally was kind of a jerk.

Bingo. Information at last. On Ancestry, I found a yearbook with Henrietta's picture from her freshman year. She didn't look much different. Huh. She was in one club—FFA, or the Future Farmers of America. That's a strange club for a city girl. It took me a moment, but I remembered that Henrietta had a specific job with Carlos. Chicken herder. I guess she put that club to use.

Unfortunately, that was all I found in her sophomore, junior, and senior yearbooks too. There were no records of her going to college, listed in the US Census, or any photos. She was almost completely off the grid.

After an hour, I couldn't find anything more on Henrietta, so I turned to Doreen. This led nowhere. Could the old woman have scrubbed all information from the web? It didn't seem like an easy thing to do. How do you live all your life in one place and never have so much as a birth notice?

"This is so frustrating!" I said to Hamlet, who was in his ball on the couch next to me, stuffing baby carrots into the pouches on either side of his face. Philby was nowhere to be seen.

"You should check the dark web." Betty's voice made me jump.

"How did you get in here?" I asked.

The kid shrugged. "Get better locks."

Well, I had to, *now*.

"Are you looking for that chick who bought it in your garage?" Betty sat down next to me.

"Yes," I said after trying to figure out a better way to say it. But I couldn't. "You're not on the dark web, are you?"

She shook her head. "My parents told me if I had any online presence at all, they'd take me out of your troop."

That brought me up short. "But you've helped Ava set up her platform."

"That's Ava, and that's for her mayor stuff. My folks haven't put two and two together on that yet, and I'm pretty sure that since it's for Ava, it's some sort of loophole."

Well, the kid had that figured out.

"Why mention the dark web?" I asked.

"Because she's not on Betty Vision," the kid said.

I glanced at Henrietta's yearbook picture on my screen. "That's up and running?"

Betty picked up the ball. "A special invitation–only prototype is. She's probably not on there since I didn't even know she existed until after she died."

"I didn't get an invitation," I grumbled.

The girl pulled out a sticker and slapped it on the side of the ball. It said, *Hamster Freedom Forever!* "I told you, you're too old. Hilly got in at the cutoff."

For a moment, I toyed with arguing with her. But it was her social media platform, so I dropped it.

"Have you asked the CIA?" Betty suggested.

"Of course. Riley looked them all up…" My voice trailed off.

But did he? He looked further into our old colleagues' deaths. But had he found more on Henrietta? I texted him. He replied back in moments that he was sending me an email.

That was a relief. Of course he'd thought of that. What had I been thinking? And why hadn't I thought about that? Maybe I wouldn't be a good PI after all.

"You're wondering if you'd make a good private investigator," Betty said.

I tried not to look surprised. "How could you possibly know that?"

"I'm experimenting with mind reading. It's part of the mind control trifecta." She held up three fingers, "One, master hypnotism…"

"You've mastered hypnotism?" I asked a bit skeptically.

The girl stared into my eyes.

"Rutabaga!" I shouted involuntarily.

Oh no! "I thought I was done with that!"

Last summer, one of the elderly Scouts who lived across the street in my old house had hypnotized me that if someone clapped a certain way, I'd yell out that word. Up until now, I'd believed it had worn off, if that's something hypnotism does.

Betty frowned. "You are. You were supposed to shout something else. I guess I have to tweak it more."

"No. Forget it. Stop." Then I got curious. "What are the other two steps?"

"Snooping. I heard Mrs. Albers suggest it. And you've been distracted a lot lately. I had a 50/50 chance that what she said was distracting you."

"That actually makes sense." She really was going to be a good spy. "What's the third thing?"

Betty put Hamlet in a ball on the floor. "You should buy me ice cream."

I closed my laptop. "I should buy you ice cream," I agreed.

"See?" Betty grinned. "That's step number three. The power of suggestion. And it worked."

I thought about it for a moment. "Nope. Still buying you ice cream. Come on."

"It really did work." Betty shook her head. "Wait till I tell Hilly!"

"It didn't work," I assured her. "I'm just a sucker for ice cream. Seriously, you know I eat it all the time. Even in the winter!"

Betty narrowed her eyes. "You do?"

I nodded, lying to the girl. "Yup. And it's something you didn't know. So I win."

I don't have ice cream all the time, but first off, I don't want her to know she's mastered mind control, and two, I really do like ice cream.

I glanced at my watch. "It's eight thirty."

"So?" Betty asked.

She had a point. I texted Rex to let him know I was heading out.

We weren't at Feeling Lucky's five minutes before Teo and Elena walked in. Without asking, they joined us. It really was uncanny how much they looked alike. Teo looked a bit tired. I guess for someone who'd been single his whole life, suddenly becoming a father was a bit overwhelming.

Kayla took their orders and then slouched back to the counter to make it up.

"Teo, this is Betty, one of my Girl Scouts," I said, introducing the kids. "Betty, this is Teo and his daughter Elena."

The twelve-year-old and five-year-old nodded at each other but said nothing. They were sizing each other up—something I'd seen spies do but never little girls. Well, except for Betty.

"How's it going?" I asked.

"Great!" Teo said a bit too eagerly. "Right, daughter?"

Elena looked at me and nodded.

"Daughter?" I whispered.

Teo shrugged. "Am I supposed to say something else?"

To be honest, I really didn't know.

Their ice cream arrived.

Elena looked at her dad. "I need to wash my hands, Daddy."

Teo looked at me in askance, probably wondering if he should go with her.

"Come on, kid." Betty got up from her seat. "I'll take you to the bathroom."

The second the two disappeared, Teo slumped in his chair.

"That bad, huh?" I asked.

"I don't know what I'm doing! This was a terrible idea. And..." He bit his lip.

"And what?" I pressed him.

Teo lowered his voice. "There's something about the kid. I don't know what it is. She seems obedient enough. But I'm kind of getting why her grandma pawned her off on me."

"That's just nerves." I waved him off. "Doreen is far too old to take care of a five-year-old. Believe me, I was nervous when I started working with my troop for the first time, and they were five. You'll be fine."

"Maybe," Teo said, sounding unconvinced. "You're probably right. I was an only child with no cousins. I could talk to adults easily but had trouble with other kids. I need to find a book or something."

"Let me ask you something before the girls come back." I glanced in the direction of the restrooms. "What do you know about Henrietta? I can't remember much or find anything online."

Teo's demeanor changed from desperately seeking my advice to dismissive. "Just an average sort of woman. She didn't tell me much about her life."

"How did you know about her mother?" She had to have told Teo something, or he wouldn't have had her contact info.

Teo was, again, dismissive. "She once gave me her information. I stored it in my cell but didn't think about it until you brought her up."

"She doesn't seem very average to me." I shook my head. "She just shows up at her estranged mother's house with a baby, drops it off, and flees?"

"She wasn't exactly the mothering type." Teo spread his hands out. "We didn't talk much, if you know what I mean."

I held up my hand to stop him. "Yeah, I don't need those details. I'm just trying to figure out who would want her dead."

The blood drained from Teo's face, and he cast a terrified glance in the direction of the restroom. "Shhhh! I haven't told Elena that yet!"

"She never knew her mother," I said. "It might not be so bad."

But Teo was in a full-on panic. "I'm not taking any chances! Don't tell her!"

I promised. "Then you have to tell me who you think would want to kill her."

He threw up his arms. "I don't know! She didn't strike me as the type who'd make someone mad enough to kill her! She just was kind of bland. Boring, even!"

I leaned back in my chair. "Well, if you didn't kill her, who did?"

Teo's eyes went wide, and he calmed down. "I see your point. Let me think. It was six years ago."

"Bird Goddess," Kayla called out from the counter, crooking her finger for me to join her.

"Be right back." I stood up. "I expect you to have some ideas when I get back."

Teo nodded, and I made my way to the counter.

Kayla chewed on her lip. She tapped her pencil quickly.

"Something on your mind?"

She froze. "You know?"

Of course I guessed what she was thinking. Maybe I've even mastered a bit of mind control. "I'm guessing this is about the schism."

Kayla gasped. "I don't use swear words. Kurt says it's beneath me."

I didn't feel like explaining the definition of schism. "This is about you and Heather leaving the Cult of NicoDerm, right?"

Betty and Elena walked past me. Betty flashed me some sort of hand signal, but since we didn't have hand signals worked out, I had no idea what she was saying.

"Yeah," Kayla breathed. "Heather says you're going to join us."

"If you guys walk out, then I will too." I turned to see the girls sit down with Teo.

Kayla smiled and started to get excited. "And help us found our own cult—a coven for witches!"

I held my hands up. "Whoa. I don't have time to start a coven!"

Her face fell. "Why not? You have Girl Scouts every other week and no job. What else are you going to do?"

Betty appeared next to me. "She's gonna be a private investigator."

"Well, that's kinda cool," Kayla said grudgingly.

"I haven't made a decision yet," I insisted. "But it doesn't matter because I really don't have the time or energy to commit to something else."

"But this will take the place of your time with the regular cult," she pressed.

"That's true," I said slowly. "Why don't you find a bunch of other girls to help you? Certainly Stewie was the only thing holding you back."

"That's a good point," Kayla said. "I'll broach it at our first meeting. Tomorrow night, in the woods. The usual place."

"But I just said…" I started.

"We'll be there!" Betty announced before dragging me back to the table.

"We will not be joining the coven," I insisted on our way to Teo and Elena.

"Why not?" Betty stopped in her tracks. "It's girl power and could be very educational."

The last thing I needed was for Betty to learn witchcraft. "We'll talk about it on the way home."

"I should've known," Betty said. "You're too old. I'll ask Hilly."

"She's only one year younger than me!" I protested as we sat down.

Teo looked at us in askance, and Elena sat there quietly.

"It's nothing." I changed the subject and nudged Teo under the table with my foot.

He jumped up. "Okay, now we're going to wash our hands!"

That wasn't what I'd had in mind. I thought we'd just step over to the counter to ask Kayla for extra sprinkles.

"You two are going to wash your hands together?" Betty seemed dubious.

"Not together, but at the same time," I corrected as I got up. "In separate bathrooms, of course."

As we walked to the hall where the restrooms were, Teo said, "I think that went smoothly."

It didn't really, but we were now alone. "What did you think of?"

Teo whispered, "I remembered that Henrietta said she once worked for a Russian oligarch in Des Moines! Is that useful?"

"Why didn't you tell me this before? Something like that could be very important!"

Henrietta was involved with the Russians? Des Moines had a large Russian community, and Betty's grandfather—also Russian—had many contacts. Aleksander had helped me with a case once. Betty had engineered the original meetup and was awfully knowledgeable about what went on in that community.

I often wondered if she was related to Putin, she reminded me of him so much.

"I'll look into it." We'd have to get back before Betty realized we were talking. "Did she say when it was or who it was?"

Teo nodded. "Just before she joined Carlos's team. Maybe eight years ago? I can't remember a surname, but the first name was Grigori Ivan…I think."

"Thanks. I've got a solid contact who can help." I wasn't going to mention that Betty was related to him.

"I'm going with you," Teo said.

"Are you guys gonna wash your hands or what?" Betty shouted.

I ignored it. We had probably thirty seconds before she came looking. "No, you aren't. You're still the prime suspect in all of this. I'll take Riley."

"I can help!" Teo said.

"So can we!" Ron and Ivan appeared in the corridor outside the bathroom. Ron was giddy as he said, "We can help little sister and new friend fight Russian mob!"

I shook my head. "I will handle this on my own."

"You do not remember, but we are your bodyguards," Ivan insisted. "Rex would be very angry with us if we did not stop them from killing you in horrible ways."

"What are you guys doing here, anyway?" I hissed.

"Wives want peanut butter and bubblegum ice cream smooshed together with raisins on top," Ron explained.

I gagged involuntarily. "Make sure they tell Rex! I can't keep this secrecy up much longer!"

Teo and I walked back to the table. Elena and Betty were just silently staring at us.

In spite of my fear that Betty had somehow been listening, I was very happy about this new lead. If the Russians killed Henrietta, I didn't need to worry about Teo or Doreen or someone else. Yay!

"You need my grandpa's help again, don't you?" Betty said on the ride to her house.

"How did you… Are you bugging my phone again?"

"Nope," she insisted. "Mind control."

Damn. I would rather she'd been bugging my phone.

CHAPTER SIXTEEN

Rex looked at me curiously across the breakfast table. "Are you alright? You kept repeating the word rutabaga over and over in your sleep."

"It's nothing. I had a nightmare," I lied.

My husband didn't look like he was buying it. "You had a nightmare about turnips?"

I nodded. "Yes, of course. Doesn't everyone?"

I'd never had nightmares about rutabagas before. Oh sure, I'd been terrified by dreams of killer watermelons, and once I woke up drenched in sweat dreaming about a head of iceberg lettuce, but rutabaga? That would be ridiculous.

"How's it going helping Sheriff Carnack?" I asked quickly.

Rex's lips were set in a grim line. "We really haven't had this kind of problem before. We might have found a couple of teenagers with a joint now and then, but Carnack says he's pulling a lot of people over on the county roads with a few pounds of the drug."

"Should be fairly easy to find the dealer," I said. "Someone from out of town would stand out."

Someone like Teo.

"How are they delivering them?" I wondered.

Rex shook his head. "We don't know. They're not coming in by vehicle. Carnack and the State Police have been watching the roads for out-of-state vehicles and running the plates. But it's almost all local traffic."

An idea popped into my head. "Drones, maybe?"

Rex's eyebrows went up. "I guess it's a possibility we shouldn't rule out. It's a recent development. Like I said, it started around the time Teo arrived in town."

Teo could very well be here to push drugs. I didn't want to admit it, but the guy was kind of growing on me. Was buttering me up an act to kill Henrietta and introduce drugs to the community? No matter how I looked at it, I didn't have definitive answers.

"How did you find out about the drugs?"

Rex ran his hands through his hair. "Carnack found a warehouse between here and Bladdersly with about one hundred pounds of marijuana wrapped up and ready to go. Did Teo ever deal with that drug?"

I shook my head. "Not to my knowledge. It was mostly heroin or cocaine."

My husband got up and started clearing dishes. "Carnack's going to bring Teo in for questioning."

"Not a very warm welcome," I muttered. "A suspect in murder and drug running."

"Yeah, well, we don't hang out the welcome mat for something like that." Rex kissed me as Hamlet ran into the kitchen in his ball with Philby and Martini hot on his heels. I got the impression the rodent was screaming *weeeeeeeeee!*

"Why do we have a hamster in a ball?" He looked at the aquarium. "I thought we had enough animals with a dog, two cats and a frog."

"It's a loaner from Kevin," I explained. "His landlord finally figured out he had hundreds of hamsters and kicked him out. He's going to move into his mom's house."

"Why not take this guy with him?" Rex picked up the ball and studied the hamster.

"He actually brought over fifty-one and asked me to hamster-sit. I divvied them up between the girls."

Rex pointed at the rodent in a ball. "What's he doing *here*, then?"

"That's Hamlet the Brave. He terrorized Philby the minute he met her." I shrugged. "I like him."

"Seems like he's the one running from the cats." Rex peered in the ball. Hamlet gave him a look that seemed to ask why the fun had stopped.

I took the ball from his hands. "Watch this."

The second the ball hit the floor, it took off straight for the cats, who turned tail and ran away into the kitchen. The ball disappeared around the corner, and we heard yowling. When we got to the kitchen, both cats were up on the counter, hissing at the ball on the floor as Hamlet did a victory lap around the table.

"I can see how that might be useful." My husband grinned.

"Have you talked to Doreen yet?" I asked.

Rex nodded. "I did. Before I went to Carnack's."

I loaded the dishwasher. "How did it go?"

Rex pulled a bottle of water from the fridge. "Remarkably easy. I guess they weren't exactly close, but she was sad about it."

I closed the dishwasher. "So she was upset about the murder."

He nodded. "She sobbed a little, but after a few minutes she accepted it. She did ask about Elena. I told her Teo seemed like a nice guy but that she didn't have to give up custody to someone she didn't know."

I felt a little guilty that I hadn't protested more when she handed over Elena. "What did she say to that?"

Rex had a strange look on his face. "Nothing. She didn't say anything. Maybe she's rethinking things, but I have to wonder if she didn't kill Henrietta herself."

I'd wondered about that myself. "Perhaps Henrietta showed up, Doreen tried to give Elena back, and Henrietta refused. That could be a motive."

"But why dump the body in our garage?" Rex wondered.

"Good point. She didn't even know me," I admitted.

Rex steepled his fingers. "Not necessarily. Henrietta could've told her about you and Doreen didn't mention it. Or maybe she thought dumping the body in the garage of a policeman in another town would throw us off."

Hamlet ran out of the kitchen, and Philby jumped down and followed him. "Hey! Take it easy!" I shouted.

Rex arched his right eyebrow. "You think Philby will take your warning?"

"I wasn't talking to Philby," I said.

"There is something I should tell you." Rex took a bottle of orange juice out of the fridge and poured me a glass.

"Carnack said something about taking over the case since it's in my garage."

I stared at my husband. "Can he do that?"

Rex nodded. "I have a conflict of interest. But then I usually do in such things because you are usually involved in these cases."

"Why hasn't he tried to step in before now?" I took a drink.

"I think he's up for re-election," Rex explained. "Solving a murder and ridding the county of drugs would clinch his job."

"Come on." I slapped his arm playfully. "The sheriff's an incumbent, and he's popular! He doesn't need this."

Rex shook his head. "Actually, he has a serious contender. She's polling higher than he is. And she's a conspiracy theorist."

"What? Who? How?" This seemed impossible! Everyone loved Sheriff Carnack!

"Medea Jones." Rex winked before kissing me and heading out to work.

No. It couldn't be. Medea Jones was a cub reporter in the area who, at one time, due to my background, believed I was her way to a Pulitzer Prize and a job at the *Des Moines Register*. Whenever I was involved in some case, she thought I was behind it.

But she wasn't a conspiracy theorist. And why would she want to be sheriff? How was she polling so high?

My cell phone buzzed, and I answered it.

"Mrs. Ferguson," a man's voice said. I recognized it as Betty's Russian grandfather.

I lost all interest in Medea Jones. "Hi Aleksander. And please, it's Merry."

"I hear you want to talk to me. Are you free this morning?"

We made plans to meet up at a children's park in West Des Moines. I wrote down the address, and after putting Hamlet back in the tank, I headed out.

It takes half an hour to get to Des Moines but a little longer to get to the western part of the city. It gave me time to think. Betty set the whole thing up without being there when

Teo and I had talked about it. I really needed to debug…everything.

The playground was a pretty little park with comfortable benches beneath big shady trees. I found Aleksander sitting on a bench, and he waved me over. We greeted each other, and I sat down.

"Betty tells me you need information on a Russian," Aleksander said, getting straight to the point.

"Betty shouldn't have known about that," I apologized.

"I have learned never to underestimate my granddaughter," said the old man. "Sometimes I get calls from the Russians asking about her." He scratched his chin. "I suppose I should talk to her about it, but she is kind of scary."

He had no idea.

"So." He slapped his knee. "How can I help you?"

I froze as I spotted Hilly hanging upside down from the monkey bars. She gave me a little nod as she swung there, back and forth, her dark braid touching the ground.

I tore my eyes off her and turned to Aleksander. "Um, do you know an oligarch called Grigori Ivan? I don't know the last name."

Betty's grandfather paled a little but nodded. "Grigori Ivanovich. Nasty fellow. Dabbles in drugs, prostitution, and murder. Why do you want to know about him?"

Great. He was the bad kind of Russian oligarch. "I think he might be the suspect in a murder back in Who's There." I left out the part that it took place in my garage.

Hilly swung until her body was parallel with the ground and then let go, her feet easily finding the ground. I guess if anyone could defy the laws of physics, it might as well be Hilly. The question was, what was she doing here? She made no effort to look in our direction, but she was causing a stir with all the kids on the playground, who were gawking at her every move.

"He goes to the Comrade Club." The old man eyed me. "You didn't do so well there last time."

"Last time you didn't tell me how strong those drinks were," I countered as Hilly took to the swings.

Hilly was swinging wildly, coming level with the top of the swing set each time. I'd never seen anyone do that. As kids we always tried but never achieved it since the swing sets here were at least fifteen feet tall. Like this one was.

"Should I meet him there or somewhere else?" I asked.

Aleksander hesitated. He was an important member of the club. I was sure he was wondering if taking me there again would hurt his reputation. "I'm not sure that's a good idea. He's usually there with his men, and approaching him in public isn't a good idea because everyone's afraid of him."

My gaze traveled to Hilly, who performed a Cirque du Soleil triple twist dismount. A herd of children ran over and surrounded her in awe.

"If you think he murdered someone, I wouldn't put it past him," Betty's grandfather said. "But I'd advise not getting involved yourself. You'd best send the Iowa State Police to question him."

"I kind of need to take care of this myself," I admitted.

"Suit yourself"— he shrugged—"but like I said, he is very dangerous."

Hilly herded all the kids to the merry-go-round. They climbed on top, and she began running alongside, spinning it. What was she doing here?

"I can get you his number." Aleksander looked at his cell. "But why don't you let me make a few calls first?"

I nodded, and he began tapping on the screen.

"Privet Feodor!" The man said hello warmly. "Yes, I still have that new vodka. No, we can't drink it now. I have a question. I've been looking for Grigori. He told me that if anyone ever asks about him that I'm to tell him right away."

What? Was he selling me out? I looked around the park. It had some good defenses, and I did have Hilly, who would no doubt mobilize a child army.

Aleksander put the call on mute. "When did this murder happen?"

I relaxed a little. He was just using what he could to get the intel we needed. "Oh, um six days ago."

He unmuted the call. "Oh yes, I will give your wife my wife's recipe for borscht. So have you seen him? I think he was at the club about six days ago."

Morning, I mouthed.

"It was in the morning, I think." Aleksander winked. "Oh? He was out of town? Did he go visit his family in Moscow?"

The merry-go-round was spinning so fast it was a complete blur. Kids were screaming with joy and terror as Hilly stopped and stood back with a smile.

Aleksander's voice interrupted. "Oh, he was still in Iowa. Is he still around?"

Grigori could be a suspect! He wasn't in Des Moines but was not far. He has been known to deal in all the old vices. And he might have known about me enough to put Henrietta in my garage. This could put Teo in the clear.

"Thanks, Feodor! See you at the club!" Aleksander hung up and looked at me. "Did that help?"

I nodded. "There's the distinct possibility that he was at the scene of the crime. I really need to talk to him. How do I find him?"

Betty's grandpa sighed. "I was hoping to avoid it. But I'll set you up. I wish you'd reconsider. You're known to the Russian community after last time. He won't be happy that the Malenki Mops wants to see him."

I frowned. "Little Pug? I'm known as the little pug?"

"Well"—he spread his hands wide—"you are tenacious… I'll arrange a meetup. Say hello to my granddaughter." Aleksander got to his feet and walked away.

I looked back at the merry-go-round, which was draped with passed-out kids. Hopefully they weren't dead. I'd be willing to bet they were happy.

Hilly was nowhere to be found.

CHAPTER SEVENTEEN

It didn't take long to find her. Hilly was waiting for me in my van.

"How did you get in?" I held up my key.

She laughed. "That's a silly question!"

I started the engine. "Why are you here?"

Hilly looked around as kids staggered like drunks toward us. "I like this playground."

"When have you been here in the past?" I asked unbelievingly.

She pointed at a dumpster next to my car. "That's Morris."

I couldn't help but look to see if there was a name on it. "You name dumpsters?"

"I give them the name of the guy I dump in there," Hilly said with a smile.

Uh-oh. That meant… "You killed some guy named Morris in this park?"

Hilly avoided the question. The CIA wasn't supposed to act on American soil. Then again, they weren't supposed to have assassins either. "Betty's grandfather seems nice."

"He is," I said. "Why are you here?"

She shrugged. "I like this park. I didn't know you'd be here."

Yeah right. "Liar."

Her eyes grew wide. "Really, Merry! You might have a little faith here."

I changed the subject. Arguing like this with Hilly was impossible. Like arguing with a rabid armadillo. "Do you know who Grigori Ivanovich is?"

Hilly cocked her head to one side. "I think so. I think his brother was a target in Moscow." She looked at Morris. "They don't have a very good dumpster system in Moscow. Not like here."

"You took out his brother?" That wasn't good. I probably shouldn't be seen with her right now if that was the case.

"Yes…" she said slowly before nodding. "I'm sure I did." She looked up and to the left. "Definitely. And I did it in front of Grigori."

"Well, that seems a bit harsh," I said.

"There was no way around it." Hilly shrugged. "Grigori was supposed to be at his dacha on the Black Sea. How was I to know he and his assistant would walk in."

My spydy senses tingled. "Assistant?"

"That's right. American woman. Blonde. Petite. Midwest accent."

In spite of the July heat, ice moved through my veins as my spydy senses tingled.

"Do you remember her name?" I said with as much control as I could muster.

Hilly frowned. "He did call her something. That thick Slavic accent mangles so much. Enry, I think."

"Henry?" I gasped. "As in Henrietta?"

Hilly smiled broadly. "Yes! I think so! Do you know her?"

"Well, she was murdered in my garage a week ago…" This seemed like information I should've had before. I just didn't know to ask Hilly the right questions.

"That's a coincidence." Hilly waved at a couple of kids who were holding on to each other to walk a straight line.

Was it possible Grigori killed Henrietta to get back at Hilly? Perhaps he knew that I was connected to Hilly and my garage was the next closest thing? While this could be great news for Teo, it wasn't great news for Rex. Taking on a Russian oligarch required resources beyond his and even Carnack's capabilities.

"Hey," Hilly said slowly. "You don't think he killed her to get back at…"

"You? Yeah, I'm thinking that."

She seemed surprised. "Not me! Hilary Clinton! It's so bizarre how we get confused for one another. Of course, she looks just like me…"

I cut her off. "No, I think it might be revenge for seeing you kill his brother."

"Why would he do that? I wasn't even dressed like me. I was in disguise. He wouldn't know who I was."

I deflated a bit. I'd thought this was a good, solid lead.

Hilly continued. "In fact, I was limited on what I could go for as far as disguises go. It was kind of funny because the agency sent me a short, blond, curly wig. Kind of like your hair."

I pulled the car over. Vehicles behind me honked their disapproval, but I didn't care. Grigori could've murdered Henrietta, not because he thought Hilly killed his brother. But because he thought *I* did.

I started thinking my thoughts out loud. "He must've found out Henrietta and I were both with Carlos and grew up ten miles from each other," I mumbled. "And if he found out I was former CIA, he might've noticed the extreme coincidence and thought Henrietta was too."

"Okaaaaaay…" Hilly laughed. "Now you're just speaking nonsense."

I ignored her. Were the pieces of the puzzle coming together? Was I solving the case?

"But do I send Rex to talk to him, or do I go…" I muttered. "However, if I go, he could kill me on the spot. I'll need to take everything I have on this one. Where did I put my bazooka?"

"It's under your bed in your old house on the right side beneath the pillow," Hilly answered, even though I wasn't talking to her.

I could take Riley, Ron, Ivan, Teo…everyone. That was more than enough backup. Then again, most oligarchs were heavily armed with lots of security. Perhaps I should just forgo my huge summing up in front of everyone and send the FBI to deal with this one.

It was as terrifying as it was exciting. I may have solved the case! And the killer had an army who could kill me! Six of one, half a dozen of the other, I guess.

"Merry?" Hilly tapped me on the shoulder. "We should get going."

"Oh! Right!" I pulled off the shoulder and entered traffic.

We got back to Who's There after half an hour of listening to Hilly once again rattle off the zillions of ways she believed she and Hillary Clinton were twinsies. I was only half listening because my brain was working on all the possibilities.

If Grigori was the killer, and it was looking pretty good, then Teo was in the clear. Well, I still thought he'd killed his colleagues, but maybe that was something I shouldn't worry about. I bounced in my seat as I pulled up to the hotel to drop Hilly off.

She stared at me blankly.

"Oh! Sorry. Are you staying somewhere else? With the twins? You haven't been staying at my old house, have you? You would've told me that."

"No. I'm staying here. I like mixing things up."

"Okay, so what's the problem?"

"My car is back at that park in West Des Moines."

It took an hour and a half to get Hilly back to her car and myself back to Who's There. I was jonesing for lunch but drove straight to Riley's office.

"Guess what?" I said as I flung the door open. "I think I know who killed Henrietta!"

Kelly and Riley exchanged looks but said nothing. I walked over to Riley's desk and plunked down into a chair, where I told them about my conversation with Aleksander.

Riley whistled. "Grigori Ivanovich? Wow! I didn't know Hilly was the one who took out his brother though."

"She wore a wig to look just like you?" Kelly was always eager for ammo against Hilly. "That's just irresponsible."

"Well," I hedged, "you're kind of at the mercy of what disguise the agency gives you."

"Regardless." Kelly held up her finger. "I do not think you should go. It would be way too dangerous."

Riley nodded. "I agree with Kelly. You've been out of the biz for a while and are out of practice for this kind of thing. I think it's a bad idea."

"I'll just set up a friendly meeting with him," I promised. "Nothing threatening."

"This is a bad idea," Riley insisted.

"What if we just met for lunch?" I didn't like that Riley was taking Kelly's side. He knew what I was capable of. Although he might have been right about the rusty part.

"You should leave it up to the authorities," Kelly warned. She probably knew what I was thinking. She always did.

"Look," I insisted. "You know the Feds would take weeks to get around to interviewing this guy. And I want to get this done and over with."

Kelly began typing away. "He's got a pool filled with sharks! And an alligator pit!"

"I'd be disappointed if he didn't," I said. "I know what I'm doing. I did this kind of stuff for years."

"Hilly should do it." Kelly narrowed her eyes. "It's her fault he thinks you killed his brother."

I rolled my eyes. "If Hilly goes, she'll just kill him and stuff him in a dumpster and we'll never know the truth!"

Riley looked at Kelly and nodded. "She's right. Hilly doesn't really do interrogation."

"You're siding with her?" Kelly asked. "You know what she's like…"

Riley held his hands up. "I worked with Merry for seven years. She's a professional who has always gotten out alive. I trust her."

"This is crazy!" Kelly pointed at her screen. "This guy is probably living in an impenetrable fortress with animals meant to eat you! He's dealing in drugs, prostitution, and God knows what else!"

Riley turned back to me. "She has a point."

"This man probably killed Henrietta and left her body in my garage. This is my concern."

"Not just your concern and not just your garage. I'll tell Rex if you even think about it." Kelly had pushed the envelope and taken this up all the way to ten.

"Okay." I threw my arms up. "I won't do it."

Kelly stared at me. "You're just saying that, and then you're going to go ahead and do it."

"No I'm not," I lied.

Kelly leaned forward for the coup de grace. "Pinky swear that you won't go."

I should've finessed it more. I didn't think she'd go right to pinky swear. Who did that? There should be some negotiation first!

"Merry," Kelly said, "I cannot lose my best friend because she did something really stupid. Now either you pinky swear that you won't contact this guy in any way, or I'm calling Rex."

Two seconds later, we were interlocking pinkies. Five seconds later, I walked out to my van.

"I'm going with you," Riley said as he joined me at my car.

"I can't go," I said glibly. "You saw me pinky swear to Kelly."

Riley grinned. "You swore you wouldn't contact him in any way. That says nothing about going there. Since you have no intention of leaving this alone, I will contact him to set up a meeting, and you and I will go."

Kelly was watching us through the window. I'd bet anything that Riley told her he'd come out and make sure I didn't do anything stupid.

I scowled and threw my arms up and down as if I was throwing a tantrum. "Great! Let's go! Meet me at the hospital parking lot in five." Then I stomped over to the driver's side, got in, and slammed the door, hard. I even pealed out just for the frosting on the deception.

Once I was out of her sight, I smiled. Riley still had my back.

I drove home first and grabbed my .45 H&K then met up with him in the hospital parking lot, where, he was checking his gun, a 9mm Browning.

"I called, and Grigori sounded thrilled to meet us. We're heading to his house just outside of Des Moines now."

That made me pause. "How did you do that?"

Riley gave me a subtle smile. "It turns out I know his niece, Ludmilla. Remember that week you followed Putin around Minsk?"

"You slept with her, didn't you?" I shook my head.

"Fortunately, no. The woman is happily married and has ten kids and a mustache. No, she lost her cat and I found him."

"Is that what they're calling it these days?"

He produced a card from his wallet. "She said if I ever needed anything to call. Back in the day, I was saving it for a favor to get you out of a Moscow prison, but this works too."

I took the card. Sure enough it said, "To Riley from Ludmilla – thanks for finding my darling CuppyCakes." It included a number with a Moscow area code. And it still seemed like a euphemism for something else, if you catch my drift.

"I called," Riley continued. "Turns out she was only too happy to arrange things with her uncle." He frowned. "I hope something doesn't come up that I'll regret using that."

I got into his black SUV. "Why didn't you try to talk me out of it first?"

Riley got in and started the engine. "I know what you're like when you get things like this in your head. Besides, I could use a little excitement."

As we drove to Grigori's place, I filled him in on Kurt, fulfilling my obligation to the kid.

"I don't need more staff," my handler said. "I'd make an exception for you, but I really can't take him on right now."

"You could give him a partial assignment now and then," I offered.

"You're really thinking about being a PI?" Riley asked.

I told him the truth. "I don't know. Not really. Or maybe. I'm not sure. I don't think I'm in the best place right now to figure something like this out."

"You'd be good at it, you know," he said without taking his eyes off the road.

That was a surprise. "You think so? I figured I'd just be a pain in your butt."

Riley laughed. "I still can't get used to you not swearing. I know you quit years ago because of the troop. But you used to be an excellent cusser. And you would've never said *butt*."

"Yeah, well, people change," I insisted. I did miss swearing. You don't spend years undercover with dudes without honing that particular talent.

"You're good at investigating, Wrath. Granted, your methods can be impulsive and a bit crude, but you always seem to figure it out."

I wasn't sure if he'd insulted me or not.

"I just don't know," I said. "I haven't been tied to a job in seven years. And even then, I didn't really have a desk or routine. I'm going to need more time."

Riley nodded. "Okay. Right now, we need to come up with a plan for this. We're going into this with nothing but a once-rescued cat to protect us."

"We go in, ask him point blank if he killed Henrietta," I said. "Then if he says yes, we run like hell back to the car and let the Feds deal with him."

Riley glanced my way. "You really do just want answers, don't you?"

I looked out the window. "I'd like to think Teo is telling the truth. He has a little girl to take care of now. Besides, Ron and Ivan love him."

"I don't know," Riley said. "I think we just go in there and talk to him. We leave with whatever information we've got and decide from there. Interrogating him seems like a terrible idea."

He had a point. "Okay. We'll just make conversation until his guys burst in. Then we'll shoot our way out, taking him hostage. We can hand him over to Rex, and that's the end of that."

Up ahead was a huge billboard. I recognized Medea Jones's scowl as she appeared to look down at us.

Carnack is Soft on Crime, the billboard said. There was a badly photoshopped image of Sheriff Carnack with his arms around inmates. They weren't even his arms…or his inmates, as the four convicts' uniforms said ANGOLA on them, which as far as I knew was still in Louisiana.

"Seriously?" Riley said. "That woman is running for sheriff?"

I nodded. "And it looks like she's going big with her campaign."

We passed two more billboards before we left the county. Both had the scowling image of Medea Jones, and both implied Sheriff Carnack was unfit for the job with badly edited images. I didn't like it.

"Can you imagine how difficult it will be to work with law enforcement with Medea as sheriff?" Riley asked.

"What does a reporter in search of a Pulitzer Prize want with the sheriff's gig?" I wondered.

"We can talk about that later," Riley said. "According to my GPS, we're five minutes away from Grigori."

"Getting in shouldn't be a problem since he's expecting us." I checked my second magazine and shoved it and my gun in my purse. "It's getting out that worries me."

"We've done this before," Riley said evenly. "We know he's well-armed and most likely well-manned. We know Russians can be difficult to get a normal conversation out of. And we know that if we make one false move, he'll bring down the house on top of us."

"That's true. Remember Yuri Andreivich? All it took for him to bring out the guns was when you called his wife Star."

Riley squirmed. "It slipped out!"

"Her name was Lara," I said. "You said the name of her tattoo, which was in a very intimate spot. We almost got killed over your carnal knowledge of the wife of a very bad man."

If we hadn't had those grenades on us, we might never have gotten out alive. I never really forgave Riley for that one. But then, he was always involved with one leggy blond or brunette no matter where we were, and this was the only time it came back to haunt us. Hopefully he wasn't sleeping with anyone important to Grigori.

We pulled off the highway onto a gravel road. Normally in Iowa you can see for miles in any direction, but it was July, the corn was up, and this turned out to be a wooded area. We turned again onto a rural route with too many numbers and then into what appeared to be a driveway.

The house that came into view was a small bungalow that looked like it belonged in a Thomas Kinkade painting.

There was no checkpoint, and the house was very welcoming with a huge front garden filled with butterflies.

A man came out onto the porch and waved happily at us. Riley and I looked around.

"We have the wrong address," I mumbled.

"Right," Riley said. "Although I'd rather it was this place."

"Me too," I agreed as the man came over to the car.

He looked like Santa Claus with a snowy white beard, a pot belly, and a jolly attitude.

"Hello my friends! Hello!" the man said as we got out of the car.

"I'm sorry," I started. "We must have the wrong address. We're looking for Grigori…"

"Ivanovich!" The man smiled warmly. "That is me! But where are my manners! Come in! Come in!"

Riley and I shared a look of confusion. This was Ivanovich? Where were the armed men? The pool full of sharks? The gator pit?

"Are you taking us to Mr. Ivanovich?" Riley asked.

The man stopped and spread his arms wide. "I am Grigori! Now come inside for some lunch. I need to feed the sharks first, but then we will eat."

We walked inside. I'd never seen a more inviting house. Two basset hounds sat up when we walked in and waddled toward us, tails wagging. There were natural hardwood floors, wall-to-wall bookcases filled to the brim with regency romance novels, leather furniture, a stone fireplace, and it all smelled like vanilla.

My stomach rumbled.

"I'll be right back!" Grigori said. "Cuddles and Fluff will keep you company."

The two basset hounds licked our knees politely.

"Um…" I started.

Riley just nodded.

What was happening? This bad Russian lived like this? Was it a game? A ruse? Were we being watched by the real Grigori Ivanovich?

As if on cue, the man reappeared.

"I thought we'd have a light lunch on the patio!" he said as he rubbed his hands together.

Riley and I followed him past a cozy dining room with an antique table and chairs into a kitchen that belonged on the pages of an expensive magazine. We helped him carry a plate of sandwiches, cheese, sausage, and cookies out to the backyard.

There was a fence around the perimeter, but you didn't notice it because of the explosion of brightly colored flowers. It was a traditional English garden! The patio was made up of stone pavers upon which were comfy, outdoor chairs with soft, chintz cushions.

The dogs wandered out to join us and then fell over onto their sides and began snoring.

"I don't get many visitors!" Grigori said. "When my niece called, I was thrilled!"

"Ludmilla is your niece…" I said disbelievingly.

Riley must've gotten the wrong Grigori Ivanovich. Granted, that wasn't a common name around here, but somehow, he found another one who was tied to a woman with the same name. I could've killed him, but the chicken salad sandwiches were genius. We might as well stay and eat.

"Mr. Ivanovich," Riley started. I could see the wheels turning in his head as he tried to figure out a way to find out if this man was the baddie we'd believed him to be.

"I think we have the wrong Grigori Ivanovich," he said simply.

The Santa man's face fell. "Oh no! I am sorry! Were you looking for someone who *isn't* his own crime syndicate?"

The looks on our faces must've confused him.

"I didn't think there was another Grigori." He smiled. "You will at least finish lunch I hope?"

"Did you say his own crime syndicate?" I managed.

"Oh yes." He nodded happily. "You do have the right man! I'm so glad. My business is so dreary, and all the men who work for me are so serious. It is so nice to meet people who aren't actively killing someone." Grigori smiled broadly. "Tea?" He held up a white porcelain pot entwined with roses.

I wasn't sure how to proceed. This could all be an act, but my spydy senses weren't tingling.

We introduced ourselves, not really knowing what else to do.

"A private investigator! How interesting." Grigori clapped. "And did you say your name was Merry Ferguson?"

"Yes," I said slowly, trying to think how to phrase this.

Most of the time, in the spy business, you have to have a cover and you have to lie. It wouldn't work very well if you told everyone you were with the CIA now, would it? Over the years, I've lied to so many people that part of me wanted to tell the truth.

"Since you're being so honest with me," I said, "I might as well tell you. My real name is Fionnaghuala Czrygy, or Merry Wrath."

I sat back to wait for recognition. Then I ran my right hand through my hair for emphasis. At any moment now, he should pull out a pair of guns and shoot us.

"Ah! The spy who was outed!" Grigori's grin grew larger. "I get to meet a private eye and a famous spy! How wonderful!"

Something buzzed nearby. Grigori pulled a phone from his pocket. The case had smiley faces all over it.

"I'm terribly sorry!" He held up his index finger. "I have to take this. Please forgive me."

He got up and walked farther into the garden, his back toward us.

"What the hell is happening here?" Riley asked.

"I'm not sure. But you're right. We expected this to be far more dangerous…"

"I mean, he could have a healthier option for lunch." Riley pointed at the spread.

I gaped at him. "You're joking."

Riley grinned. "I'm joking. But seriously, are we about to die? Is he playing this nice Santa thing to take us unawares?"

I shrugged.

Grigori was speaking in a happy voice and then shouted, "I don't care what you do! That shipment of AKs won't move themselves! Get on it, or I'll feed you to my sharks, Oleg!"

He must've hung up, because he spun on his heel and turned to us with an apologetic smile. "I'm so sorry. Business, unfortunately, calls sometimes, but I don't want it to ruin our little luncheon!" Grigori looked at me. "Now, you were saying, you're that poor spy the vice president outed on CNN. I felt very badly for you. So unprofessional."

"Yes…it…was…" I couldn't figure out what to say next.

Riley gave him one of his most charming smiles. "Well, it's very interesting for us too! It's not every day we get to meet a Russian oligarch right here in the middle of Iowa."

Grigori laughed. "I get that a lot. You probably thought I was this super-violent and dangerous criminal." He spread his hands. "But I'm just a person like everyone else. I like people. Always have. And it's hard to make new friends sometimes, in my line of work."

"I'll bet," I said. "I felt the same at first when I got home. I didn't want people to know who I was because I wasn't sure how they'd take it."

Grigori nodded vigorously. "That's it! Exactly! You'd be surprised to see how many people find what I do a bit off-putting."

Riley agreed. "I worked with Merry before she left the CIA. I was worried that moving here would make socialization difficult."

Grigori slapped his knee. "And you saved Ludmilla's cat! I should thank you for that. I gave her CuppyCakes when he was a kitten. She may have ten kids, but that cat is her baby!"

"Do you really have a pool filled with sharks?" I asked. "Or is that for show?"

Maybe all of this was for show. I still hadn't figured that out.

"Want to see?" Without waiting for an answer, Grigori jumped to his feet and went to the back gate.

We followed him through the gate into another building. There was a large glass pool in the middle of the floor, the size of a large kiddie pool. In it were five fish—all about the size of my thumb.

"Sharks!" he said. "Oh, I know, it's a bit misleading and I could just lie, but I feel like you should always tell the truth when you can."

"Are they man-eaters?" Riley wondered.

"They are! And freshwater sharks at that. Colombian sharks." He looked at them and then at us. "They'll get bigger.

"And there's my alligator pit." Grigori pointed to a small tank with two tiny caimans inside.

While it was truth in advertising, it wasn't threatening at all. Grigori led us back into the garden, and we sat down at the table once more. I devoured another chicken salad sandwich. Seriously! What was in these things that made them so delectable? Fruit maybe?

The phone buzzed again, and once more, Grigori excused himself and walked away to take the call.

"I am completely lost," Riley said. "It's like a Jekyll and Hyde scenario.

As if on cue, Scary Santa began shouting at someone on his phone for the caller to "make an example of" someone who'd disappeared with a suitcase full of cocaine.

"I know." I reached down to scratch one of the bassets between the ears, and he groaned appreciatively. "I don't know how to handle this."

"Take it slowly," Riley said. "We'll feel him out to see what's going on."

I nodded as Grigori screamed, "Well, just kill him, then!"

He hung up and joined us once more.

"I turned it off. Now that we don't have any distractions, how can I help you?"

There's a moment, when you work in clandestine intelligence, when you have a split second to make a decision on how you will answer and hope that they don't pull out a gun and shoot you on the spot.

"Mr. Ivanovich," I started, but he held up his hand. I spotted something I hadn't noticed before.

"Grigori. Please. And I hope I can call you Merry and Riley?"

I nodded my assent. "We wanted to talk to you about Henrietta Herschmann."

This might have been a terrible idea, but I leaned forward and looked him in the eye. "And we want to know if you murdered her."

CHAPTER EIGHTEEN

———

The happy gleam in the eye disappeared and hardened. "I don't know if we can be friends after all."

Well damn. I was really starting to like him. I mean, of course I couldn't be friends with someone who pushed drugs and trafficked humans. But he did make an awesome chicken salad.

Riley stepped in. "Let's take a step back, shall we?"

"Too soon?" I asked.

Riley gave me an imperceptible nod and turned to Grigori. "What my friend wanted to ask was did you remember that she worked for you? We are just trying to find answers in her death. The deceased former employee of yours was killed in Merry's garage, and we were wondering if you knew who might want to do that?"

And did you kill her?

Grigori softened. "Henri hadn't worked for me for years. I knew she was from Bladdersly, but beyond that, I knew very little about her life in general. I'd last heard she was working in Prague, but my intel might have been wrong."

I didn't regret laying my cards on the table. It has and remains the quickest way to find out, even if it ends with a shoot-out.

"You do understand why I asked," I said plainly. "We are trying to find out what really happened. Some innocent people might end up going to prison for the murder."

The Russian gave a little shrug and relaxed. "I haven't seen her in years. And we left on good terms. In fact, I'd recommended her to Carlos the Armadillo. Gave her a glowing reference."

But that didn't mean Grigori didn't kill her. This man was a stone-cold killer. He'd as much as ordered an assassination while we were having tea and sandwiches.

"Is there anyone else in your organization who might not have gotten along with Henrietta?" I asked.

The man thought about this for a moment while I surreptitiously took another sandwich. If I was going to get shot by this man, I might as well die with a full stomach.

"Maybe. I might have something for you. But it will have to wait. I have an appointment I'd forgotten about."

Likely story.

Grigori stood up, and we did the same. I was taking my sandwich with me.

At the door, he smiled again. This one was friendly but didn't have the warmth from earlier. "I will contact you tomorrow with my thoughts, Mr. Andrews. Now, thank you for coming. It was lovely meeting you both."

And with that, he closed the door.

Back in the car, Riley let out a long sigh. "You know, for a moment there, I thought we'd made a new friend."

"We can't be friends with a criminal like that," I said before taking a bite. "In fact, when this is all over, I might have to see what I can do about getting his trafficked women out of there. Wherever they are."

As we pulled out of the driveway, I wondered if Grigori was the one flooding the county with weed. I told Riley my suspicions.

"I've been hearing some talk of that through my informants," Riley said.

"The informants again? How do you have informants in Who's There? It's not a seething hotbed of criminal activity."

"A small town is perfect for that because everyone knows everyone else's business and there are always a few who are more than willing to make money off of that."

"Do you think Grigori is behind the drugs?"

"Did you think of Teo as a suspect?"

I nodded. "He says he only ever peddled in heroin and cocaine."

Riley thought about this. "That's true. Dealers often stick to what they know."

"But they also adapt to demand. I don't recall a time people around here did the heavier drugs, but I could see a demand for marijuana."

"Do you think Grigori killed Henrietta?" Riley asked.

"I definitely think he's a major suspect. We have no reason to believe he told us the truth."

"He showed us the sharks and gators. Obviously he threatens people with his pool full of sharks and his gator pit. I'd be willing to bet he did that on good faith so we'd think everything else he said was true."

"That only makes him more suspicious in my book," I said. "And there's something else. He was wearing a ring just like the one I found in my garage. The one with the arrow? Well, Grigori's had a target etched on it. I think he's lying when he implies that he and Henrietta weren't close."

"That does seem like a strong clue. Have you gotten any word on fingerprints from Soo Jin?" Riley asked.

I took out my cell and called her. The call went straight to voice mail. I left a message asking about prints on the note and ring.

Riley waited until I put the phone away. "Who are your main suspects?"

"Grigori, obviously. She worked for him, and he lives nearby. Doreen had a very strange relationship with her daughter, and I could see that there's resentment for dumping Elena on her. And then there's Teo."

"And it could be someone else," Riley reasoned.

I nodded. "And it could be someone else. There could be someone we haven't met or considered."

We passed one of Medea's billboards, and it wasn't even in our county. This one had a picture of me, and it said, *Sheriff Carnack is Soft on Repeat Offenders!*

"Is it too much to hope that it's her?" I pointed at the scowling face.

That's when I noticed in smaller print: *Paid for by the committee to imprison Merry Wrath.* Damn. Ronni was organizing.

"Kelly's been working a lot of overtime trying to get more information on the five deaths Teo was present for." Riley acted as if he hadn't seen that last part.

"Has she found anything new?"

He shook his head. "All of these deaths took place in South America, and there's a bit of a language barrier, so nothing yet."

Kelly didn't speak Spanish. I did. But I didn't want to spend all day on the phone translating.

"Do you have anyone you can use to translate? One of your *informants*, perhaps?"

"I should make you do it," Riley said. "My Spanish is too rusty. But I'll bet you've still got it."

"I don't know. I haven't spoken it in years. My Russian is far better. I'll see if Rex knows of anyone. I'd say Inez's parents, but I think asking them to translate the gruesome details of five deaths that could be murders might just be too much."

We rode the rest of the way in silence. Riley dropped me off at my van in the hospital lot and drove away.

I sat for a while, trying to think this through. I'd really hoped we'd go see Grigori and he would say, *yes, of course I killed her. And I'm flooding your home community with drugs. So what?*

What was that all about, anyway? The super nice guy at first, then the cold-blooded criminal after? Which part was an act? I'd had the feeling that the Santa Grigori was genuine, until I saw the look in his eyes when I mentioned Henrietta.

Wasn't it interesting that he didn't have to think about who she was? The woman hadn't worked for him for years, and yet he didn't have any hesitation when I mentioned her. Part of that could've been the name—it was unusual. And he didn't seem surprised when I said she was murdered. That may have been the most telling part of all. That and the ring, that is.

Or did Henrietta lead the kind of life that made others believe she'd eventually meet with a sticky end? People in the drug business didn't live as long as a plumber or teacher. The job was dangerous. Look at Chloe the Clownfish or Sharkface Shawn.

Rex texted to ask about dinner, and I suggested Oleo's. Even though I'd just had three chicken salad sandwiches, I figured I could always eat some fries. I removed the .45 from my purse and put it in the center console and closed the lid.

When I got to the table, I found that Sheriff Ed Carnack was with him.

"Hi Ed!" I gave him a quick hug before sitting down.

Ed Carnack was a tall, large-framed man and an excellent sheriff. He was competent and smart and didn't mind me investigating now and then. At least, I think he didn't. He'd never really said. I'd better not mention it.

"I'm glad you're here," I said as the waitress delivered two bottles of beer for the guys and a glass of wine for me. "Riley and I went to see a possible suspect in the murder, and turns out he's in the drug biz."

I told them the whole story, leaving out that Riley and I thought we were headed into a gun fight or that we took our guns at all. They were amused by the sharks and caimans, but the atmosphere had grown more serious by the end of my story.

"I feel that, for the record," Rex said, "I need to remind you that this isn't your job and you put yourself at risk."

Carnack said nothing.

"I know," I agreed. "But he's definitely a viable suspect in both investigations, right?"

The sheriff rubbed his chin. "I've heard of Ivanovich. Keeps his hands clean, stays out in the country by himself to distance himself from his work."

"I'd heard something about a Russian crime boss but didn't know more than that," Rex admitted. "You said he had a ring matching Henrietta's?"

"Not matching, exactly." I picked up my glass. "But the same metal and size. I think her having one with an arrow and him having one with a target is pretty interesting."

"Soo Jin doesn't have any forensic evidence back from the lab, I'm afraid," Rex said. "Things are really backed up, and there's been some turnover in the staff. I don't know when we'll have that."

I filed this in the back of my mind. "If you don't mind my asking, how are you finding out about the increase in marijuana usage?"

The waitress deposited three plates with the best burger in Iowa, surrounded by fries. Rex must've ordered for me. I'd have to eat it. Letting an Oleo's burger go to waste would be criminal.

After a few bites, the sheriff answered my question. "I assume Rex told you about the warehouse. We're arresting a lot of folks on possession. As you know, in Iowa any amount is illegal. But that won't stop people from trying to get their hands on it."

"The mayor and the city council are considering options," Rex added. "I might even get that new police officer I've requested."

We ate in silence for a few minutes. I didn't want to get involved in their drug investigation. Murder was kind of my thing, really. But it was convenient that two of my top suspects were in the trade.

"I'm going to bring Teo Manteo in for questioning," Ed said as he pushed back from the table. "I think I can get Ivanovich to come in, just to answer a few questions."

"I want you to know you have my total support for your campaign," I blurted out.

"You've seen the billboards," the sheriff surmised.

I nodded. "I don't see how she can win. She fails at practically everything she does."

"You never know in these cases." Carnack took off his hat and ran a hand through his hair. "I've been in law enforcement for twenty years, all in this county. I have the experience, and folks know me. But sometimes a candidate comes out of nowhere and takes things by storm."

"One with a loud mouth," I added. "She's just awful. How could someone that brash and obnoxious win any election?" I kept my thoughts on Ronni's involvement to myself. I didn't want to bring up Rex's sisters in case I accidentally blurted out their news.

"It has been known to happen," Rex said. "Say Ed, did you know Merry is considering becoming a PI?"

I shot him a look. "Well, I didn't really want that out there. I'm not making any decision soon."

"You might be good at that," Carnack said. "And if that doesn't work, you could be my deputy."

Rex froze, his bottle halfway to his lips. Then he appeared to regain his composure and finish drinking.

"Thanks, Ed," I said sincerely. "I don't think I want to go into law enforcement. I don't even think I want to be a PI. But that's nice of you to say."

"Well, whatever you decide to do"—the sheriff winked—"I think you'll make an impression."

Rex and Ed laughed.

The question was, good…or bad?

CHAPTER NINETEEN

———

We weren't in the door five seconds before I got a call from Carol Ann, Betty's mother.

"Hey Carol Ann! What's up?" *Please let this be nothing!* Betty was inserting herself more into my life than usual, and I really needed a break.

The woman sounded frantic. "Merry, we think Betty has joined a cult or something! She just left the house wearing a white bathrobe, and before she walked out, she asked if I had any eye of newt!" There was a pause. "Is that something I should have? Do you think the aliens would like it?"

Carol Ann had long labored under the idea that she'd been kidnapped by aliens who'd taught her to play the bassoon instead of the usual *you know what*. To keep her happy, Ava allowed Betty's mom to start a welcome wagon for the aliens she knew were coming, called Helping Hands and Tentacles.

"I don't think you need eye of newt," I soothed as I suddenly pictured a lot of eyeless newts sitting helplessly in the woods. "I'll go find her and take care of it."

"Oh good." The woman sounded relieved. "We've been so nervous lately because our back door has been reminding us not to forget our keys every time we go out. Thanks!"

Betty's parents were also often the victims of some of Betty's more creative pranks.

I grabbed my keys and ran out to the van. I had a coven meeting to attend and break up.

"Bird Goddess! You made it!" Heather jumped up and down.

"Where's your robe? You need a white robe," Kayla chastised.

"'Sup?" Betty asked.

"You really *have* split from the Cult of NicoDerm and started a coven," I stated. "Well, more power to you, but Betty's parents are more alarmed than usual, so I think you'll need a cutoff age. She's too young."

I left out that mentally, she was smarter than these girls.

Heather's face fell. "But we need her to teach us magic and mind control and stuff."

Betty nodded. "And they're going to teach me how to summon a demon *correctly*." She turned to the girls. "I did it wrong once. I don't want to mess that up again."

The two teens nodded as if they totally understood.

"Betty does know some magic," I admitted. "But she doesn't know mind control, and I don't think anyone should be summoning a demon."

"I do too know mind control." Betty's eyes narrowed.

I made a conscious effort not to look at her but still couldn't help myself as I shouted, "Rutabaga!"

"Stop that!" I turned on the girl, and for a split second I thought I saw disappointment in her eyes. I turned to the others. "Why do you want to know that anyway? I thought you wanted to do white witch magic."

"We do," Heather said. "But we need to teach Stewbutt and Mikey a lesson in how to treat women."

I had to agree with that. "Still, let's make this as benign as possible."

"So you're in? Yay!" Heather cried out.

Kayla agreed. "You are so getting a lifetime twenty percent discount at Feeling Lucky's!"

"I didn't say I was in…" It hit me what she'd said. "Wait, a lifetime discount?"

Heather elbowed Betty. "You were right! That worked! You really do know mind control!"

Kayla piped up, "I need to know some tricks to use on my boyfriend, Kurt."

I needed to dispel the idea that Betty could control me. "That's not mind control. It's more like extortion. Besides, everyone knows I love ice cream."

"Do the rutabaga thing again!" Heather cried out, drunk with power.

"I'd better not," Betty said in a tone I didn't recognize. Was she concerned about my snapping at her? This was either great news or terrible news, and I wasn't sure which.

"Are you guys sure you want to leave the Cult of NicoDerm?" I asked.

Heather and Kayla looked at me strangely.

"Oh, we're not leaving the cult," Heather said.

Kayla laughed. "Not without the Chapel of Despair. That place is too cool."

The Cult was wealthy in their own right because they owned the rights to the Beetle Dork franchise, which was built around a comic book Hilly wrote about a superhero named Beetle Dork. She had given the kids the rights, and they'd bought the Chapel of Despair, which was known to most folks as the old Lutheran church.

"I've got plans for that place," Heather said. "We're gonna redecorate and stuff."

"I can recruit the other girls in the troop," Betty suggested. "Then it's like we have our own clubhouse."

While this was an interesting idea, I did promise Carol Ann I would do something about Betty joining a cult. Besides, I didn't think I could convince all of my troop's parents that it was a good idea for their girls to become witches.

"How about this," I offered. "I'll talk to Stewie and get him to see the light. You can still have your coven within the cult. Deal?"

Betty nodded. "And if he doesn't agree, you can always kill him with one finger."

Believe me, there were times when I'd thought of doing just that.

Kayla and Heather gaped at Betty.

"Can you teach us how to do that?" Heather asked.

"Sure," Betty said. "But it'll cost you. Cosmic manipulation ain't cheap."

I left them to negotiate the terms of Betty's totally made up whatever and headed to the Chapel of Despair.

Despair was the right word for it, because I found Stewie and Mike slumped in the office, surrounded by five empty boxes of Twinkies and two dozen empty soda cans.

"Bird Goddess!" Stewie squirmed to get upright. "You're here! You're staying with us!"

Mike's Adam's apple bobbed in agreement. "Those girls can suck it!"

"No, I'm not staying with you unless we talk and you see the error of your ways," I said with less zeal than I should've mustered.

Stewie sniffed arrogantly. "I'm a dread demon. I never make errors."

Mike nodded then paused. "That's not true. There was that time when you gave two thousand dollars to that Nigerian prince."

Stewie turned red. "He was real royalty, and he needed money from us to get his money in Nigeria!"

Mike didn't let up. "And then there was that time you blew a circuit breaker downstairs trying to set up lighting all over the chapel that would make you look taller. That took out half the city's grid for two days."

I stared at the redheaded demon. "That was you? I had to re-chill all my wine!"

Stewie raised his arms over his head and wiggled his demon fingers. "You will not tell the Bird Goddess embarrassing things about me! The Dred Demon commands you!"

Mike rolled his eyes. "Whatever."

Was there dissension in the ranks…of…two?

"I don't care about that," I assured them. "What I want to do is find a way to bring the rest of the cult back."

"Why?" Stewie stuck out his double chin. "We don't need them. In fact, with all that estrogen gone, Mike and I have become more powerful!"

"I sincerely doubt that," I said.

"It's true," Mike said. "Stewie actually had the strength to slam the door to the chapel yesterday. Normally he needs one of us to help him."

"Stop telling her that!" Stewie waved his arms around like he was attempting to make a spell, but it just made him look like a nerdy octopus with spasms.

"And he actually almost won a video game against his cousin Sherman," Mike continued.

"He cheated! Or I would've won!" Stewie squeaked.

"Guys!" I held up my hands. "You've been acting like misogynistic jerks lately."

"Demons outrank witches!" Stewie stamped his little foot.

"That's misogyny," I put my hands on my hips. "You have to treat the girls like equals and let them have a say in…whatever weirdness you guys are doing."

"She might be right," Mike said. "Heather and Kayla just wanted to do some white magic. I don't see why that's a bad idea."

"Because…it…just is!" Stewie was turning an alarming shade of red. "We are men! We have to act like men!"

"Real men don't act this way," I pointed out. "Real men respect women and treat them like equals."

"They do?" Stewie eyed me dubiously.

"That's not what it says in the manual," Mike added.

"What manual?" I asked.

Mike left the room and came back with an old book. It was written by someone named Dred Demon Arthur and was titled *How to Recruit and Control Hot Chicks into Your Cult*. It was dated 1954.

I handed it back, refusing to look at it. "Nope. Toss that crap out. That's old, male chauvinist stuff, and you're better than that."

"I am?" Stewie blinked at me.

"Of course you are. I wouldn't have been part of your group all these years if I didn't think deep down that you are a good guy."

Stewie beamed at Mike. "She said I'm a good guy!"

Mike nodded as if he always believed this was true.

"Listen. Girls are equal. You can't only give them ranks subordinate to you. Heather's got all these ideas on branding." I didn't know what they were, but she was always talking about it.

"And Kayla's got a real job. These two women have skills you could use to make this place better."

"Well, I don't know about better. We are druids, after all. Can they make it more druidy?" Stewie asked.

"Sure," I responded, not really understanding what he meant. "Just call them back, grovel at their feet, and give them whatever they want. I don't have any more time for this. I've got a murder to solve."

I was at the door when I turned back. "And you need to install age limits. No one under the age of fifteen. Got it?"

I didn't wait for an answer.

Back at home, I told Rex about the whole cult schism thing while Hamlet raced around the floor in his ball.

"Where are the cats?" Philby and Martini were nowhere to be seen.

"Hamlet managed to lure them into the closet. Once they were inside, he rolled out and slammed into the door, closing them in."

"What?" I scooped up the ball and stared at the animal inside. "He's a genius!"

"I saw the whole thing." Rex smiled. "I think we should keep him."

I carried the ball into the kitchen and dropped a baby carrot inside. Hamlet shoved it into his right cheek pouch and took off running into the dining room. He stopped short of Rufus the frog's aquarium. For a moment, it looked like the frog gave him a thumbs-up.

"Any news on the case?" I asked Rex.

"Soo Jin should have the full report tomorrow. But I doubt there's anything new. I'm going to bring Teo and Doreen in again for further questioning. I don't like how those five deaths in Colombia are tied to him."

"You still think Doreen did it?" I sat down next to him on the couch.

"Well, I don't think it's you." He pulled me against his chest. "Then again, you are pretty suspicious and were in the CIA, so…"

"Wow," I said. "When you say it like that, I do look suspicious. Should I turn myself in?"

Rex kissed the top of my head. "Or you could throw yourself on the mercy of the court."

I looked up and kissed him. "Sounds good. We might as well get started."

CHAPTER TWENTY

Kelly called me the next morning and asked me to come in. I was there first thing.

"I have some information on the five mysterious deaths in Colombia." She handed me a folder and then sat back in her chair.

"Inconclusive?" I paged through the file. "In every case?"

"Yup. The authorities did not think they were accidents but had no evidence that they weren't. Mateo the Matador was gored by a bull, but they found Ambien in his system and concluded it made his movements and reaction time slow."

"Lots of people take Ambien." I studied the rather gruesome crime scene photo.

"And he had a prescription for it, in his name. But his mother said he never had one before and in fact wouldn't have taken it because it would've conflicted with his job." Kelly frowned. "Did Mateo use heavy machinery?"

"No"—I shook my head—"he was the head cocaine tester. Taking Ambien would've thrown his instincts off."

"That's a thing? Head cocaine tester?" Kelly looked shocked.

"It was with Carlos's outfit." I shrugged.

Kelly decided to continue. "Then there's One-Handed Tim." She looked at me. "Why was someone with only one hand cleaning a gun?"

I knew the answer to this one. "He was very independent. I think he was afraid Carlos might fire him if he thought he was unable to complete certain tasks. Tim was terrified of the prospect."

"But why? Firing isn't so bad, and he could've found something better."

"Ah," I said. "There's where your error lies. Firing to most people means losing your job. Firing to Carlos meant at the end of a gun. You lost your life. And Tim was pretty sensitive about his nickname."

"What happened to his other hand? Gun accident?" Kelly asked.

I shook my head. "He lost it in a poker game." When I noticed she looked confused by this, I added, "literally."

"Okay." Kelly bit her lip but went on. "His death is suspicious because when he ejected the magazine, he didn't check the chamber."

"Look at you, talking about guns and stuff!"

Kelly grinned. "Anyway, he was looking down the barrel, and it went off in his face."

"That happens," I said. "Sadly, more than you think."

"Yes, but the weird thing was the entry wound was in the side of his head, not the front, where he would've been looking."

"That is suspicious," I agreed. "Let me guess, those around him then said it was suicide."

Kelly nodded. "But why didn't the report just say suicide instead?"

"Because Tim was a devout Catholic," I said. "He couldn't have been buried in the church cemetery."

"So, that really could've just been a suicide, then," Kelly reasoned.

I shook my head. "Tim was the most upbeat and optimistic guy you'd ever meet. And he'd never want to put his parents through a scandal in the church. What about Pedro the Pimple and his flesh-eating bacteria?"

Kelly frowned. "He'd been in a spotless, climate-controlled room for a week. There's no way he could've been infected."

"Carlos kept his money room like that. He thought money had diseases. He should've been more worried about all the chickens running around," I said. "Nobody else had it?"

"No," Kelly said. "In fact, he'd been alone the whole time."

I nodded. "Of course he was. Carlos was always paranoid about his money, and often Pedro was the only one allowed into the room. It was nice for a sterile room. Had a shower, a big-screen TV outfitted with a thousand movies and cable, a bed, and a fully stocked kitchen. Are they sure he didn't go to the hospital for something else and contracted it there?"

Kelly shrugged. "They didn't know the answer to that. Which was why it was considered inconclusive."

"Last two," I said. Chloe and Shawn.

"Chloe had a fatal allergic reaction to an anemone sting and died. Same thing with Shawn. He wasn't bitten by a shark but stung by a Colombian Shark. He had a reaction and drowned immediately. Chloe was pulled from the water and died on the beach."

Grigori Ivanovich had Colombian sharks. Could that be a coincidence too?

"That is bad. So what's the catch on those two?"

"They found no anemones in the area. The police decided that the anemone became detached when it stung her, or she pulled it loose and it washed away. But the oceanographer was suspicious. And for Shawn, Colombian Sharks are freshwater fish, not found in oceans."

"One of those scenarios could be explained, and the other not so much?" My eyebrows went up. "I'm not sure that's unusual with the police in a South American country."

Kelly sighed. "That's all I've been able to find. I wish there was more."

"It's not your fault. I doubt we can use any of this. Yeah, there's some suspicious stuff and Teo could've killed these people. But he really was friends with all five. Then again, if he's a psychopath, friends are a disposable commodity." I paused for a moment. "Did the reports say anything about Teo being in the proximity of those killings?"

"No." Kelly thumbed back through her notes. "But Riley said the CIA insisted. They might've had access to information the locals didn't."

"Can I borrow your file on this?" I asked.

Kelly handed it over then came around the desk and folded her arms over her chest. "By the way, I know you broke your pinky swear and went to see the Russian guy."

There were two ways to play this—really shocked that she would suggest such a thing, or come right out and tell her. I wasn't really sure what the consequences were for breaking a pinky swear. The girls said something about a needle in your eye, but I wasn't sure this would hold up in a court of law. Maybe in North Korea, but not here.

And I really, really didn't want this getting back to the girls. If they thought a pinky swear was breakable, then they might break their promises, and since I held such a tenuous grip on troop justice as it was, I felt this was too risky.

Of the two options, I opted for cowardice.

"Riley made me go at gunpoint," I explained. "Did you know he does stuff like that? Has he made you do something like that? Probably not. It's too early in your working relationship."

She wasn't buying it. "Riley. Held a gun to your head. And you expect me to believe that?"

"How did you hear about it?" I hedged.

"Rex told me. He called this morning. He still wonders if you're pregnant and wanted to know what I had to say about it. I think he told me the truth in hopes of getting me to admit to it."

Was that why he was so romantic last night? "Why don't you just tell him I'm not?"

"He's your husband. You tell him." was all she said.

I grabbed my keys. "That's right. Randi and Ronni are just going to have to deal with it. This is my husband, and I don't want him feeling bad that I haven't told him!"

I marched out to my van and got in. This was the right thing to do. My sisters-in-law were making me lie to my husband for them. Well, enough was enough! I drove straight to the station and marched into his office and shut the door.

"I'm not pregnant!" I announced and turned around to see that we were not alone.

Rex sat at his desk with an amused look on his face. In the chair opposite him was a young woman I'd never seen before.

"Oh, uh, hey. Sorry to interrupt." I gathered up my remaining dignity and reached for the door.

"Merry, wait. I want to introduce you to someone. This is Joanna Priestly. She's interviewing for the new officer position."

"Oh! Hi!" I walked over and shook her hand. "Are you Troy's friend?"

The woman laughed. She looked to be around my age, an African American with shoulder-length, wavy brown hair and a friendly smile. "Officer Wallace and I worked together a few years back. I've been a police officer in Des Moines for years. I wanted to move someplace quieter."

Should I tell her about all the murders? I opted not to. "Great! Rex can really use the help."

There was a crash outside the office, and we watched as Kevin Dooley emerged from the break room holding the front glass from the vending machine.

"Machine's broken again," he said before stuffing a Ding Dong in his mouth.

"Like I said." I turned to Joanna. "Rex really can use your help.

Rex stood. "Well, Officer Priestly, when can you start?"

The woman stood as well. "How about in two weeks?" She looked at Kevin, who was trying to set the front of the vending machine on his desk with mixed results. "Or sooner, if you really need me.

Rex asked me to stay and walked Joanna Priestly out. I plunked down in the chair and waited. He was back in a few moments.

"I'm so sorry," I apologized. "I didn't mean to barge in here like that. Kelly just told me about your conversation, and…I just didn't think."

Rex held up a hand. "It's okay, Merry. I'm sure Officer Priestly will forever remember the day she got the job."

Outside the office, Troy was trying to help Kevin maneuver the glass off his desk.

"Look, I just wanted you to know, I'm not pregnant. I'm sorry about all the subterfuge."

"It's fine," Rex said. "I know Randi and Ronni are pregnant. I was just messing with you because you weren't telling me."

"I wanted to, believe me." The words gushed out of me. "But Randi kept making me promise, and it took longer and longer and…" I sat straight up. "How did you find out?"

"Ivan and Ron told me weeks ago."

My hands curled into fists. "I'm gonna kill them."

"No, you're not," he ordered. "Those two are freaked out by the twins' behavior, and I had to talk them down a bit. That's all."

"Yeah, well, those two haven't had a lot of experience with women. Back in Chechnya, they asked me the dumbest questions about female anatomy. I'm not going to tell you because I won't insult your intelligence."

"Thank you."

I continued, "But they were convinced that women had four belly buttons, where the baby came out. And they thought the uterus was a musical instrument we kept in our marsupial pouches."

Rex held up his hands. "I don't need to know that."

I looked toward the doorway. "So the funding came through for that additional officer! Yay!"

Rex looked excited. "This is going to be great. And it means I'll have more regular hours and be home most evenings and weekends. We can take that trip up to that house you inherited in Behold if you want."

This was good news! I jumped up, ran around the desk, and threw my arms around my husband before remembering he didn't like that. But then, Rex didn't push me away, so maybe hiring Joanna was a great thing.

When I stood up, I asked, "Hey, are Joanna and Troy like, *friends* friends? Or just work friends?"

"Work friends. Joanna is married." Rex's lips twitched.

"Oh good, because I was thinking of hooking Troy up with Soo Jin sometime."

His right eyebrow went up. "That's interesting. I'll see what he thinks of Dr. Body. Now, you'd better go. I've got a ton of paperwork and have to make a presentation to the city council about our new hire. See you at home!"

"Okay! And Rex, don't let on that you know around Randi. She seems very keen on telling you herself."

"My lips are sealed."

I walked past a guy from the vending machine company, shaking his head over the glass door on Kevin's desk.

"I was trying to spy on the candy," Kevin was explaining. "Wanted to know why the Hershey bars with almonds and the plain Hershey bars switched places overnight."

He wanted to spy on the candy? Someday I was going to have to sit that man down and explain to him where candy comes from…

An idea popped into my head. I could do that. No, not spy on a vending machine, but I could spy on Teo. Maybe I could find out exactly what he was up to. And I had just the right piece of equipment for it.

CHAPTER TWENTY-ONE

I sat in the van watching the pink-sequined drone as it lifted off the curb and into the air. This should work. Easing up on the remote, I sent the drone up and over the small house where Teo was staying, hoping from that height, no one in the backyard would notice it.

More than once in the last fifteen minutes, I'd questioned myself as to why this was a good idea. To be honest, I was kind of at a standstill in the investigation. Doing a little spying on Teo might knock the case loose a little bit in my head.

The screen on the remote showed me an empty backyard. Great. He wasn't there. How was I supposed to spy on him if he didn't come out in the open? Suddenly, the screen went black. Uh-oh. I manipulated the controls to bring the drone back to me but was flying blind. I couldn't dodge trees or even the roof without the camera.

The drone rose into the air and started back toward me. At least I could see it to control it now. Trying not to rush it, I guided the drone back to me and landed it on the ground. I picked it up to see that the camera was missing. Broken bits of wire and plastic led me to believe that the drone had been damaged. The preciseness of the damage made me think that it was shot out. And since I didn't hear a gunshot, it had to be an air rifle or silenced weapon.

This was a bad idea. The camera probably broke on a branch or something.

I put the drone into the van and started to drive off when I heard a whirring motor. In my rearview mirror, I spotted a very large black drone. It was following me.

No, that was crazy. Of course it couldn't be following me. Why would it do that? It was probably some kid in the neighborhood playing with his own drone. Hopefully it wasn't Betty, and hopefully it wasn't armed with acid lasers.

I turned left, and the drone followed. At the next block, I turned left again and found it still on my tail. The third left turn confirmed my suspicions. I was being followed. By a drone.

But who was it, and why?

I hit the gas and sped out of the neighborhood. The drone still hovered there, right behind me, in my rearview mirror. Crap.

For a moment I entertained the idea that the girls were following me. That would be a relief. But this was a plain black drone, and the girls had decorated theirs with glitter—and it sat on the passenger seat next to me.

It could be someone just messing with me…like Hilly, or maybe the cult got a drone in the short time since I'd last seen them. Still, half a mile later, it seemed like whoever it was would have run out of range by now. Unless there were two of them and one was driving.

It had to be Teo. Who else would chase me with a drone? His plan to move here and be my best friend was a lie that he was exploiting to torment me with Henrietta's murder, blow up my garage, and now chase me with a drone.

A ding from my dash told me I was dangerously low on gas. I'd have to stop soon. That was the last thing I needed—to have a drone blow me up while I was loading up with something as flammable as gas. What were my options? I could go home and give it nothing to work with. Then again, it might follow me home to dump whatever its payload was. It was certainly large enough to carry weapons.

Why did I let the gas get so low? I don't usually do that. Normally, I keep my tank no lower than half full. It's a strategy from my spy days. The best bet would be to always have a full tank so I could go on the run if I had to. But I'd gotten soft since I'd retired, and half a tank was more than enough to get me to Omaha at least.

Maybe someone siphoned off my gas! No, I would've known if the gas cap had been tampered with. I'd just made a mistake.

Pulling into the first gas station on Main, I jumped out of my car and started fueling. The drone hovered in the air, ten feet from me, waiting. It was unnerving to say the least. It just held its place while I topped off.

I took a couple of steps toward it, but it flew backwards. Looking around, I couldn't see anyone in a car nearby, operating it. I turned and walked back to my van. The drone followed. Spinning on my heel, I tried to grab it, but once again, it danced out of reach. So I went back to the pump and waited.

The drone continued to hover. It was literally waiting for me to move on.

What was its endgame? To find out where I was going? It wasn't operating discreetly, which was what I would do if following someone. Of course, I'd just sent an obnoxiously sequined drone into the backyard of Teo the Tapir.

This thing wanted me to know what it was doing. It could be trying to intimidate me. Instead, it was annoying me. Well, to be fair, I was a bit worried. Being stalked by a person sucked, but a machine? Ten times worse. There was no way to see who it was.

I could take out its camera. I looked around for some sort of weapon…a rock or something. All I could find was the windshield squeegee. Still, it packed a lot of heft. I picked it up and flipped up the wipers on the windshield, to give the impression that I wasn't going to take out the drone. In a flash, I turned and hurled the long-handled weapon.

The drone neatly ducked it, and the squeegee fell onto the cement. Now it was onto me. I couldn't do that move again. I picked up the squeegee and returned it to the bin. The gas pump stopped, and I finished up, got in my car, and started to drive.

A normal, small drone could only go a few hundred feet. A medium had the capacity to travel up to three miles. I was going to put that to the test. *Let's see what kind of range this thing has.* Turning onto Main Street, I made a beeline for the edge of town.

Once I hit gravel, I knew I could go faster than I had in town. The drone stuck with me. We had to have hit the three-mile mark, but the drone showed no sign of slowing up. I drove farther. The drone kept pace.

This was no hobby-bought-at-Walmart drone. This was professional. My problem now was to figure out how far it could go. Granted, I could've driven straight to the police station and let Rex deal with it. But what could he do? I wasn't sure this thing was breaking any laws.

I hit speed dial and speaker. She answered immediately.

"Betty," I said, keeping my eyes on the rearview mirror. "Are you following me with a drone?"

"No," her voice said. "But that sounds awesome."

I heard girls asking what was going on, and Betty said, "Mrs. Wrath is being hunted by a drone."

There were ooohs and ahhhs. Seriously, I did not need this.

The miles were passing quickly now, and the drone still hadn't slowed up. I hung up on Betty and called Hilly. She answered before the phone rang.

"Hi!" the assassin said brightly. "What's up?"

"I'm being chased by a drone," I replied. "It's been following me in the car for miles and is still going."

"And you want to know how that's possible," Hilly said.

"Yes. Have you heard of that happening?"

"Only with military drones, which are huge. Is it armed?"

"I can't tell. Not with anything big anyway."

"Why don't you shoot it?" Hilly wondered.

"I don't have my gun. I'm driving in the country, but the damn thing is keeping up." I checked the rearview window. Yup, still there.

"Hmmm…" Hilly mused. "I've heard that there are some modified drones out there, but I've never seen one."

I swerved to avoid hitting a turtle. "Who would have something like that?"

"Bad guys…spies…Feds…Guatemalans."

The drone wasn't showing any signs of slowing down. "I don't think it's Guatemalans."

"You could lure it to the Radisson, and I could take care of it," Hilly offered.

"And run the risk of blowing up the hotel? It's the only nice one in town!"

"Good point. I've already paid in full. Talk to you later! Bye!"

She actually hung up on me. Which was good because something dropped from the drone, lowered about five feet, and then launched at me.

"Missiles?" I shrieked as I quickly turned right on a conveniently available gravel road.

The missile passed me by. After a few seconds, I heard it hit something as a thin whisp of smoke rose above the corn. Okay, that was good. It wasn't able to turn corners. But still! A drone was firing missiles at me!

My cell went off, and I answered as the drone dropped another one.

"Mrs. Wrath, what brand of drone is that?" Betty asked. "Hypothetically, of course. In case we're in the market."

The missile headed straight for my rear window. I swerved to the left, and it glanced off the side of the van. That was going to leave a mark. Would my car insurance cover a random drone attack? I watched as the missile kept going and hit a stop sign, blowing it up.

That's it! I spun the van around—a tricky endeavor on gravel, but I'd been practicing this move since I was sixteen. The drone panicked and started to back up. I drove straight toward it.

"Was that an explosion?" Betty asked.

"Yes!" I shouted. "And now we're playing chicken."

"I hope you win," Betty said. "I'll stay on so I can help the cops identify your body from the twisted, smoking remains. Would you prefer a huge funeral at the zoo or a small one in your backyard? And can you be buried in your backyard?"

"It's a bit soon for that," I said through clenched teeth. I was gaining on the drone, which seemed to be in a bit of a panic.

Then it dropped another missile. This one came right toward me. The road had ditches on either side, so there was no chance of swerving. This sucker was going to hit me square in the windshield. If only I had my gun…wait! I took it to see Grigori! I groped the middle console and found it. My fingers clasped around my .45 H&K. Nice.

This was going to suck, but there was nothing I could do. I slammed on the brakes and fired several shots into the windshield. Then, twisting myself into an improbable position, I kicked out the glass. I fired at the back window and grabbed a duffel bag full of Scout gear and flung it at the window. It fell to the ground below. Then I ducked.

The missile made a whistling sound as it breezed overhead through my car and out the back window. Then I sat up and fired two shots at the drone. They all hit, and the drone crashed to the ground. The missile exploded against a tree in the distance.

I got out of the car and went running toward the drone. As I stood over it, the machine detached one more missile that just fell to the ground. I fired two shots into the guts of the thing, and once it was really and truly dead, I scooped it up and carried it with the missile to my now windowless van. I picked up the duffel bag and sat inside the van, waiting for my heartbeat to return to normal.

I pulled up to Riley's building. He was standing outside, talking to Kelly. Their jaws fell open when they saw me.

I got out, grabbed the drone and missile, and walked over. "What? Like you've never seen a minivan with both windshields shot out before?"

"Not since Afghanistan," Riley said.

I paused. "When were you in Afghanistan? I was never in Afghanistan."

"After you left. For like a week."

Inside, I set the wreckage on a table with the missile beside it. "This thing chased me all over the countryside." I explained what had happened.

Kelly stepped outside to make a phone call, but Riley began examining the pieces. "Chinese parts," he said. "I'm not sure about the missile."

"I think it's Teo's," I said. "I was spying on him with my troop's drone, and as I was driving away, this one popped up and chased me."

"And it shot the windows out of your van?"

I shook my head. "No. I did that so the missile could pass through without blowing me up."

Kelly returned, holding her phone. "Drones that big have to be registered with the FAA. Does it have a serial number?"

I smiled at her. "Nice detective work!"

Riley studied it but shook his head. "It looks like it did, once, but part of it's been shot off and the other part was filed away.

Kelly said something into the phone and hung up. "I thought I really had something there."

"It was really good investigative work." I patted her on the back.

Since it was an attack, I called Rex and the sheriff. They agreed to meet me at Riley's.

Riley held out a candy bar. "Here. You look like you need it."

I tore open the wrapper and devoured it before Rex, Troy, and Carnack pulled up. Soo Jin arrived seconds later.

"Are you alright?" Rex walked over and put his hands on my shoulders, eyeing me up and down.

I nodded. "I'm fine. My van, however, needs a little work."

To his credit, my husband didn't look shocked. Sheriff Carnack shook his head.

"Rex filled me in," Soo Jin said breathlessly. "Can I see it?"

We all went into Riley's office, where the drone was sitting on a table. Soo Jin put on some latex gloves before lightly touching the drone. I looked over at Troy, who was watching her with an impassive face. How was that possible? Soo Jin was so pretty it hurt to look at her.

"I've never seen one of these before," she said after a minute. "Armed with missiles too."

"Soo Jin has a new hobby," Rex said.

The medical examiner nodded. "I needed something to do on weekends, so I took it up." She gave me a wry smile. "The nightlife here is pretty limited, and I got tired of going to art exhibits in Des Moines by myself."

Troy's eyebrows went up. "You like art? Did you see the Magritte retrospective last month?"

Soo Jin acted as if she was seeing him for the first time. "I went opening night! You?"

Troy nodded. "Well, not opening night, but the next day."

Rex and I exchanged meaningful looks.

Soo Jin blushed after a moment of silence. "Are you interested in the Koons show next week?"

Troy beamed as if he'd seen her for the first time. "Actually, I bought two tickets, hoping to find someone to go with me. Let's go together."

They held each other's gaze a bit too long before they realized the rest of us were standing there.

"We can discuss details later," Soo Jin said. She looked down at the wreckage. "I don't know if I can find out who the owner is. But I'll take it back to my lab and see what I can do."

"Here." Troy put on gloves and scooped the large machine up. "I'll carry this for you."

"Can you show me where this happened?" the sheriff asked.

Rex, Riley, and I rode with him out of town to the spot where I'd had my altercation.

"You know these fields pretty well," Carnack said as he studied the stop sign that had blown up.

"When you're sixteen and have your license, you look for places to drive. I drove all over these roads."

"We will try to find out who did this," Carnack said.

Rex looked at me. "Do you think it's Teo?"

"It came from his house," I said. "Or was it the neighborhood? It started tracking me there."

"I'm going to bring him in as soon as we get back." Rex looked grim.

"That might be a while," Carnack said. "We have to secure the area."

Just then, a huge pickup truck with large tires arrived and Ron and Ivan climbed out. "We were following the police scanner and heard about this!" Ron exclaimed.

"Hello Merry and Rex!" Ivan added.

I was just about to give them a tongue-lashing for telling Rex about their wives when my husband commandeered a ride for himself, Riley, and me. A pair of deputies showed up as we were leaving.

"Someone else might have an expensive drone like that," Riley said quietly.

I understood what he was trying to say. "Grigori Ivanovich."

CHAPTER TWENTY-TWO

Ron and Ivan dropped Rex off at the station, where he and Troy got in a squad car to go pick up Teo. Back at Riley's, Ron and Ivan stared at my van.

"Looks just like vans back home!" Ron said. "Were you homesick for Chechnya?"

"Yes," I said wearily. "I decided to totally destroy my van for want of nostalgia."

Ivan nodded. "I do know what you mean. I asked wife if I could make house look like back home, but she said she did not want it burned to the ground." He made a face. "Wives are so silly when pregnant!"

"You should surprise your wives with goats," I suggested. I wasn't feeling particularly charitable toward my sisters-in-law right now. "They can rough up the exterior, and it will be just like home."

"Good idea!" Ron said. "And everybody knows that babies love goats."

Riley pulled me aside as the Chechens began debating how many goats to get.

"It could be Grigori," Riley said. "He would have access to something like that."

"He did seem pretty angry when I mentioned Henrietta," I mused. "But he's not going to tell us anything. He'd probably shoot us on sight."

We thought for a moment, and I had an idea.

"We should talk to Doreen. She might know something about Grigori. Henrietta might've been in touch with her mother or even living with her when she worked for the Russian. Let's go," I added, walking over to my van. I stopped in front of it. "Let's take your car."

We stepped over the Chechens, who were now rolling in the grass, punching each other while arguing about how many goats to get.

I called Doreen on the way, telling her I wanted to stop by. She seemed more than willing for my visit. Riley and I rehashed what we knew but realized until we had new intel, we were spinning our wheels.

I introduced Riley as we went in. Henrietta's mother was very welcoming and brought us a tray of lemonade and cookies.

"So, how is my granddaughter?" Doreen asked.

"Fine. I saw her and Teo getting ice cream the other night. They seemed okay." I waited for a moment. "Teo has a huge learning curve."

Doreen shook her head. "I am so sorry to dump Elena on you both like that, but I think that's what Henrietta would've wanted."

"I'm sure you're right." Riley flashed his panty-melting one-thousand-gigawatt grin.

The old woman beamed. Flattery worked with her. "You're very understanding of an old woman. Henri was difficult at times to live with. But she was my daughter, and Elena is my one and only grandchild. I'm sure I behaved rashly, but I think Henri would've chosen a good man to have a baby with. I'm sure she trusted him."

What's not to love? A romance between two dangerous drug runners always has a happy ending.

"I still think it's such a crazy coincidence that Henrietta and I were both from this area and we worked halfway around the world."

"Isn't that something?" Doreen slapped her knee. "Why, I was born and raised here. Did you know that?"

"I did! Herschmann…" I pretended to consider the name as if trying to recollect something about it. "I apologize for not knowing anything about your family."

She waved me off. "Oh well. They're all dead now. It doesn't matter."

"Must get pretty lonely with no family around." Riley's words dripped with charming sympathy.

"Oh, I don't think so. I've got my church Altar Guild, and that's enough for me. I don't like going out around people. To be honest, I'm glad Teo has Elena. I was dreading kindergarten in the fall. I'd have to get involved with people, and I like my life the way it is."

"Doreen," I said carefully. "I'm trying to get a picture of who Henrietta was. She passed away in my garage. It seems important that I know who she was before we worked together."

The old woman smiled expectantly.

"Did she do any work locally before she went to Colombia?"

Doreen thought about this. "I think so. I think she worked for someone in Des Moines, actually. It was the beginning of her career in the drug trade," she said proudly.

I leaned forward. "Do you know if it was Grigori Ivanovich?"

Doreen's eyes snapped to mine.

"I'm sorry," I said quickly. "I did a little work for him too. Not at the same time and all that."

"Oh yes." She clapped her hands. "Gregory! Lovely man! Wonderful gardener. Weird obsession with sharks. I liked him."

"Did they get along?" Riley asked. "Were they friends?"

"I think so." Doreen seemed confused. "We were always invited to his lovely little home in the country for Thanksgiving! I always brought pumpkin pie." She paused. "I did think there were too many people standing around with guns. It doesn't seem fitting for the occasion. Now Arbor Day! That's a proper gun holiday!"

"Oh of course," I said. "I've always thought, plant a tree, fire a gun!"

Riley nodded but turned his head away slightly to avoid laughing.

"Gregory was a lovely man," Doreen said. "But he was very jealous. When Henri left him to go to Colombia, he stopped inviting me to Thanksgiving. Of course, I had the church Altar Guild after that, but still. He did carve a nice turkey."

"Jealous of Henrietta?" I ventured. "How?"

"Oh no, they weren't romantically involved," she laughed. Then she paused. "At least, I don't think they were. Maybe they were. What was it Henri told me…?"

We waited to hear what she had to say. If Grigori had been in a relationship with Henrietta and was jealous and angry when she left, was that enough, all these years later, to kill her over? Lovers had murdered each other for far less than that.

"You know what?" Doreen rose to her feet, her joints creaking. "I think I have something you might like."

She vanished down the hall.

Riley whispered, "She's not all there, is she?"

I shook my head. "At least we're getting some intel and we don't have to hang her upside down off a tall building or tie her up and play emo music until she talks."

Riley smiled. "Tashkent! Those were the good old days."

"Here it is!" Doreen emerged with a shoe box. "Those are Henri's things from about that time. I was just going to throw them out, but maybe it will help you understand the kind of woman she was." She looked at the tray to see the cookies gone.

"Oh dear. Should I go get more?" she asked worriedly.

Riley and I rose to our feet.

"No, thank you. You've already been too kind. Would you like me to give this box to Elena after I've looked through it?"

Doreen shook her head. "Oh no. It's best she doesn't…know too much about her mother."

"Well, I'll give her a hug for you," I said.

We showed ourselves out. I held the box on my lap while Riley drove.

"Let's get something to eat," I decided. "Those cookies did nothing for me."

We drove a few blocks to Ella's. I left the box in the car, and we went inside. After ordering two hot beef sandwiches, we tried to make sense of what we'd learned.

"I can't figure her out," Riley said. "She was proud of what her daughter did, handed her granddaughter over to a man who was a complete stranger, thought it was normal to have

Thanksgiving at a Russian mob boss's house every year, and gave away her daughter's possessions."

"I wonder if she didn't give Elena to Teo because she knows her mind is slipping." I took a drink of water. "Besides, some families are just weird."

"Didn't you say that she never goes to the church altar committee meetings?" Riley asked.

"Maybe she says it so that people won't think she's lonely and try to help her. Some people just want to be left alone." I looked around. "Our only other suspects are Teo and Grigori. Do you feel like we're missing someone?"

Riley leaned back in his chair. "I do. I just don't know who. I'm trying to remember what you told me back in Colombia about Henrietta but keep coming up with nothing. I remember you telling me she had some hernias, but that's it."

I shrugged. "She was nice and all that. Maybe nicer than some at Carlos's compound. Definitely nicer than Teo. Then again, I liked Mateo, Tim, Pedro, Chloe, and Shawn too. I don't know why, but I can't get the thought that Teo killed them off my mind."

Riley flexed his fingers. "Kelly told me what she learned. It does seem plausible that Teo killed them. Then again, coincidences happen."

Speaking of coincidences… "Did you realize that Shawn was killed by a Colombian shark and Grigori has a tank of Colombian sharks?"

Riley stared at me. "I hadn't thought of that. This case is riddled with coincidences. Doesn't that make Grigori a stronger suspect?"

I sighed. "Yes, I guess. Except why would he kill Sharkface Shawn? He didn't know anyone on Carlos's crew except for Henrietta."

"That could literally be the only real coincidence in this case." Riley echoed my sigh.

I leaned back and sighed. "Teo is still our best suspect, isn't he?"

Riley nodded. "We have to face facts. Teo never liked you. He even tried to kill you back in Colombia. Now he turns up out of the blue to be your best friend and live where you live?"

"I don't know what his motivations would've been to kill the others, but he had a relationship with Henrietta, which could be a motive. And leaving her in my garage to frame me makes sense. So does blowing up my garage."

I told him about the drawing and note Kurt had found.

"Oh, and by the way, Kurt is awesome and wants to work for you."

Behind Riley, a strange-looking woman who looked a lot like Kurt gave me the thumbs-up.

"Sounds like he did some good work," Riley said.

The woman two booths back gave a fist bump to the air. I glared at him, and he stopped.

"The drone came from Teo's house, I'm sure of it. And it tried to kill me. Another thing," I added. "He could've killed Henrietta to get custody of Elena."

Riley thought about this. "You said he was shocked by Doreen handing her over so quickly."

"I would be too. He probably thought it would take time." I rubbed my eyes. "I guess Teo is our guy."

Our food came, and Riley frowned at it. "How do you eat this thing?"

I knew Riley had seen a hot beef sandwich before. "It's an open face roast beef sandwich on white bread, topped with mashed potatoes and gravy, and it's awesome."

"It doesn't look very healthy." Riley poked the mashed potatoes with a fork.

"Of course it is! It's meat, a vegetable, and grains. Eat it."

He dropped the fork and sat back. "Why does it bother you that Teo is the killer? You hated him."

"I know, right? I can't explain it either. Maybe it's because he's looking to change his ways. Maybe I feel sorry for him. I have no idea, but I've become more sympathetic for some reason."

Riley dug his fork in and took a bite. He frowned.

"You don't like it?"

He looked like he didn't want to answer. "I love it. I don't want to love it."

"Anyway…" I brought us back around to the main conversation. "I guess I just wanted to believe he'd changed."

"He might be behind the drugs flowing into this area." Riley pointed the fork at me. "It's just too far-fetched to think he's innocent of all these things."

"I know." I slumped. "Maybe we just leave this completely in the hands of the police."

Riley took another bite and winced. "I hate that I love this."

"You're the only person I know who flinches while eating food they love."

We finished our lunch in silence, me realizing Teo was the only possible suspect in all of these very connected cases. Riley was probably trying to figure out if he could make a healthier version of this or whether or not the waitress was bangable.

We paid the check and got back into the car as Kurt texted. *What did he say? Do I have a job or what? Does he have a dental plan?*

I shoved my phone back in my pocket and stared out the window until we were out in the country.

The box Doreen had given us sat on the floor between my feet. I picked it up and opened it.

Then I opened the window and threw it out while shouting "*Go!*"

Riley automatically hit the gas hard, and we put precious time between us and what was in the box. Aww…he still had the killer instincts. Back when we worked together, we'd agreed to trust each other implicitly, and if one said, *drop, go,* or *stop,* then the other would act immediately.

An explosion rocked the ditch, and the car wobbled slightly. Riley came to a stop in the middle of the lane and looked at me.

I shrugged. "Sorry. I didn't have time to say it was a bomb."

"You could've said *Bomb* instead of *Go.* Those words both would've worked."

I threw my arms in the air. "I just reacted, like in the old days. You did too. Which was good, by the way."

We got out of the car and slowly approached the ditch. Not too close, in case there was a second bomb. There were papers burning all over the place and little bits of envelopes with stamps.

"I think Doreen bombed us," I said.

That was the second time in one day that someone tried to blow me up. And it was getting a little old.

CHAPTER TWENTY-THREE

———

"Hello Merry," Sheriff Carnack said as he arrived on the scene with a bomb squad. "Eventful day."

Riley told him what had happened while my brain raced. A crummy, white conversion van pulled up and over, and the sheriff went over to the driver.

"Sorry ma'am, this is a crime scene…" he started to say.

"Merry!" Kurt shouted. "It's okay! I know her!" He walked over to Riley and stuck out his hand. "Nice to see you again, sir!"

Riley looked at me.

"It's Kurt Hobbs…in disguise," I somehow felt the need to add.

"I'm sorry, Mr. Hobbs," the sheriff said. "You can't be here."

"But I can! I saw something that might help!" Kurt reached up and took off his wig and earrings.

One of the bomb squad members shook his head. "I hate doing work in Bladdersly. So many weirdos."

Sheriff Carnack gave the man a sharp look, and he went back to work.

"What do you mean, you saw something?" I pressed the young man.

"Well, I think I saw something. You guys weren't facing your car, but I was."

Riley's eyebrows went up. "You were in the diner? Looking like that?"

"Of course!" Kurt seemed surprised by his reaction. "I'm usually in disguise because everyone knows me here."

"What did you see?" I asked.

"A silver sedan pulled up on the other side of your SUV. I couldn't see who was in it, But I saw the top of the car door through your car's window. It opened and closed, but I never saw anyone get out. Then I thought I saw the SUV door on your side open and close. Then the sedan's door opened and closed again. It backed out, but not far enough to expose the front seat. Then it left." Kurt frowned. "Or maybe it was just a ghost and not anything significant at all."

"If the bomb wasn't put in there by Doreen, someone else did it while we were in the diner."

Riley nodded. "Do you remember what was under the bomb?"

I thought for a moment. "Letters. A stack of letters. Maybe the killer didn't want anyone to read those letters."

"I want to work full-time, sir," Kurt said to Riley. "For you."

Riley nodded absently. "You've done a good job yet again. Come into the office tomorrow and we'll talk."

Kurt put the wig back on. "In disguise or…"

"Absolutely," I said. "Now you should go. I'm sure the sheriff wants to close down this road."

Kurt gave us a proper Paraguayan military salute and fled.

"I've got something for you, sheriff." The man who'd spoken earlier about Bladdersly handed Carnack a stack of letters. "I don't know how they escaped the blast, but we found them several feet away."

The sheriff took the letters and put them in his back pocket. "Good job."

The two men walked back to the ditch.

"I need to get those letters," I whispered. "There might be something in there that seals the deal for Teo."

Riley stared at the two men. "Leave it to me. I'm better at pickpocketing." He pulled a pen out of my purse and walked over, calling out to Carnack that he'd dropped it.

I walked over to the SUV passenger door and inspected it. No prints were visible. Had Kurt seen what he thought he did? I was going to have to rule out the whole ghost thing. I texted Kurt to check and see if Ella's had a security camera. He said they didn't, but he'd recommend it for next time someone puts a bomb in my car.

"We've been given permission to leave," Riley said before walking around to the other side of the car and getting in.

I climbed into the passenger side, and he handed me a stack of envelopes.

"Carnack is going to be upset when he finds these missing."

"No, he's not," Riley said.

"He stuffed them in his back pocket," I started.

"I asked him for them," Riley finished.

I looked up from the letters. "Huh."

"He said you have to get them back to him tonight, but since Doreen gave them to you, possibly along with the bomb, you should see them."

"Sounds like that goes entirely against protocol," I mumbled.

The scrawl on the front of the envelopes was illegible. The letter inside showed that they were correspondence Henrietta had sent her mother, and the date was from when she met Teo in Colombia. I began to read.

Dear Mom,

I'm sorry we fought before I left. But you know how Grigori is. I just had to get out of there. His jealousy is too much. I've met some nice people here, but a lot of them are pretty strange. I've made a couple of friends named Chloe, Shawn, and there is this one girl I could swear has an Iowa accent, but I could just be homesick. She's okay but one of the weird ones.

Was Henrietta calling me weird? Okay, that's fair, but still, it seemed a little mean.

Tell Grigori I'll call him when I'm ready. Yeesh. Russians. Am I right?

Gotta go. Carlos is hosting the annual Cartel Chicken Charades with several other drug lords, and I'm one of the judges.

Bye,
Henri

"I remember that!" I said eagerly. "All of the cartel leaders had to provide a team and a chicken. The chicken would act out the suggestion, and the team would have to figure out what the chicken was pantomiming."

Riley kept his eyes on the road. "I don't remember you ever mentioning that. How does the chicken read the suggestion?"

"The suggestion is whispered to the chicken, who then acts it out. Of course, this is an industry based on lies, so all the teams cheated since no one knew what the chicken was doing other than walking around clucking. It eventually evolved into whoever came up with the most creative guess. Our team won when I was there because we said the chicken was obviously the Transformer, Optimus Prime, trying to buy a toothbrush in Ulaanbaatar. I have to say, Chuckles the Chicken was very talented."

"What did the winner get?"

"The other drug cartels couldn't attack you or your shipments for a month. And we got a chicken trophy."

Riley laughed. "Okay, back to the detective work. So from this letter, we know that Doreen and Henrietta fought. That Grigori was jealous, and we can guess they left on bad terms, and you were weird—which is something we already knew."

I opened another letter and read. "Ooh! This one mentions Teo!"

Mom,

I've met a guy. And he seems nice. Sure, he's a bit scary, but what bad guys aren't? He makes me laugh, and he's pretty gorgeous to boot. I helped him prank that weird chick with the Iowa accent. We blew up her bed with explosives. It was fun.

Grigori called again about you know what. I need to do some thinking. I'll write later.

Henri

I stared at the letter. "She helped him blow up my bed? Seriously? That bitch!"

"Maybe she wanted you dead too?" Riley asked.

I shook it off because I'm a professional, and besides, Henrietta was dead. "Well, we know there's still something going on with Grigori. She doesn't put it in her letters. Probably to avoid detection of whatever it was."

"I think this makes Grigori more of a suspect. He could've killed Henrietta when he found out she was in the area."

"Why was she in the area?" I wondered. "And why was she wearing fatigues, and why had she dyed her hair? I think you need to use your connections to find out why Henrietta was here, when she got here, and more about Grigori."

Riley pulled up in front of his office. "Okay. What are you going to do?"

"I'm going to sit at home doing absolutely nothing."

"You're going to talk to Grigori, aren't you?"

"Yes." I shook my head no. "Don't worry. I'll take Hilly, Ron and Ivan with me."

"Now I'm really worried," Riley said.

"All right, guys," I said to Hilly, Ron, and Ivan, who were in my backyard with me. "Let's review."

Hamlet the hamster had discovered the great outdoors, and who was I to stop him? Leonard ran happily alongside the ball, wagging his tail, while Philby and Martini watched plastered against the kitchen window.

"This is so great!" Ron said. "The B Team is back together like last time to do a mission!"

"The B Team?" I asked. "Why aren't we the A Team?"

Ivan rolled his eyes. "Because we do not have BA Baracus. How do we have A Team without Mr. T?" He twirled his finger next to his head to indicate I was crazy.

"Fine." It wasn't worth arguing over. "B Team. Whatever."

"Do I get to *spank the naughty lemur*?" Hilly asked.

I groaned. "Oh no. Tell me we're not back to those stupid euphemisms for killing someone."

Ron raised his hand. "That is fun! I want to try! How about if we *use angry words on a spider monkey*?"

Hilly nodded, which seemed like encouragement.

Ivan jumped up and down. "We can *overfeed the livestock*!"

That wasn't half bad…

Ron tried again. "Or *de-shed a buffalo*!"

That one made me smile.

"*Ex-communicate the ostrich*!" Ivan shouted.

I couldn't resist. "*Give mannequins to the goats*!"

The joy stopped like the needle being slid across a record.

Ivan shook his head. "That is not very nice."

These guys were a little too into goats. I probably should've known better.

"Everyone knows goats are afraid of mannequins," Ron said solemnly.

"Okay, bad choice of words," I said. "Let's review the plan." I pointed at Ron.

He folded his arms over his chest. "Take back words against goats."

"Fine." I was re-thinking using them at all. Especially if the Russian had goats. "I take it back."

Ivan shook his head. "You have to mean it."

"I mean it!" I shouted.

"Mean what?" Betty said.

I looked down to see Betty, Inez, and two Kaitlyns in full camo, with face paint and everything.

I pointed at one of the Kaitlyns. "That's not the way you do it."

She smiled up at me with a pink kitten nose, whiskers, and a heart-shaped beauty mark. The other girls' faces were also painted as a pony, a puppy, a koala, and Betty was an angry emu.

"Word on the streets is you're taking on a dangerous Russian guy," Betty said. "We're here to help." She pulled a grenade out of her pocket.

"Whoa!" I snatched it from her. "Where did you get that?"

The girls looked at Hilly.

She shrugged. "What? They're twelve now. It's time for them to start handling grenades."

"No it isn't! I'm their leader, and it is up to me to decide when to train them on grenades." Kelly would be proud. Well, probably not about the last part of that sentence. I looked around just in case she was near.

I collected the grenades from each girl.

"Now we're weaponless!" Inez said. "What kind of leader sends little girls into battle unarmed?"

"The kind who won't let you go with her, that's who."

"Yes," Ron said. "Merry is right. Is too dangerous for little girls."

Ivan added, "But we will help with your grenade training tomorrow."

"No," I said. "No grenade training. Got it?"

"Face it, Wrath," Betty said. "You need us as backup. We can flank them, cut the power, and keep them pinned down so you can *whack the weasel*."

Hilly shrugged. "Maybe they can shoot anyone who gets past us?"

"No. Now you girls need to go. No fighting with Russian mafia today. Got it?"

Inez perked up. "So you're saying we can fight them another day."

"And," one of the Kaitlyns said, "you are going to teach us how to use live grenades later…like tomorrow."

"I did not say those things. Well, not directly. Now head out before I call your parents."

The girls left the yard.

"We are to have your back," Ron said, finally answering the question I'd asked a while back in this bizarre conversation. "If Russian tries funny business, we will not laugh."

"Russians are not funny anyway," Ivan said. "So it will be easy."

I stared at them and then turned to Hilly, who said, "Relax. I've got these guys."

"Yes, but you gave the kids live grenades."

"Not really. Those are really old." She looked at them in the grass next to me. "They're probably not even active anymore."

I gave up and checked my phone. Aleksander had given me the address of a warehouse just off I-80 outside of Des Moines before asking me never to contact him again. That was fair.

"Let's go," I said.

Hilly and the Chechens sang every song from the Disney movie *Frozen* while I reviewed the plan in my head over and over. We were taking the Russians by surprise. That could go badly for us. But I wasn't in the mood for messing around anymore. I needed answers, and I needed them yesterday. Grigori was going to give us what we needed, at gunpoint if necessary.

It could be certain death. I'd been in that situation before. But I was hoping the element of surprise would give us an edge. Maybe we'd even catch Grigori alone. We could get that lucky. Then again…we probably should've brought the grenades.

"This is where Betty's grandpa sent us?" Hilly peered up at the broken windows on the second story of an old brick building.

This place was more isolated than the Corn Hole. An old building that used to be some sort of manufacturer, the warehouse was supposedly a front for the Russians and the location of Grigori today. Why go here? Because I didn't want to wait any longer. And I'd already seen his house.

We got out of the car, and I stuffed my .45 into a hidden holster inside the waistband of my jeans. Then I pulled my Girl Scout polo shirt over that. I probably should've gone with a 9mm. They were easier to hide. But this was what I had.

Ron and Ivan did the same thing with their guns. Hilly pulled a pair of nunchucks out of her pants and began twirling them.

"Where's your gun?" I asked.

"I didn't bring it," Hilly said. "I thought these were better for this situation."

"We may be walking into a shootout," I growled. "And you brought a close-combat weapon?"

Hilly looked at me. "I don't get it."

"Never mind." The Amazon was deadly with a pencil eraser. This would have to do.

"Remember the plan," I said before turning around and walking up to the door.

I knocked.

"Who's there?" a man growled from the other side.

"Merry Wrath Ferguson here to see Grigori Ivanovich," I snapped.

"Wait here." I heard footsteps walking away.

"You know what?" Ron said happily. "We could walk into certain death!"

Ivan agreed. "I should have brought my machine gun."

I was regretting this already.

Too late. The door swung open, and a seven-foot-tall man with facial scars and a sneer that could wilt flowers glared at us. He scowled when he saw Hilly and the guys but let us in anyway.

There was a moment where I was sure they would take our weapons. To my surprise, no one asked. We followed Scarface Gigantor into the main room, where Grigori was sitting at a table with ten other men who were all latch hooking rugs. Ten guns sat on the table, and more than a few men were sticking their tongues out.

"No no, Yuri!" Grigori leaned over a bald man with a bandolier of ninja stars strapped to his chest. "You need the *gray* yarn for the kittens!" He turned to another man who had two crossed machetes strapped to his back. "Boris, don't force the hook or you'll tear the fabric." He stood up. "Seriously guys! We've been working on these rugs for weeks, and you're still not getting it."

The others muttered apologies, and Grigori noticed me for the first time.

"Merry!" He smiled like he did the first time we met. "And more friends! That is wonderful!"

The men dropped their rugs and grabbed their guns, surrounding Grigori in a semicircle that looked pretty rehearsed to me.

"Is nice to meet you too, Mr. Oligarch, sir." Ron waved.

Grigori's eyebrows went up. "Chechens? You boys are a long way from home." He turned to look at Hilly. "And an Amazon! How delightful!"

Hilly smiled and nodded. For a moment I was afraid she'd go all quirky and tell him she killed his brother in front of him years ago.

"To what do I owe the honor of your visit?" Grigori set the rug aside.

There were ten guys, plus Scarface and Grigori. We were outnumbered. I'd suspected as much, but I wanted this over.

"I have a few questions about Henrietta," I said plainly. "Just some intel that's come to light recently."

He gave a short nod, but his expression remained pleasant.

"Mr. Ivanovich," Scarface said. "I don't think you should…"

Grigori raised a hand, cutting him off. "It's alright, Jerry. I've got this." He turned to me. "My relationship with Henrietta was a personal matter, and I am grieving her death. I will answer a question though. But there is a condition."

"What's that?" I wondered.

"One of your men has to fight Jerry here. If you win, I will answer one question, no matter how unpleasant it is for me or if it implicates me."

"And if you win?" I was trying to size up Lurch to figure out which one, Ron or Ivan, would be better to take him on. He was taller and looked more dangerous. But I knew my guys could probably hold their own.

"You"—Grigori tilted his head forward as he looked up over his glasses—"will visit me at my house on a weekly basis for tea. It does get so lonely out there sometimes."

Seriously? "That's it? You'll make tea once a week for me?"

"Of course," Grigori said.

I bounced lightly on the balls of my feet. "Make it chicken salad, and you've got a deal."

"There's one other thing," the Russian said.

Of course there was.

"I get to shoot you if I win. I won't make it a fatal shot, but it will be a good one. It might make a weekly tea inconvenient, and I will have to install ADA-approved ramps…maybe widen doorways to make room for your wheelchair, but that's it. Take it or leave it."

To be honest, I didn't know if I could come up with a question that was worth the risk of getting shot.

He waited for me to accept the offer. Why didn't I bring my bulletproof vest?

"One shot only? And if you miss, you can't fire another," I warned.

"Absolutely."

I turned to look at my team, who nodded back. Of course they did. They weren't running the risk of getting shot.

"Fine." Now I needed to come up with a question where the answer would bust this investigation wide open. "With one condition. If I win, then you have to stop the flow of drugs into my county."

I didn't think he'd accept that. Especially since accepting the deal would implicate him in the current crisis.

He shrugged. "Okay. You have two minutes to decide who fights Jerry." He turned to the bald, ninja star guy. "Can you please bring me my heart pills? It's that time of day, and I don't want to miss the window. Thank you."

"But sir," the man said, "you need me here."

Grigori narrowed his eyes. "I need my heart medication. The sooner you get them and a glass of water, the sooner you can watch my back. Okay?"

The B Team huddled up.

"You should pick me!" Ron said eagerly. "I want to fight the giant!"

"No!" Ivan shoved him. "I should do it. I want to fight the biggest man I have ever seen."

Ron frowned. "I said it first, and according to American children custom, I called dibs, so I win."

Ivan poked Ron in the chest. "Merry needs someone good so she will not get shot. I do not think you are good enough to win."

The men started shoving each other back and forth before dropping to the ground, wrestling and punching.

"I'll do it!" Hilly shrugged simply.

"What? No!" I disagreed. "You're too valuable an asset. Why do you think I brought those idiots?"

Hilly shrugged. "I can do it and win."

"You have one minute left!" Grigori said as someone set down a glass of water and a handful of pills.

Ron managed to get Ivan in an arm bar. Ivan elbowed Ron in the knee and freed himself.

"Those two are gonna kill each other before the fight," I sighed.

"I'm going to do it." Hilly stepped away from me toward Ivanovich.

Ron and Ivan scrambled to their feet and began to protest, but I silenced them with a look.

"I need you two to watch the other guys," I hissed.

"You?" Grigori's eyebrows went up in surprise. "A woman?"

Hilly walked over to Jerry. He was a whole foot taller than her and had at least fifty pounds of muscle on her. She looked him up and down before turning to Grigori.

"Piece of cake," she said with a smile.

Jerry the Giant looked at Grigori, who gave him a nod.

Hilly was an excellent fighter. And if brute strength, what she had in abundance, failed her, she was insane enough to become very creative. This didn't mean I wasn't completely apprehensive about this turn of events.

What did I think? That I'd just be able to walk in and ask him anything? And that he'd answer? I'll admit this wasn't well-planned. I looked at the Chechens, who were pouting like toddlers. Yeah. Hilly was the best choice.

I'd been in a lot of fisticuffs over the years. My personal philosophy was to approach it knowing you're going to get hurt, so don't flinch or cower. Go whole hog. Yes, you'll get some bruises and possibly a broken bone, but you'll inflict at least the same amount of damage on whoever you're fighting, whether it's the brother of a Yakuza boss or Melbert Dolan, who tried to grope me in a bar in Tucson.

Hilly and Jerry squared off, facing each other about six feet apart. Then Hilly closed her eyes, brought her hands together as if praying, and gave a deep bow. It looked cool, some sort of martial arts ritual to pay respect.

Jerry froze, unsure what to do. Maybe he thought he should do the same thing too. He copied her movements, closed his eyes, and bowed…and she closed the distance and threw him about six feet away.

You know the phrase, the bigger they are, the harder they fall? Well, Jerry fell pretty hard and was struggling to bring his solid wall of muscle upright.

"I do not think Hilly should do that," Ron said quietly.

"What are you talking about?" Ivan said. "She got advantage of much bigger man."

"Guys!" I pointed at the men on either side of Grigori. "Focus!"

Jerry ran at Hilly and lunged for her. She stepped out of the way, gave him a kick to the kidneys. The man groaned but stayed on his feet. He turned around and ran at her, this time grabbing her long braid and yanking.

Hilly grimaced but didn't cry out in pain. Instead she did the strangest thing I've ever seen. I always wondered why she wore such a long braid. I never grew my hair out because I didn't want it used against me.

Hilly jumped up onto the man's back, grabbed her own braid, brought it around his neck, and pulled it tight, strangling him with her own hair.

A couple of Grigori's men looked impressed. One or two lowered their guns. That was good because if things changed and this fight went south for us, we needed to be able to take them out quickly.

Jerry went down on the ground. As he got low, he grabbed her by the back of the head, brought his knee up, and smashed it into Hilly's face.

She didn't even blink. I was starting to wonder if she was a robot. Hilly fell onto her back and, using whatever leverage she had, threw Jerry up and over her head behind her. While he tried to recover, she got to her feet, jumped into the air, and landed full body on top of him like a WWE wrestler.

Jerry gasped and pushed her off him. He reached down to his boot and pulled out a knife.

"That is cheating!" Ron shouted.

Hilly smiled. Jerry got up and came at her, knife in hand. He was smiling until he noticed she was. She was getting inside his head. He slashed and she dodged, dancing around him as if she was toying with him.

At one point, Jerry's knife slashed at her side. She started to bleed, but it didn't look like a dangerous cut. Hilly didn't even seem to notice. Jerry got lucky and landed a punch to Hilly's face. She reeled backward from the blow, staggering but staying on her feet. Her cheek started to discolor, but Hilly ignored it.

The assassin danced around Jerry, and with his size, he couldn't keep up. Hilly landed two quick punches to the back of his head. He grabbed her wrist and pulled her around, her back up against his abdomen. With both of her arms pinned between them, Jerry wrapped both arms around her in a crushing bear hug and began to squeeze.

Hilly gasped and squirmed, but her face never showed fear. I thought that was telling. Her face turned red and then purple as she wriggled in his grip. I put my hand on my gun, and I saw Ron and Ivan raise theirs. Three of us against eleven. We just needed to shoot four each, which would mean one of us shooting someone twice. I smiled. Just like the hamster math.

Grigori smiled and reached out to the ninja guy.

"I don't have a gun," he told him. "I'm the ninja star guy."

Grigori scowled and turned to the machete guy on his other side.

"Nope. Machetes only," he said.

Grigori shoved him out of the way, and the next guy handed over his gun then looked sad and mumbled, "That's my only gun."

I tore my eyes off the Russian long enough to see Hilly's eyes starting to roll up in her head. Jerry was grinning through a split lip. Then his expression changed. An abject look of fear crossed his features before his eyes went wide. He let out a long scream before he passed out onto his back.

Hilly slid from his grip, got to her feet, and stepped over to me, holding her nunchucks.

"What happened?" I asked.

"I tied these around his…well, you know, twisted, and pulled." She looked at the prone giant. "I might have castrated him. I told you these things would come in handy. It's a good thing I stuffed them into the back of my pants."

Grigori stood there blinking like a fish, staring at his best man, out cold on the floor.

"We had a deal, Grigori," I shouted a little louder than I needed to.

Grigori nodded and handed the gun to Machete Guy, who held it like with the tips of his fingers and handed it to the original owner.

"You are right," Grigori acknowledged. "I'm sad you won't be visiting me, but a deal's a deal."

"I'll still come visit you as long as you make chicken salad," I said. "But not every week because, you know, that would be weird."

The man brightened at that. Who knows? It might be good to have a Russian mob guy in my pocket. Take that, Riley and your strange Whovian informants.

"What is your question?" Grigori called back.

I'd thought about this while Hilly was fighting. If I'd had more time, I could've constructed the perfect question that would tell us everything we needed to know and tie up all loose ends. I came here thinking I was going to have to drag every tidbit out of him over a lot of questions.

This was my only shot.

"Who killed Henrietta Herschmann?" I called out.

Ninja star guy turned to him and asked, "Henrietta the Hernia's name was really Herschmann? That's too many *H*'s."

Grigori smiled and held up his index finger. He left the room and returned with a leather-bound journal. "This will tell you what you need to know. Take it and go."

"Oh. Uh, thanks," I said. "This has the answer?"

He nodded and turned to Hilly. "If you ever want to take on a side hustle, I could use a woman like you."

She waved him off. "Nah. No thanks. Bye!"

We backed out of the room as Grigori and his men stepped over Jerry, went back to the table, and picked up their latch hook rugs.

"Do you think that has the answer?" Ron asked as we got into Hilly's SUV.

"I hope so." I stared at it. "If it doesn't, I have to go back and beat it out of him."

"Can we go with you to tea? I like that man," Ivan said.

I looked at Hilly as she turned on the engine. "Are you alright?"

"Oh yeah," she said. "Totally. Now all that's left is for you to look in that book, find the answer, solve the case, round up everyone, and tell us who done it!"

"That would be nice," I said as I opened the book and a piece of paper fell out. It had a coiled snake watermark. I kept reading.

By the time we got to Who's There, I knew what had happened. Well, almost all of it. But I was pretty sure I was right. I'd need to call Soo Jin about a couple of things, but I believed I knew what was going on.

Who knew you could find the killer by reading a book?

As if on cue, Soo Jin called.

"Hey Soo Jin!"

"Merry, the lab results came back on the drone, the letters, and the shoebox bomb. There's something you should know."

I smiled. "I think I already do."

CHAPTER TWENTY-FOUR

"Why is Joanna here?" I asked Rex, who'd just finished arranging chairs. "She doesn't start for two weeks, right?"

We'd decided to have the big reveal in the community center. It was a neutral location, and in spite of our new, I-guess-I-won't-shoot-you friendship, it didn't seem like a good idea to let Grigori or anyone else in his outfit know where I live. Okay, that and the hammering from the guys building a new garage across the street from the murder site was a little loud.

"I thought our new officer might as well get to know your dramatic style of revealing who done it." Rex smiled. "She was very curious. She'd never heard of anything like this except for in mystery novels."

"I'm sure," I grumbled, "that other amateur sleuths do this in other places."

Rex ignored me and went over to greet the sheriff and his deputies. The room was filling up, and I was starting to regret not having some sort of snack. What would you put on a sheet cake commemorating the solving of a murder? All I could think of was an image of the crime scene, which might put people off their appetites. But that would mean more cake for me! Now I really regretted it. If there ever was a next time, I would have to try that.

I looked around the room. The B Team of Hilly, Ron, and Ivan stood along the back wall, arms crossed as if they were hoping for some action. Soo Jin and Troy were talking animatedly in the second to back row. Sheriff Carnack and his deputies held up the wall on the right. Kevin was in the community center kitchen, scrounging for food, while Joanna stood with Rex on the left.

Kelly and Riley were in the front row with Kurt, who was dressed as himself…I think. I didn't remember him having a goatee and monocle. The rest of the group found seats. It included Grigori, who came with Jerry the giant, who kept glancing at Hilly, who ignored him completely. Doreen sat with Teo and Elena, the little girl holding her grandmother's hand while the old lady beamed at her.

Seconds before I was about to begin, Medea Jones burst through the door wearing a huge campaign button. She took a seat in the middle and glared at me. How did she find out about this? I didn't invite her! I looked at Rex, who mouthed, *Community center*. Oh. Right. It was for general public use.

"Okay." I clapped my hands as Betty and Ava came in and sat down in seats I'd just noticed were labelled *Mayor* and *Shadow Master* in blue crayon. "Let's get to it."

"Why are we here?" Grigori asked. He was sitting in the middle, crocheting.

After a nervous glance at the Russian, Doreen held up her hand. "Yes, I don't understand. What's going on?"

Teo frowned but said nothing.

Rex came over and stood next to me. "Merry has solved the case. I realize it's unusual, but this sort of thing seems to help her think through it, and it does make it easier to tell everyone all at once what we know." He stepped back and gave me a little nod of encouragement.

I faced the room. "I think everyone here knows about Henrietta's murder in my garage, but here's an abbreviated recap. A week ago, two things happened. The first was that Teo the Tapir was in town and looking for me. Since he and I'd had an acrimonious relationship when I was undercover within his cartel, I assumed he was here to find and kill me."

Elena looked at her father, who stared stonily ahead. Doreen drew her granddaughter a little closer to her.

"The second thing that happened was that Henrietta Herschmann was found murdered in my garage in the house I share with Rex, while at the same time, the garage in my old house across the street blew up."

Jerry raised his hand. "Why do you have two garages across the street from each other?"

Grigori and Doreen nodded. Teo leaned forward looking interested. Perhaps he thought that this was something all Americans did.

"Because she's a Communist!" Ronni shouted rather unhelpfully. She and Randi were sitting in the back. I hadn't even noticed that they'd come in.

Medea seemed to agree with my sister-in-law.

"My first house is across the street from my husband's first house and…" I shook my head. "You know what? I realized it sounds strange, but it isn't really important. And no, I'm not a Communist." I wasn't at all sure why two garages would make me one, but whatever.

I continued, "Since Teo was in town and he'd been in a relationship with Henrietta and had tried to blow me up once before, he was our main suspect."

Ron went over and sat next to Teo, patting his back.

"Later, Kurt Hobbs—" I began.

"The Third, Esquire," Kurt called out.

I ignored him. "—found a note detailing my address with a little stick drawing of me deceased. He found this note where Teo had dropped it earlier. We also found out that five of Teo's colleagues from the cartel had died under inconclusive circumstances and that Teo had been in the vicinity of each death at the time."

Teo's lips formed a hard line. Elena's eyes grew wider as she stared at him. Doreen put Elena on her lap.

"In addition," I went on, "there's been an influx of drugs coming into the county since Teo's arrival, and I was attacked by a drone that came from his house. All of these things would be more than enough to arrest Teo and possibly gain a conviction."

Medea jumped to her feet and pointed at the Colombian. "Teo did it! See? I solved it before Wrath did and definitely before your lame-o sheriff did! Medea for sheriff!"

"Sit. Down." I narrowed my eyes at the young woman until she did.

After hearing no more outbursts, I started again. "Since then, Riley and I were the recipients of a bomb, and there was a fight with Russians. I've read Henrietta's letters"—I held up the book Grigori gave me—"and a journal. Other clues included matching rings that Henrietta and Grigori had. It's been a long, confusing road filled with half-truths and lies."

"You might need to move it along," Rex whispered. "We only have the room for thirty minutes."

He pointed to the doorway, which was filled with little girls dressed in pageant dresses and wearing way too much makeup. A man entered, wheeling a rack of theatrical lights.

"Okay if I set up, folks? We've got the Little Miss Whorish Pageant," he asked.

I nodded my approval, thinking that the word Whorish and little girls were an unfortunate combination.

"More than a week later," I continued, "I know what happened. I know who killed Henrietta, has brought drugs into our town, and who blew up my garage. Unfortunately, I can't give you too much information on the drug investigation, as that is ongoing. Sheriff Ed Carnack…"

"Boooooooo!" Medea shouted. "Medea Jones for sheriff!"

I wanted to walk over and kick her ass, but Ed Carnack seemed unfazed. The pageant man started setting up the lights and made a lot of noise doing so.

"Let me tell you what really happened," I called out, voice raised over the din.

I paused dramatically, and Soo Jin gave me the thumbs-up while Troy beamed at her.

"Teo is innocent," I declared. "Of everything. He didn't kill Henrietta, attack me, or blow up my garage. He also has nothing to do with the marijuana that is flowing into the county." I smiled at the man, who sighed with relief.

Another man came into the room with a cart loaded with sound equipment. "Don't mind me," he said.

This was the last time I would let Ava book the community center for me.

My voice was louder still as I continued to tell the story. "This case was tricky. Everything pointed to Teo. Whenever I considered ruling him out, five more reasons popped up to implicate him. The killer went to great lengths to make it look like Teo was our man."

Two more men came in with what appeared to be a folding stage. They set up behind me and started to work.

"But he wasn't the killer!" I shouted. "The killer is smart, ruthless, and someone who doesn't stand for anything getting in their way. The person who murdered Henrietta Herschmann was her mother, Doreen." I pointed at her.

The old woman startled. Elena walked around to the other side of her father, and he put his arm around her.

The men behind me stopped making noise. I turned to see that they were staring at Doreen.

"You did it? Why?" Teo was incredulous.

Doreen's shaky hands went to her chest. "But I didn't do it. Why would I kill my own daughter?"

I had to hand it to her. She was playing the confused little old lady pretty well.

Grigori nodded as if he'd suspected this all along.

I wasn't falling for it. "*You* also are the one bringing drugs here. In fact, I believe you are blackmailing Grigori to manipulate his business. You're the mastermind, not him."

Doreen opened her mouth and then closed it.

The sound guy yelled, "What was her motive? They have to have a motive. I've seen it on *NCIS*!"

Once again, I ignored an outburst. "Let's go back to the earliest deaths. Teo didn't kill his friends from the cartel. Henrietta did."

Teo sat straight up, and he stared at me with an undecipherable expression.

"I've forwarded my thoughts to the Colombian authorities," I explained. "It's up to them to pursue it further. I believe Henrietta was enraged that Teo wasn't interested in any sort of commitment. And if she's anything like her mother, that explains the scorched earth campaign that I believe she used to frame him. She's not here to give us the details, but I can guess it infuriated her to no end that he was never arrested."

One of the guys setting up for the pageant said, "Hell hath no fury like a woman scorned, right guys?"

"Good one, Harry!" another one chuckled.

"She did have a terrible temper," Doreen said.

Like mother, like daughter, I thought to myself. "When Henrietta found out Teo was moving here to live and that I lived here, she decided to try to kill me and frame Teo." I looked at him. "You found out what was going on and confronted her, didn't you? That's why you had the note with Henrietta's fingerprints on it."

I gave a silent thanks to Soo Jin for coming through with the fingerprints at the last moment. It was the piece of paper that had fallen out of the journal that made me realize Henrietta wrote the instructions to detonate my garage. The paper was a handwritten note from Henrietta to Grigori, with the same watermark of a coiled snake on it.

"I'm sorry," Teo apologized. "I was shocked when she showed up. She actually believed I was pursuing you romantically. I was looking for you and found her snooping around your old house. We argued and I left. I found the note later in my pocket, where she'd planted it."

"And you didn't tell me," I reasoned, "because Henrietta's body was found soon after in my other garage across the street."

Teo hung his head. "I didn't want you to think it was me. I was going to destroy the note, but I lost it."

"And Kurt found it," I added. "Henrietta went to a lot of work to frame you. And Doreen didn't help when she murdered Henrietta later and put her body in my garage."

Jerry raised his hand again. "Why did she murder her own daughter?"

My eyes turned back to the killer. "I believe Doreen murdered her because Henrietta wasn't going to let her mother control her or her daughter anymore. Granted, Henrietta killed a lot of people and tried to kill me, but this is a control thing, and I believe Doreen controlled nearly everything Henrietta did. From working with Grigori, who worked for Doreen, to giving up her own baby."

"What evidence do you have?" Doreen asked.

I smiled. "The shoebox bomb had one, good print. It was yours."

Kevin Dooley, his arm deep in a bag of tortilla chips, said, "You shouldn't put bombs in shoeboxes. You might blow up your feet. Then where would you be?"

"That's ridiculous!" Doreen laughed harshly. "I've never been fingerprinted in my life!"

"No," I said, "but you'd handled the letters Henrietta wrote home. We found some of them miraculously intact after the bomb detonated. And we were able to lift a print off that. You gave us the box with the bomb inside it. The only person who could've touched that bomb is the bomber."

Rex stepped forward. "There was also a matching print on one of the missiles found with the drone that attacked Merry."

I turned to him. "There was?"

Rex seemed surprised I didn't know this.

"There was!" It was great that he made my case stronger. "That should be enough to lock you away. You see, if only you'd had some sort of presence in the town where you'd lived all your life. That really bothered me. It's too strange for someone your age to not have any documentation or participation throughout your years there. Only bad guys or spies go out of their way to avoid records. But you couldn't live completely off the grid. People knew who you were over the generations. I was suspicious of why you would do that. When the fingerprints came back, my suspicions were confirmed."

"We also found traces of marijuana on the drone you attacked Merry with," Sheriff Carnack spoke up. "We believe that's how you delivered the drugs. It's only a matter of time before we round up your dealers."

"Fake news!" Medea, the newspaper reporter, shouted. "The sheriff manufactured the drugs to make Medea Jones look bad!"

Nobody paid attention to her.

"What about Grigori?" Hilly called from the back. "What was he involved with?"

Grigori gave me a tiny nod.

"Grigori Ivanovich was being blackmailed by Doreen. That's how she was able to dominate the drug trade. Henrietta worked for Grigori and, I believe, gave her mother the ammunition to blackmail him."

"What did she have on him?" Jerry looked his boss up and down as if the answers would sprout from his clothing.

The men behind me started making noise again, which reminded me that I needed to wrap this up before I had to tell the rest of the story on a catwalk.

"Well, that's classified and part of the sheriff's investigation," I said. "You can ask your boss that."

"No thanks!" Jerry waved me off. "Forget I said anything." He glanced at Hilly, who was cleaning her teeth with a pocketknife.

To be perfectly honest, I didn't even know what the blackmail was. The journal that detailed everything Grigori had experienced with Henrietta and Doreen had some parts blacked out and redacted. But it was inadmissible because just this morning, it disappeared from my house. I'd have to look into that later.

The sound of tap dancing came from the doorway as several little girls began practicing what must be their group routine. They smiled huge, fake grins at me, looking like deranged circus clowns. I shuddered.

"Anyway," I said, trying to wrap it up, "due to her and her mother's problematic relationship and the fact that Doreen was muscling in on Grigori's activities and becoming dangerous, Grigori was worried about what Doreen might do to her daughter. He's the one who convinced her to take up with Carlos's cartel in Colombia.

"But Henrietta couldn't cut all ties," Grigori said sadly.

"Grigori gave me his journal, detailing all of this." I left out that the journal was now missing. "I'm sure he'll be a witness in these events that led up to Henrietta's murder." I was actually pretty sure Grigori would refute this later.

Rex walked over to Doreen and gently helped her to her feet. He didn't use handcuffs, probably out of deference to her age, and the sheriff followed them out.

"Finally!" a little pageant girl shrieked, and they pooled into the room.

"You have an interesting way of doing things here," Joanna said with a smile.

I looked around. Medea was handing out flyers and talking loudly how, as sheriff, she would support having me extradited—which was weird because this was my hometown. Grigori was showing Ron and Ivan photos on his phone of his latest latch hook rug. Jerry asked Hilly for her number, and she responded by flipping him onto his back before writing her number on his arm in Sharpie. Kevin had found a tube of cookie dough in the freezer, and he was trying to gnaw through the wrapper. Betty and Ava walked over, waiting patiently.

Joanna turned back to me. "Who's There isn't what I expected. Is it always this…unique?"

"Oh yes," I finally answered her. "This is pretty par for the course in Who's There. By the way, have you met our mayor?"

Ava stepped forward and offered her hand as Joanna, to my delight, shook it and said it was an honor.

Betty looked the newcomer in the eye. "If you need any informants, I can hook you up."

It hit me like a lightning bolt. "*You're* Riley's informant?"

The girl shrugged. "Of course we are."

"We?" I asked.

"The whole troop," Betty said. "You didn't know that?"

I had to admit, I never saw that coming.

CHAPTER TWENTY-FIVE

———

Once faced with the overwhelming evidence, Doreen, to everyone's surprise, confessed to everything. Turned out, she had moved in on Grigori years ago, thanks to some very creative blackmail with Henrietta's help. She was responsible for drug trafficking all over the state. The one place that hadn't been touched before now was her home county.

The greed got to be too much for her, and she recruited two men to be her dealers. Once she found out the sheriff was watching county roads, she began experimenting with drones. In fact, the one that attacked me was just there to spy on Teo and Elena to make sure her granddaughter was okay. The fact that I turned up was icing on the cake, since I'd worked with Henrietta in Colombia. The woman thought I might be onto her.

As far as Grigori's involvement in bringing her down, he'd managed to hide everything that would implicate him. He'd been plotting Doreen's downfall for years and, over time, erased all traces of his own criminal activity. Rex and Carnack were sure there was more they could do until a Fed in a black suit with sunglasses that he never took off showed up and told them not to get involved.

For someone I hadn't paid much heed to years ago, Henrietta turned out to be very different than I'd thought. My former colleague had been a vicious killer who'd take out people just to frame the father of her child…a child she may not have had much interest in anyway. It appeared that she'd liked Grigori but also helped her mother blackmail him. She even used the idea of his shark collection to kill Sharkface Shawn.

Teo may not seem like the ideal parent to raise Elena, but considering her grandmother and mother, I thought she stood the best chance of growing up somewhat normal.

Teo ended up buying a big Victorian house with a wraparound porch in a neighborhood with lots of kids. Elena is already running a little gang, and Betty checks in on her now and then—which makes me a little nervous.

Oh, and the thing Doreen warned us about Elena and sharp objects? Turned out not to be as ominous as we'd thought. Elena was just extremely clumsy.

The days of hamster-sitting the awesome Hamlet the Brave came to an end when Kevin finally moved into his mom's house and asked for all the hamsters back. I reluctantly said goodbye to the little guy. Kevin said I could have visitation rights, and I might take him up on it. Hamlet had just mastered locking the cats in the closet and was working on getting the ball up the stairs. I kind of wanted to see if he could do it.

Riley was so impressed with Kurt's work (although decidedly not impressed with his disguises) that he opened a branch of his PI firm, Andrews Investigations, in Bladdersly with Kurt handling things. It's a tiny office, but Kurt's ordered one hundred acrylic business cards and is bursting at the seams with pride. Kayla's even been bragging about him.

As for Kayla and Heather—Stewie and Mike begged them to come back to the Chapel of Despair and the Cult of NicoDerm. They promised the girls could do white magic, but I sensed something was up. I'd need to keep my eye on Stewie for a little while. The kid was mostly harmless and usually a danger only to himself. But my spydy senses told me he was plotting revenge, and there was no way that was happening on my watch.

I'd made a date in the near future to visit Grigori for tea. I'd turned down joining his latch hook rug group, which seemed to disappoint him.

A week later, Rex's parents returned from Greece, and Randi and Ronni had everyone over for a cookout and made the official announcement. My husband did a great job of appearing surprised, and the twins were thrilled with the response. Well, Ron, Ivan, and Randi seemed thrilled. Ronni mentioned a couple of times in her speech that I should be locked up for "creating a hostile fertile environment." Not sure what that meant, but I thought I'd better avoid whatever that was.

"Thank you," I said to Randi as she flipped burgers on the grill. "That was a hard secret to keep."

"We are just thrilled that you are going to be an aunt!" Randi patted my hand.

"I'm not!" Ronni shouted as she walked past. "The only aunt my kid's going to call her is Auntichrist!"

Ivan and Ron were in the corner, arguing animatedly in a way I knew would soon come to blows. I went over to see what was going on.

"Stop it!" I hissed. "Your wives are doing all the work, and you're over here bickering!"

The two looked like naughty schoolboys who'd been caught cheating at math—which, by the way, I was very good at.

"He started it." Ron pointed at Ivan.

"No!" Ivan retorted. "You started it." He cuffed Ron in the head.

Ron responded by pulling Ivan into a headlock.

I held up my hands. "Stop it!" I waited until they did. "What is the argument about?"

"Names," Ivan said. "He does not like boy name I like."

Ron nodded. "And he does not like boy name *I* like!"

"Why does that matter?" These guys were so confusing sometimes. "You each get to name your baby the name you want!"

The two Chechens looked at each other.

"I do not think that she understands," Ron said.

"Maybe we should use small words," Ivan suggested.

"Look." I put my hands on my hips. "It's simple. Ron may not like the boy name Ivan picked out for his baby, but it's Ivan's baby. You can each pick out different names, and it doesn't hurt anything."

Ron and Ivan burst out laughing.

"You do not understand," Ron said.

Ivan nodded. "We are not picking name for one baby."

"We're picking one name for both!" Ron finished.

"What?" was all I could think to say.

"Both babies will be born on same day!" Ron said.

"Which means both babies must have same name!" Ivan said.

"You've got to be joking," I said.

"Is tradition back home in Blasto Blasto," Ron said. "I want to name boy Ivan."

Ivan nodded. "And I want to name boy Ron."

I threw my arms in the air. "You guys are fighting to christen your babies with each other's names, and that's a problem?"

"Yes!" both said at once.

"Now she gets it!" Ron said. "It was exhausting to explain to her. I have idea! Why don't we name them Ivan?"

"No!" Ivan crossed his arms. "We should name them Ron!"

I walked away as they started wrestling. I hoped they had girls.

The yard was crowded with well-wishers that included Hilly, Teo and Elena, and my troop for some reason.

Ava got up on a bench, and Betty made a trumpet fanfare noise with her mouth. "The mayor is going to speak!"

All eyes turned to the girl.

Ava held out her arms. "I would like to congratulate the happy families and welcome two new voters to Who's There!"

"Okay!" Betty yelled. "That's it! You can go back to talking about boring adult stuff now."

Teo joined me. "Thank you for everything, Merry. I'm so happy to be part of your family."

"I'm glad it worked out." And it turned out I was. "Whole new life, right?"

He smiled and looked relaxed for the first time since I'd seen him at Feeling Lucky's. "Oh yes! I don't have to run a business that makes me worry about whether I bribed the right police. I don't have to plot to kill any rivals. Life is going to be so much easier."

"Word of advice," I cautioned. "You should never bribe police in this country."

"Huh." Teo rubbed his chin. "Good to know."

I looked around for his daughter. "How is Elena doing?"

Teo cast a quick glance at the girl, who was talking earnestly with the four Kaitlyns. "She's an interesting child. I think. I haven't been around many. I had to invest in rubber forks. She tripped and fell yesterday, and the fork ended up embedded in the wall. It was a steak knife the day before. I really need to work on this with her."

I wasn't sure I wanted to know more about that. "I'm sorry about Henrietta and Doreen. How is Elena taking it?"

"She seems fine," Teo said. "I have to say, there is a little something off about her."

"Maybe it's just moving in with a father she didn't know existed, after her mother who she never knew died and her grandmother, the only family she's ever known, is going to prison for her murder," I advised.

Teo smiled and nodded. "Perhaps. She's already planning to join a Girl Scout troop in the fall when she starts kindergarten. Maybe you can be her leader too?"

I shook my head immediately. "I can't. Believe me, I've got my hands full with this troop. But someone will step up."

Teo walked away as Hilly and Jerry joined me. I didn't even know he was here.

"Hey Merry," Hilly said brightly. "You remember Jerry. He's that guy I fought in that warehouse."

I looked up and smiled at the extremely tall man. "Of course I remember Jerry."

"The one who works for Grigori? The Russian mob guy?" Hilly continued.

"Yeah." I held out my hand. "I remember. It wasn't very long ago."

Hilly bit her lip. "Ron and Ivan said you were kind of slow today. I'm talking about the big guy I fought so you wouldn't get shot."

I closed my eyes and counted to three.

Jerry shook my hand. "Sorry for all that. I brought you something as an apology for thinking about killing you."

He handed me a package wrapped in brown paper.

"You really don't have to…" I started to say.

Hilly turned to Jerry. "She loves it!"

I had no choice. I tore off the paper and unfurled a large latch hook rug of a hamster in a ball.

"I love it," I agreed with Hilly. "Thank you!"

Jerry's eyes opened wide. "Really? That's great!" He reached and took Hilly's hand.

Hilly twisted his wrist until he fell to the floor. Then she gave him a tiny kick in the ribs.

"Sorry." Jerry stood up. "She doesn't like PDA." He smiled broadly. "Isn't she wonderful?"

"Let's get some cake!" Hilly dragged him by his now sore wrist toward the table on the other side of the lawn.

The girls came over and flooded around me to see the rug.

"I like him." Inez looked in the direction of the assassin. "But I give them two months, tops."

Lauren agreed. "Maybe less."

"Why don't you think they'll make it?" I asked, in spite of the fact I thought it would be more like one month.

"He's too needy," two of the Kaitlyns said simultaneously as the other two nodded.

"Hilly's a lone wolf," Betty added. "You can't pin down a lone wolf."

The girls were smarter than I thought.

"Are you going to be a PI?" Betty asked as the rest of the girls followed Hilly to the cake.

We sat down on a bench, even though I was seriously worried there wouldn't be any cake left.

"Not at this time." To my surprise, I felt a whoosh of relief. "I don't know if I'm cut out for a nine-to-five job."

"Makes sense," Betty seemed to agree. "You were a spy. Most investigating seems to be sitting around waiting for something to happen. That's boring."

That reminded me. "Why didn't you tell me you're an informant for Riley?"

The little girl shrugged. "I didn't think it was important. Besides, it gets me to my endgame."

For a moment, I was afraid to ask. Then I realized that as her troop leader, I should probably know. "Which is?"

"Total global domination," she said matter-of-factly. "Ava being mayor is just the start. I'm going to help the Kaitlyns run for class president, vice president, and student council next year."

"That's three positions, and there are four Kaitlyns," I said.

Betty shrugged. "What's your point?"

"My point is that I'm good at math," I insisted.

Betty said nothing about this.

"And I'm not old," I added. "And when Betty Vision is up and running, I want in."

The girl studied me for what felt like eons. "Okay."

My curiosity got the best of me. "So tell me, what's the next step after dominating school politics?"

"Isn't your dad up for re-election soon?" Betty asked. "I could work on his campaign. I've got a great secret weapon to make Iowans vote for him."

"He's the most popular senator Iowa has ever had," I laughed. "What could you do to make him even more dominant?"

"Mind control," Betty said. "While you've been out running away from killer drones and getting Hilly to do your fighting for you, I've been perfecting my skills."

"I didn't get Hilly to fight for me." I may have been a smidge defensive. "She volunteered."

"That might be true," the kid allowed.

"How have you been perfecting it? Are you going to get me to say some other vegetable?" I teased. "Or would it be an upgrade to fruit?"

Betty got up and stood in front of me. Her face was inches from mine, and I found myself staring into her eyes.

Without knowing why, I suddenly shouted, "All hail Betty the all-powerful overlord!"

Betty grinned and walked away. The others all stared at me for a moment.

Hilly nodded to Ron and Ivan. "You're right about her. I wonder why I didn't see it before?"

Everyone turned back to what they were doing.

That seemed like a dangerous new development. Then I put it out of my mind and got in line for cake.

ABOUT THE AUTHOR

Leslie Langtry is the *USA Today* bestselling author of the *Greatest Hits Mysteries* series, the *Merry Wrath Mysteries,* the *Aloha Lagoon Mysteries,* and several books she hasn't finished yet, because she's very lazy.

Leslie loves puppies and cake (but she will not share her cake with puppies) and thinks praying mantids make everything better. She lives with her family and assorted animals in the Midwest, where she is currently working on her next book and trying to learn to play the ukulele.

To learn more about Leslie, visit her online at:
http://www.leslielangtry.com

Enjoyed this book? Check out these other reads available now from Leslie Langtry:

www.GemmaHallidayPublishing.com